devil's bargain

RACHEL CAINE

D1343707

HARLEQUIN®

entertain, enrich, inspire™

All the characters in this book have no existence outside the imagination of the author, and have no relation whatsoever to anyone bearing the same name or names. They are not even distantly inspired by any individual known or unknown to the author, and all the incidents are pure invention.

All Rights Reserved including the right of reproduction in whole or in part in any form. This edition is published by arrangement with Harlequin Enterprises II B.V./S.à.r.l. The text of this publication or any part thereof may not be reproduced or transmitted in any form or by any means, electronic or mechanical, including photocopying, recording, storage in an information retrieval system, or otherwise, without the written permission of the publisher.

This book is sold subject to the condition that it shall not, by way of trade or otherwise, be lent, resold, hired out or otherwise circulated without the prior consent of the publisher in any form of binding or cover other than that in which it is published and without a similar condition including this condition being imposed on the subsequent purchaser.

Harlequin MIRA is a registered trademark of Harlequin Enterprises Limited, used under licence.

Published in Great Britain 2012
Harlequin MIRA, an imprint of Harlequin (UK) Limited,
Eton House, 18-24 Paradise Road,
Richmond, Surrey, TW9 1SR

© Roxanne Longstreet Conrad 2005

ISBN 978 1 848 45156 8

60-1012

Harlequin's policy is to use papers that are natural, renewable and recyclable products and made from wood grown in sustainable forests. The logging and manufacturing processes conform to the legal environmental regulations of the country of origin.

Printed and bound by
CPI Group (UK) Ltd, Croydon, CR0 4YY

BC
939927923

Rachel Caine was born at the ultra-secure White Sands Missile Range—site of the first atomic bomb tests—and has kept that non-traditional attitude ever since. She's been a professional musician, accountant, accident investigator, web designer and graphic artist...all at the same time. She currently works in corporate public relations and maintains a full schedule of writing, with her successful Morganville Vampires series. Visit her website at www.rachelcaine.com.

For all my kick-ass girls.
You know who you are.
Everything you do matters.

Chapter 1

Sol's Tavern was a place for serious drinkers.

It had no elegant decor, no pretty people sipping layered liqueurs. Sol's had a bar, some battered stools, a couple of slovenly waitresses, and a surly guy to pour drinks. There was a dartboard with Osama bin Laden's face pasted on it behind the bar, and for a dollar a throw, you could try your luck; the proceeds went into a faded red-white-and-blue jar that promised—however doubtfully—to go to charity.

But the best thing about Sol's, to Jazz Callender, was that it wasn't a cop bar, and she wasn't likely to run into anyone she'd ever known.

Jazz pulled up a bar stool and set about her business, which was to get so drunk she couldn't remember where she'd been. She caught the bartender's eye and nodded at the empty spot in front of her. Their conversation consisted of a one-word order from her, a grunt from him, and the exchange of cash. Sol's wasn't the kind of place where you ran a tab, either. Cash on the barrelhead, one drink at a time.

I could get to like this place, she thought. And knew it was a little sad.

As she leaned her elbows on the bar and picked up her Irish whiskey, Jazz scanned the bar's patrons in the mirror. She didn't actually care who was there, but old habits were hard to break, this one harder than most. The faces clicked into her memory, filed for later. A couple of unpleasant-looking truckers with bodybuilding hobbies; a fat guy with a mean face who looked as if he might be trouble after a few dozen drinks. He was drinking alone. There were two faded night-blooming women in low-cut blouses and dyed hair, years etched as if by acid at the corners of their eyes and mouths.

Jazz was still young—thirty-four was young, wasn't it?—but she still felt infinitely older than the rest of them. Seen too much, done too much...she wasn't going to attract a lot of attention, even from the bottom-feeders in here. Especially not dressed in blue jeans, a shapeless gray sweatshirt with an NYU logo, and clunky cop shoes left over from better days. Her hair needed cutting, and it kept falling in her eyes. When she looked across at herself in the mirror she saw a wreck: pale, raccoon-eyed, wheat-blond hair straggling like a mop.

Her eyes still looked green and sharp and haunted.

Sharp...that needed to change. Quickly.

She tossed back her first whiskey, clutched the edge of

the bar tight against the burn, and made a silent *again* gesture at her glass. The bartender made a silent *pay me first* reply. She slid over a crumpled five, got a full shot glass of forgetfulness and slammed it back, too.

The door opened.

It was gray outside, turning into night, but even the glimmer of streetlights was blocked by the man coming in. Tall, not broad. Her first thought was, *trouble,* but then it turned ridiculous, because this guy wasn't trouble, he was about to be *in* trouble. Over six feet and a little on the thin side, all sharp angles, which would have been okay if he hadn't come dressed in some self-consciously tough leather getup that would have looked ridiculous on a Hell's Angel. He didn't have the face for it—lean and angular, yeah, but with large, gentle brown eyes that scanned the bar skittishly and looked alarmed by what they saw.

His badass-biker leathers were so new they creaked.

Jazz resisted the urge to snort a laugh and repeated her pantomime with the bartender. Behind her, she heard the *squeak, squeak, squeak* of the new guy's leather as he walked up, and then he was climbing onto a bar stool next to her.

"Love that new-car smell," she told the bartender as he poured her a third shot. He gave her a cynical half smile and took her five bucks. The fool did smell like a new car— also some kind of expensive aftershave that reminded her of cinnamon and butter—*very* nice. So maybe he did have some sense after all, biker leathers notwithstanding. Idiot.

She imagined what kind of welcome he'd have gotten if he'd walked into a bar like, say, O'Shaugnessey's, over on Fourteenth, where the cops congregated. They'd have probably directed him—with velocity—to the gay leather bar down the block.

Her comment hadn't been any kind of invitation to talk, but the guy swiveled on his bar stool, held out a big, long-fingered hand, and said, "Hi."

She looked at the hand, which was well manicured, then glanced up into his face. His soulful brown eyes widened just a little at the direct contact. Now that he was closer, she could see that he looked tired, and older than she'd thought, probably close to her own age, with fine lived-in lines at the corners of his eyelids. He had a nice, mobile mouth that looked as if it wanted to smile and didn't actually dare to try under the force of her stare.

Normally, she might have thrown him a break. Not today. And not in that getup.

She turned back to her drink. The whiskey was setting up a nice nuclear fire in her guts; pretty soon, she'd start to feel relaxed, and after throwing a few more peat logs on, she'd start feeling positively good. That was why she was here, after all. It was a private kind of ritual. One that didn't involve making new friends.

"I'm James Borden," he said. "You're Jasmine Callender, right?"

The hand was still out, holding steady. It occurred to her a half second later that he shouldn't know her name.

Especially not *Jasmine*. Nobody called her Jasmine. She felt tension start to form in a steel-hard cable along her back and shoulders.

"Says who?" she asked the mirror. No eye contact. He was staring at the side of her face, willing her to turn around.

For a second, she thought he was going to answer the question, and then he reverted to a lame-ass pickup line. "Can I buy you a drink?"

He shoots, he misses by a mile. "Got one." She nudged her full glass with one long, blunt-nailed finger. "Blow, James Borden."

He leaned closer, into her personal space, and she smelled that aftershave again. The urge to move into that warm, inviting scent was almost irresistible.

Almost.

"Jasmine—" he began.

She turned, stared him in the eyes, and said, "If you don't want to get blood all over that nice new outfit, you'd better back your biker-boy wannabe ass off, and *don't call me Jasmine, jerk.*"

He leaned back, fast. His expression was one of shock for a second, then it shut down completely. His eyelids dropped to half-staff, giving him a belligerent look. Good. He matched the leathers better that way.

She held his gaze and said, "If you have to call me anything, call me Jazz."

"Jazz." He nodded. "Got it. Right. Like the—okay. I was sent to deliver something to you."

And the cable along her spine ratcheted tighter, tight enough to crack bone. *God.* She wasn't carrying a gun, not even a pocketknife. Even her collapsible truncheon—a girl's best friend—had been left on the hall table at home. Great. Of all the nights to tempt fate...

He must have read it in her face, because he smiled. *Smiled.* And the smile matched the eyes, dark and gentle and completely not right for a guy pretending to be a Hell's Angel reject.

"Don't worry, it's nothing bad," he assured her. "In fact, I think you'll find it pretty good. Not a subpoena or anything."

He started to unzip a pocket on his leather jacket. The zipper was stiff. As he tugged at it, she asked, "How'd you find me?"

He didn't look up. His head stayed down, but she saw tension accumulating in *his* shoulders for a change. "Sorry...?"

"How'd...you...find...me." She kept her voice cold and flat. "You follow me from home? You watching my house?"

"Nothing like that," Borden said. "I was told where to find you."

She rejected that one out of hand. "I've never been here before, asshole. How could anybody tell you to come here to find me?"

He conquered the pocket's zipper and wrestled out a red envelope. "Here," he said. "I'll wait until you read it."

"Because?" She didn't take the envelope.

"Because you're going to have questions once you do."

He gestured with the envelope again. Big, red, square,

like a thousand Valentine cards she'd never gotten over the years, but it was long past Valentine's Day and she was in a far-from-romantic mood.

She let him hang there for a good thirty seconds, watching his outstretched hand slowly sag with rejection, and thought, *Well, what the hell, at least I can throw it back in his face if I actually take it.*

She was reaching for it when Borden lowered the envelope and sat back, staring over her shoulder.

She felt alarms going off in the back of her head and risked a look. A shadow loomed behind her.

Two shadows, actually. Big ones.

The weight-lifting trucker twins had taken an interest.

"Ain't that sweet?" one of them said in a high, girly voice. He was wearing Doc Martens boots, battered blue jeans and a faded T-shirt that read Kinnison's Feed & Supply. A three-day growth of straggly beard. Watery eyes. "Faggot's giving the lady a *card*." He made wet kissy noises.

His buddy was a grimy Xerox copy, except his T-shirt read Highway to Hell and was ripped at the sleeves to show off massive biceps. Tattoos, of course. You could never have too many of those. His mostly involved thorns, blood drops and naked women. The AC/DC fan ambled around Jazz and followed up his buddy's comment with a shove to Borden's shoulder. Borden rode the motion and slid off the bar stool. He wasn't a small guy, and he had good bones, but he wasn't a fighter, Jazz could see that at a glance.

"Hey!" Jazz said sharply, standing up, as well. "Back off, guys. I don't want any trouble."

"*You* don't," Borden said under his breath. "Right. What was I thinking?"

"Yo, leather boy, shove your cute little Valentine card up your ass, you're bothering the *lady*," said the one whose T-shirt advertised Kinnison's. He was the power of the two; Jazz knew that from a half-second glance. He had intelligence in those narrow light eyes, and a kind of lazy satisfaction. This was what he'd come here for, to find somebody to pound over a few drinks. She was just a convenient excuse. *Lady*. Yeah, right. She looked the part.

Borden's voice had gone dangerously soft, his eyes closed and dark again. "Is that right? Am I bothering you, Jazz?"

"Woman like this don't want no candy-ass butt boy," Kinnison's said over her shoulder to him. "Fine piece of ass like this, she needs some real companionship." He was deliberately staying behind her, pressed close. His idea of courtship would be asking what kind of condom she'd like, flavored or ribbed. If he was even that considerate.

"Funny," Jazz said, and downed the last glass of whiskey she'd ever drink in Sol's. "I started out a *lady* and now I'm just a *fine piece of ass,* and you haven't even bought me a drink yet."

"Shut up, bitch, nobody's talking to you," AC/DC snarled, and put one hand the size of a canned ham on Borden's chest and shoved. Borden, who must have been seduced by all that over-the-counter toughness he was wearing, shoved back.

Mistake.

"Stay out of it," Jazz said, brisk and succinct, to Borden. She needn't have bothered; Kinnison's stepped around her and landed a fat punch to Borden's jaw.

Ouch. She heard the crack of bone on bone, and Borden staggered back, off balance.

"Hey!" she snapped. "Give the *bitch* some attention, why don't you?"

Kinnison's, pulling back for another punch, hesitated and turned back around to face her. Grinning with unholy glee, he said, "Yeah, okay, baby, let's play."

He shot a sideways look at AC/DC, who went after Borden. No doubt in Jazz's mind that he was thinking he'd backhand her and put her in her place, then get on with the serious beat-down of his only real opponent—the man.

She smiled. "Yeah," she said softly. "Let's play."

She spun on the bar stool, clocked him with an elbow hard to his nose and felt the sharp crack of bone and cartilage. She didn't stop to let the pain register; she straightened her arm and muscled into a spin as her feet hit the floor. Kinnison's twisted away from her in a corkscrewing spiral, off balance, and as he came around roaring, she sidestepped his rush, grabbed a handful of greasy hair and slammed his forehead into the tough oak bar. Twice.

When she let go, he slithered limply down to the floor. It had taken all of about two seconds, and he was bloody and utterly unconscious.

Borden was just now gaining his balance, shaking off

the punch and staring at her as if he'd never seen her before. Tactical error, because it gave AC/DC the opportunity
to pound a fist straight into his gut, double him over and
send him flying at the far wall, hard. AC/DC followed him,
wading in with lethally steel-toed Doc Martens to the ribs.

Jazz, blood already pounding red-hot, didn't hesitate. She
left Kinnison's limp body and leaped over a fallen chair,
landed flat-footed as a cat in front of AC/DC. He yelled
something obscene in her face; she didn't even note the
words, just the reek of bad breath, bad teeth and alcohol.

Watch him. Watch...

He rushed her like a charging bear. She swept out of his
way and left him to trip over the fallen chair, but he was
fast, faster than she'd thought and not nearly as drunk as
she'd hoped. He swerved. Before she could turn she was
engulfed by his brutally strong arms, rippling with thorn
tats and overendowed girls.

Borden, down on the floor, coughed out a mouthful of
blood and tried to get up.

"Stay down," she said. Weird, how calm her voice could
sound at times like these. She might have been asking him
to pass the salt. "I'll be done in a second."

AC/DC's breath pistoned her ear, and she felt the sugges-
tive grind of his hips against her.

"In your dreams, asshole," she said, and simply let her
knees go, dragging him over. When his center of gravity
was higher than hers she flowed forward, then quickly reversed, whipping his own momentum against him into a

shoulder roll. He grabbed a handful of her hair on the way over, and she ended up on his back. He flailed and bucked, trying to throw her off, but she had her arm around his neck and she applied pressure, cutting off blood flow until his body went slack.

And then she kept on holding the pressure, fury mounting. *Stop it, you'll kill him,* something told her, but it was a small voice, and she wasn't really in the mood to listen anyway.

She kept choking him until a baseball bat slammed splinters out of the wood floor right next to her.

She looked up to see the bartender/owner—Sol himself?—his face purple with fury, pull back for a straight-for-the-bleachers swing at her head. She let go and held up her hands. He didn't lower the bat as she got to her feet.

"Cops are on the way," he said, which was the longest speech she'd heard from him yet. "Take your boyfriend and get the hell out. Don't come back."

Jazz fought off an adrenaline-hot wave of dizziness and went to where Borden sat crumpled against the wall. He was probing his bleeding mouth and looking dazed. She grabbed a leather-clad elbow and dragged him to his feet.

"Let's go," she said, and guided him toward the door. He yanked free after a couple of steps and staggered back for something.

The red envelope, lying on the floor.

He tucked it into his jacket and followed her out, stumbling over the two prone bodies.

* * *

Outside, the night was cool and quiet, stars shining in a cloudless sky. A blurry bass beat thumped from a dance club down the street, and the sidewalk was thick with teenagers trying to look sullen while they waited their turn at the red velvet rope. Jazz turned left, heading uptown. Borden caught up with her in a couple of long-legged, stumbling steps. He was wiping blood from his face with a clean white handkerchief.

"Are you okay?" he asked her.

"Why wouldn't I be?"

"Your lip..."

"It's nothing," Jazz said, and tasted blood. She dabbed at the cut on her lip and couldn't remember when she'd picked it up. "How about you? No broken bones?"

"Bruised ego. Among other things."

"You know, the tough-guy act? Really not all that convincing." She stepped out to wave down a cab, but it sped up and passed her by. Maybe the problem was the ad for Armor All lurking next to her. He really did look like he'd been whomped pretty good. She muttered a curse and took the handkerchief away from his face to inspect him with merciless authority. "You'll live. You'll have a nice shiner, though. And you should see a dentist, he popped you in the mouth pretty good. What about the ribs?"

He winced when she probed them, but they didn't feel broken. Just bruised, probably. She pulled up his shirt to see bruises forming across smooth, trembling lines of muscle. His skin felt flushed and velvet soft.

"Hey!" He smacked her hands away. "I'm all *right*."

"You were lucky," she said, unapologetic. "If you've got a perforated lung, fine, go aspirate blood in peace. And don't bother me anymore. Thanks for ruining my night. I was starting to like that bar."

She hailed another cab, but it passed her by. Probably a bad block. She decided to keep walking, put some more distance between herself and Sol's. Any cop with half a brain would be able to pick Borden out of a crowd from a description, wearing that stupid Harley ensemble.

Speaking of which, Borden wasn't going away. As she started walking again, he fell in behind her, her own personal black-leather shadow.

"Stop following me."

"I can't."

"Trust me, you can. Just quit putting one foot in front of the other."

He kept following. She walked faster. That wasn't an issue for him, considering the length of his legs. She rounded on him after another half a block, fists clenched, knuckles wincing at the pressure. "Are you deaf? Get lost, idiot! I know you speak English!"

His nose was still bleeding, but only a trickle. He wiped it absently and held out the envelope. "Take it."

"Oh, *Jesus!*" she yelled, out of patience, then grabbed it and waved him off. "Fine, whatever."

He didn't move.

"Oh, for God's sake—look, you've done your duty, I've got it, whatever the hell it is, now would you *please* just—"

"Open it," he said again, and this time he sounded like he meant it. "I'm not going anywhere until you do."

She eyed him for a few seconds. His gel-spiked hair really was stupid, but the leather might have looked halfway decent on somebody it suited; he'd probably bought it because he'd been spooked at the prospect of coming to the bad side of town and trolling tough streets. Leather had probably seemed like a smart choice. And hell, it had probably kept his ribs from breaking, so maybe he'd been right after all.

"Lose the jacket," she said, and turned and walked away. She heard the sound of metal zippers and jingling chains, and glanced over her shoulder to see that he'd taken off the jacket and had it draped over one shoulder. A black stretch shirt, black leather pants...yeah, that was all right. Maybe the leather pants were little more than just all right, not that she'd ever admit it.

"I mean it," she said. "*Lose* the jacket. Dump it, unless you want us both to get picked up for assault."

She pointed at an alley, where a homeless guy lay rolled up in newspaper.

Borden stared at her. "You're not serious."

"You want to talk to me, get rid of the thing. The cops will be all over us if you drag it around."

"Do you know how much this thing cost?"

"Don't care." She resorted to flattery. "You look better without it."

He hesitated, then walked over and handed it to the homeless guy, who clutched it in utter shock and hurried off into the shadows, probably intent on selling it, because he knew he'd never be able to hang on to it on the streets. Jazz wished him the best deal, a warm bed and the rest of the Irish whiskey she knew she wouldn't get to drink, at least tonight.

She wished Borden would move closer so that she could lose herself in that smell again, warm and cinnamon-soft. The tide of adrenaline was dropping, and it left her feeling weak and shaky.

The paper felt stiff and warm in her hand.

Borden silently trailed her as she took a right turn at the corner, up Commerce, and headed for a Starbucks half a block up. He'd look all right in a Starbucks, she wouldn't look wrong, and nobody looked for fugitives among the latte-and-mocha set.

The place was packed, full of chatting couples and groups of friends and a few dedicated, lonely laptop users looking pale and focused in the glow of their screens. She pointed Borden to a side table, near the corner, and ordered two plain coffees from the barista. He'd probably prefer a soy half-caff mocha-something, but that wasn't her problem, and she wasn't that committed to the conversation. Even the regular coffee cost an arm and a leg, and she hardly had a lot of money to burn, considering her state of unemployment didn't look likely to end soon.

Besides, since she couldn't go back to Sol's, she'd have to save her booze allowance for a more expensive bar.

Settled at the table, drinking hot strong coffee and feeling the whiskey start to retreat from the field, she turned the envelope over and over in her hands. Plain block printing on the outside read "Jasmine Callender." She didn't recognize the hand, and held it up to Borden. "You write this?"

He shook his head.

"You know what's in here?"

"Nothing that will blow up or infect you," he said. He sounded tired. Adrenaline fading. She knew the feeling. "Hey, by the way, thank you. But I could've—"

"Taken care of them? Yeah, I know." Male ego stroking. She was an expert on the subject, after years with McCarthy...no, she wasn't going to think about McCarthy. She didn't take her eyes off the envelope. If she'd still been on the Job, she'd have bagged it and dusted it for prints, but there was no point. She no longer had access to those kinds of toys. "Who gave this to you?"

"My boss."

"Who is...?"

Borden sighed and sipped his coffee. He made a face—she'd been dead right about his preferences—and watched her without replying.

Just get it over with. She slid a fingernail under the envelope flap. Tugged experimentally. It was only lightly sealed, and came open with a crisp *pop*. Despite his assurances, she lifted the flap carefully.

No booby traps. There was a thick parchment sheet of paper inside, folded to fit the envelope. She extracted it, using her fingernails, and put the envelope aside. *Wish I had chopsticks,* she thought as she made do with a couple of coffee stirrers to hold down the edges and smooth it out.

"What are you doing?" Borden asked. He sounded annoyed but interested. The table creaked as he leaned his weight on his elbows, craning for a look.

"Not getting my fingerprints all over it," she said. "Just in case."

The letterhead was Gabriel, Pike & Laskins, LLP, with an address in New York City, on Central Park West. Nice, old-fashioned raised printing, none of that inkjet stuff. The cream-colored paper had thickness and texture.

It read:

Dear Ms. Callender:

Our firm has been engaged by a nonprofit foundation to offer you a business opportunity. Our research has shown that you have made inquiries with lending institutions toward opening a private investigation agency, which inquiries have been denied. The nonprofit agency wishes to make funding available to you, under the condition that you accept a partnership agreement with another qualified individual.

The terms of this agreement will be discussed in a separate communication should you indicate a desire to proceed. As a good-faith gesture, the firm has provided the name and vitae of the individual our client requires you to accept as a partner in this start-up business, as well as a check made out in both of your names in the amount of one hundred thousand dollars (U.S.), which should be used to defray expenses related to establishment of the partnership, including but not limited to rent, office equipage, and hiring of staff, as well as an advance against salary.

Please communicate your reply via the individual who has been entrusted to deliver this communication. We thank you for your attention.

Sincerely,

Milo Laskins, Partner

Gabriel, Pike & Laskins, LLP

Jazz read it again. Then again.

And slowly tented the envelope to look in it again.

"It's there," Borden said. "The check, I mean."

"How do you know?"

"I put it in myself."

She reached in and pulled out...a business check. Thick, official stock, emblazoned with the Gabriel, Pike & Laskins, LLP, name and address. Private bankers. Printed with a neat, computerized "one hundred thousand and no/100."

Made out to Jasmine Callender and Lucia Garza.

"Here," Borden said, and slid over another envelope—slightly bent from the beating he'd taken, but bloodstain-free—that when opened proved to have some kind of résumé with the name Lucia Garza in bold at the top. She didn't read it.

Her eyes went back to read the check again.

One hundred thousand and no/100.

Borden was still coming up with things, like a magician without a top hat...a business card, this time, in cream-colored stock that matched the letterhead and the check. Gabriel, Pike & Laskins, LLP. Under that, in smaller letters, James D. Borden, Attorney-at-law.

Jazz couldn't help it. The whole thing was so absurd, so downright idiotic, that she started laughing, and once she had, she couldn't stop. She clutched Borden's card and laughed until her sides hurt and her eyes watered, with his frown grooving deeper every second.

"You're—" She finally managed to gasp it out. "You're a *lawyer?*"

He folded his arms and sat back. He looked tougher in the black knit shirt than in all that load of leather and zippers; he actually had some biceps to flex, though nothing like the trucker twins back at Sol's. She remembered the washboard-tight abs, and thought he was probably more of a boxer or a runner than a weightlifter. Some strength in him, though. Not that the trucker twins wouldn't have kicked his ass until it fell off, but...

He derailed her train of thought by saying, in an aggrieved tone, "Yes, I'm a lawyer. What's so funny about it?"

Which set her off again, gulping down giggles, wiping tears from her eyes. His vanity hadn't just been wounded, it was on life support, but she couldn't help it. The idea that a *lawyer* had come all the way from New York City, dressed in Harley make-believe, to deliver some ridiculous, asinine *joke* was...

"Was it Brown?" she finally asked, once she was sober enough to get through the question. "Welton Brown? Big guy, snappy dresser, terrible sense of humor?"

"Excuse me?"

"I'm asking who put you up to it. Was it Brown? I knew he'd go to extremes for a prank, but..."

James Borden, attorney-at-law, wasn't just looking wounded now, he was starting to look pissed off. She preferred that, actually. Vulnerability was something she always found disturbing. Aggression, that was right up her alley.

"Lady, were you in the room back there when I was getting my ribs kicked in? Would I do that for a practical joke?" Borden skidded his chair back from the table and stood up, leaning over with both hands flat on the wood. "All right. Look, I've just about had it. I caught the crying-baby express flight from New York. I've been insulted, hit, kicked, lost a jacket I spent a thousand dollars on..."

She swallowed another giggle. "Seriously? A thousand? Damn. Why'd you go and listen to me, then?"

"...and all to hand you the chance of a lifetime. If you don't want it, fine. I'll just go home and tell my boss you're not interested." Borden grabbed for the check. She slapped her hand down hard on it.

"Don't get cranky, Counselor," she said, and nodded at the chair. "Sit."

He stared at her, leaning close, for long enough that she thought she might have pushed him too far, but then his elbows unlocked and he lowered himself down to the seat again. All was not forgiven, but he was willing to give her another chance.

Which she promptly screwed up by saying, "So who's Lucia Garza? Some scumbag client of yours that you suddenly need to move out of town, set up with a new identity, and find a place to launder her drug money?"

He actually blinked. "Are you *always* this unpleasant with people trying to do you a favor?"

"Only when they're lawyers."

Borden stared at her for a long, long moment, then stood up again. "Thanks for the coffee," he said. "I'm going to the hospital to get my ribs taped now. If you don't want the check, fine, tear it up. If you don't cash it, we'll assume you're not interested. If you do, Miss Callender, please be advised that we consider cashing the check a binding good-faith contract, and believe me, we have the resources to enforce it. Call the number on the card and talk to Mr. Laskins before you do anything stupid, since you obviously don't think I can advise you." He pushed the chair in, neat and courteous. "And hey. Have a nice day."

He was walking away when she said, "Hey. James Borden. Get back here."

And for once, somebody didn't follow her orders.

She stared, bemused, as he walked up to the door. He actually opened it.

He was going to just…leave.

She fidgeted with his card, drummed her fingers on the down-turned check—one hundred thousand and no/100—and made a split-second decision.

"Borden," she called again. "Hey, Counselor. Come back. Please."

He was already going. He really was *leaving*. She couldn't believe it.

She got up and went after him, caught his arm and dragged him to a stop just outside the door. "Seriously," she said, and let go of him when she caught sight of his face. "I'm sorry, okay? Can we talk?"

"You going to insult me again?"

"Maybe," she said. When he gave her a disbelieving look, she shrugged. "What, you want me to lie to you?"

"You're unbelievable."

"Yeah, well, so's this whole situation, if you don't mind me pointing it out. Look, come on back, we'll talk it over. Okay? Besides, you barely touched your coffee."

"I hate black coffee."

"Fine. Get whatever you want."

She watched in bemusement as he ordered a half-caff caramel *macchiato*, but restrained herself from making any jokes about it. Barely. He walked back over to the table with her, carrying his cup, but he didn't sit. He said, "This isn't going to work if you don't take me seriously, Jazz. I need you to do that. Can you?"

He sounded deadly earnest. She looked up into his eyes

and saw somebody looking back with a surprising amount of will and dignity.

"Can you?" he repeated. "Because I'm one taxi ride away from being out of here for good."

"Yes," she said softly. "Sorry. I'm a little freaked out."

"Me, too," he admitted. "It's been a long day. Even without getting rescued by—" he stepped on what he'd been about to say, which proved he had some brains, and substituted "—by a client."

She was just about certain he'd been going to say *by a girl,* and he wouldn't be the first. McCarthy had been furious, the first, oh, ten times it had happened. It had taken him a while to get over the hurt macho feelings, but then he'd realized what kind of a weapon his partner could be, when pointed in the right direction, and they'd worked together like a finely tuned machine.

Until everything had broken beyond repair.

Stop thinking about McCarthy. Just stop.

Borden sat down in the chair on the other side of the table. His body language was still tense and guarded, but they'd reached détente again. She read the letter again, then slid the sheet of paper out that had the name of Lucia Garza at the top of the page.

Experience
Former Special Agent, Office of Special Investigations, USAF. Accomplished over 800 criminal investigations with a primary focus on drug enforcement.

Former USAF Security Police Officer, Law Enforcement Supervisor. Duties involved military law enforcement, traffic investigation, crime-scene processing, and a member of several Special Weapons & Tactics Units.

Former Security Manager, Helios Aircraft—Special Projects Division. Security oversight of 300 scientists and engineers working on "Black" Top Secret Projects.

USAF OSI Academy, Washington, D.C.
FBI Special Weapons and Tactics (SWAT), Ft. Riley, KS
Federal Polygraph School, Ft. McClellan, AL
Texas State Police Certification, Ft. Worth, TX
Federal Undercover Agents Course, Washington, D.C.
Antiterrorism and Defensive-Driving Course, Summit Point, WV

"Damn," Jazz murmured. "If you made this up, you've got some balls, James Borden. These are serious credentials. I think they stick you in prison for even thinking about making this stuff up."

"She's good," Borden agreed, blowing on his pseudocoffee. "You should talk to her."

"Assuming she's not made of—" Jazz waved the résumé "—paper."

This time, he refused to take the bait, and just smiled. Slightly. "From everything I've read about you, you're supposed to be one hell of a detective. Call her up. Judge for yourself."

"I'd rather talk to her face-to-face." Always a better read off of people, looking in their eyes, seeing their body language. She realized that by saying it, she'd admitted she was interested, felt a bolt of anger at herself, and watched Borden take a noncommittal sip. "Unless that's a *problem*." Her voice had taken on that mutinous edge again. She didn't like being manipulated.

He didn't seem to care. "You'd need to work that out with Lucia. Look, my flight back's in about three hours, and you know what security's like these days. I need to clean up, get my ribs checked, change out of this—" he gestured at the outfit, which really, now that she'd gotten used to it, wasn't half-bad "—and get to the airport. So, Jazz, in or out, please. Laskins is going to want an answer when I hit the ground at JFK."

"I'll call you."

"Seriously. The minute I touch down, my boss will be bugging me for an answer."

She flicked the card with her fingernail. "Your cell phone's on here?"

"Yeah. But..."

"I have to check it out and think about it."

"Can I at least tell him—"

"You can tell Mr. Laskins that I think he's probably full of crap, but I'll check the information out," she said. "And if anything—*anything*—doesn't smell right about this, I'll shred this check, send you the remains, and come to do the same to the both of you. How's that?"

She saw a genuine spark of humor flare in his eyes and liked him a lot, in that second.

"It sounds like a threat," Borden said. "And I take it seriously. I saw you put those guys down. That took, what, ten seconds? Maybe fifteen?"

She took a big gulp of coffee to sober up from the wattage in his smile. "The whiskey slowed me down."

Chapter 2

Borden left, heading for the airport or the hospital or maybe going to shake down the homeless guy for his thousand-dollar leather jacket; she was actually sorry to see him go. Maybe. A little.

She caught herself taking deep breaths, soaking up the remaining few hints of his aftershave, and mentally kicked herself. *You don't need this,* she told herself. *Really. Your life is way too complicated as it is.*

And it wasn't like she didn't have other things to think about, for God's sake. A sister she hadn't talked to in six months after their last fight. A father puttering around on the family farm, still vital but growing old. A brother in the Navy who deserved a few more letters at the very least. She had a life.

Come on, Jazz. Having a family doesn't mean you have a life. Only relatives.

She eyed the letter again, fingered the check, reread the résumé. Folded everything together and stuck it back into the red envelope, then tucked it in her waistband, under the sweatshirt. She worked her knuckles experimentally and found that the bruising was pretty minimal—funny, she didn't even remember throwing a punch, but that was how fights worked—and the abraded skin would be okay after a day or two. All in all, not the worst bar fight she'd ever had.

Kinda fun, actually. She wondered if that made her dangerous, or just masochistic.

She fished her cell phone out of its cradle on her belt, hesitated, and then dialed the number on the résumé.

Two rings on the other end. Three. And then a brisk, contralto voice said, *"Diga-me."*

"Lucia Garza?"

"Yes. Who's this?" The tone was courteous but not welcoming.

If I hang up now...hell, she'll still have my number. Jazz took in a breath and said, as professionally as possible, "My name is Jazz Callender. I got a letter from—"

"Gabriel, Pike & Laskins?" Lucia finished. "Yeah, me, too. It said you'd be calling. Something about a partnership agreement."

Jazz went still and felt her eyes half close as she thought it through. "You must have gotten my résumé, then. I got yours."

"I did." Nothing in the voice at all, and certainly no approval or offers of friendship. Lucia liked to keep her feelings to herself. "I apologize, but this is very strange for me. I'm uncomfortable with talking to a stranger on the phone about—"

"You're *uncomfortable?* Join the club. I just had my evening interrupted by some lawyer with a cock-and-bull story and a nice-looking—" she edited her usually street-worthy vocabulary with a conscious switch "—presentation. How do you know these people? You owe them money, or what?"

She didn't mean to lash out, exactly, but Lucia's careful, measured voice had pissed her off.

"I don't," Lucia replied. The voice was still level and calm, but there was a floor of steel underneath. "And I don't know them any more than I know you, Detective."

"Former detective," Jazz shot back. "Which you'd know, if you'd read the damn résumé."

There was a brief, dark silence, and then Lucia's cool voice. "A word of advice, *Former Detective,* there's no need to take your anger out on me."

"What?"

"You're obviously angry at being manipulated, and—"

"Great. A fucking psychologist, you are."

"Don't interrupt me."

"Excuse me?"

"Apparently no one's ever explained that it's rude," Lucia said. "Like your general attitude."

"Are you done? Because I don't want to interrupt your apology, which I'm sure is coming any second now."

"This isn't going to work for me."

"Why not?"

"Because I don't like you."

"Well, I don't find you a bowl of cherries, either, *Lucy!*"

She was talking to dead air. Lucia Garza had hung up on her.

Shit.

Jazz angrily slapped the cell phone back on her belt, tossed the coffee cups and headed home. It was a six-block walk, and night had well and truly fallen; overhead, stars struggled to outshine the blank glare of streetlights. Kansas City wasn't much of a walking town in this part of the city; it was a mostly industrial area, and while there were plenty of cars, she was the only one on the sidewalk.

That was all right, she was probably better off on her own just now. She walked faster, burning off adrenaline and anger, feeling the red envelope hot against her stomach.

Just as well, she told herself. *This was a total waste of time, anyway.* Why the hell would a lawyer from New York fly all the way out to the sticks to hand-deliver something like this? And get the hell beat out of him in the process? What had he *really* been after? She hadn't given him anything, except a promise to think it over and call him.

A nonprofit organization? What the hell was she, some kind of charity case? What did they want?

He'd been told where to find her. How was that even remotely possible? He had to have followed her...but if she'd failed to notice a guy in that outfit following her on a deserted street, she was worse off than she'd thought. The jingle of chains alone should have given him away. He sounded like Santa Claus's sleigh.

But if he hadn't followed her, then how had they known where to find her? She'd never been to Sol's. They—whoever they were—couldn't have just sent him there, it was impossible. No, he must have followed her, she decided. Either he was a lot better than she thought, or she'd been preoccupied with her own distress and had just plain dropped the ball.

Mystery solved.

Well, not quite. What had all that drama achieved, exactly? Why would they have put on the whole dog-and-pony show in the first place?

To get me to call Lucia Garza.

She stopped walking, frozen in her tracks as her mind raced. Maybe that was all they'd wanted. If Garza was dirty, she'd just had a minutes-long conversation that was on her cell phone records, and dammit, this could have been a setup, couldn't it? The cops who'd put away McCarthy were still on her ass, looking for any reason to pull her in for questioning. She'd had the fight in the bar. Borden—if his name was really Borden—would be tough to find, if all this was just an elaborate scheme. Maybe the paper and the check weren't genuine. Shit, for all she knew, they'd had them printed up under her own name.

Paranoia, she told herself, and forced herself to start breathing again. *You just saw McCarthy today. That makes you paranoid, and you know it.*

Ben McCarthy had told her to watch her back. She should've listened to him. *Yeah, listen to the convicted murderer. Good plan.*

She wished the sarcastic monitor in her head would shut the hell up. McCarthy was no murderer. The case had been a crock of shit, and in time, they'd figure it out, have him exonerated and released from that hellhole. McCarthy had been a good partner and a hell of a cop, and he wasn't guilty. Couldn't be guilty, because if he was, that meant she was a poor enough judge of character not to have realized that her own partner, her friend, had calmly pulled the trigger on three people and then walked away, covered it up, and lied for nearly a year. And used her to do it.

Stop thinking about Ben. That was why she'd gone to Sol's. It was a kind of punishment she meted out to herself for making the trip to Ellsworth. She always felt safer and stronger there, talking to him; he could always make her believe that the world was wrong and the two of them were right.

It was only after she got out into that wrong world again that she began to doubt, and the darkness started to creep in, and she felt the guilt and shame and horror again.

And went in search of something to drown it in.

Even if McCarthy was right, that didn't improve things for her, because if they could get to him, they could get to anyone. She wished she could call him. If his enemies had set this up, then she needed McCarthy's clarity of mind to tell her what it meant.

Right now, it was just a heap of fragmented facts looking for context. McCarthy had always been the logical one, the one to meticulously pick through the pile and fit pieces together until the picture started forming....

Her cell phone rang. She grabbed for it, startled, and checked the number before thumbing it on.

Lucia Garza was calling her back.

"Yeah?" she asked cautiously.

"Look, I'm sorry. It's Jazz, right?"

"Yeah," Jazz said, and started walking again.

"I got out of line, and I apologize. It is strange, though, don't you agree?"

"I do." She struggled with it for a few seconds, and admitted, "I was out of line, too."

Another brief silence. "You think you're being played?"

"Probably."

"Yeah, me, too." The sound of papers rustling. "I don't like this phone thing. It's a paper trail. They can interpret it however they want."

"They, who?" Jazz asked.

"They anybody."

"You're not paranoid—"

"If they're really out to get you," Lucia finished. "Sorry for interrupting."

"Hey, that's your freak, not mine. Me, I hate being lied to."

This time, she did hear an emotion in the voice. "We have something in common after all."

"So." Sol's was ahead. Jazz quickened her pace to get past it faster. "You want to do this thing? Talk face-to-face?"

There was a long, silent pause, and then, "I don't know. Yes. I think so. Otherwise—"

"There's a check," Jazz said. "I have it, it's made out to us both. For a hundred grand."

"For a *what?*"

"One...hundred...thousand...dollars."

"I didn't think you meant cents," Lucia said. "Is it good?"

"I'll check it tomorrow, but yeah, I'm kind of leaning toward the idea it is."

"Why?"

She couldn't really say, until she tried to put it into words. "The guy they sent. He was...credible."

"Really," Lucia said doubtfully. "If we're thinking about any of this, I will insist on seeing the law firm. In New York. And talking to this lawyer you met, face-to-face."

Something lightened in Jazz's guts, because those were the exact same steps she would have taken, in Lucia's position. "Yeah," she agreed. "Sounds good."

"But first, we need to meet. In person."

"When?"

There was a pause, and then Lucia said, with a hint of a laugh in that smooth, professional voice, "What're you doing tomorrow?"

"Wait...you're in Washington, right?"

"I travel," she said. "Happens that I'm in transit right now after a case in Dallas. I can reroute through K.C. Can you meet me at the airport?"

"Sure." This was moving a little fast, but hell, Jazz's schedule for tomorrow had mostly been devoted to sobering up from tonight. "Call me with the flight number."

"Jazz," Lucia said. "You hate Jasmine, right?"

"Wouldn't you? Fucking Disney movies."

Lucia laughed and hung up without saying goodbye.

Jazz clipped the cell phone back on her belt and walked the rest of the way to her apartment in silence, thinking.

Then she wrote her brother a letter.

Just in case.

The call came at seven-thirty the next morning. Jazz was already up, showered and dressed, making her shaggy hair look a little less like a mop and more like an actual style. In honor of Lawyer Borden, she'd used hair gel. She'd chosen a plain brown shirt, blue jeans, and her ubiquitous cop shoes, deliberately unimpressive but clean and neat. ID and the red envelope in her purse, along with paperwork that showed she'd been a decorated Kansas City police detective, until six months ago.

She'd included the paperwork about the retirement, too, but she figured that if Garza was anything like she sounded, she'd already have the full story from three credible sources.

At the first chirp of the cell phone, Jazz picked it up and said, "Garza?"

"Hola," the other woman responded. She didn't sound awake. "It's early."

"And here I figured you for a morning person."

"Not even close. Look, my plane's landing at ten-thirty. Meet you at baggage claim, right?"

"Flight number?" Jazz wrote it down, clicked the on-off switch on the pen nervously, and then said, "How will I recognize you?"

"I'll be the one standing on one leg, singing 'The Star Spangled Banner,'" Lucia said grumpily. "We're cops, right? We've got to have a sign?"

True enough.

Jazz put out food for Mooch the Cat, petted her on the way out the door, and went to bail the car out of the parking prison where she stored it.

The drive out to Kansas City International was about fifteen miles, but it took longer, of course; traffic on Broadway, then on I-29. Jazz hated driving. Other drivers made her crazy. McCarthy had always gotten behind the wheel when they'd gone on calls, picked her up at her apartment, navigated the streets with casual ease and no sign at all of irritation. When she'd been forced to do it, she'd been a snarling bundle of nerves, arrived at crime scenes angry and wired. It had been a job for McCarthy to calm her down....

She flicked the thought of Ben out of her head, hit the turn signal, and exited for MCI. Parking was a nightmare, of course. She hated that, too. And parking garages. She ended up taking a distant spot, because she damn sure wasn't cruising the lot for anything closer. The walk would help her calm down, anyway; she didn't want to meet Lucia Garza looking sweaty and wild-eyed.

She checked her watch. Ten-thirty on the dot. A couple of jets were coming in for landings; unless there had been a miracle and the plane was early, she should be right on time.

Jazz followed the signs to baggage claim. She arrived at ten-forty, just as the flight number flashed on the screen and one of the carousels began to clunk out luggage to a growing crowd of travelers.

She scanned the group without focusing on anyone in particular. Nobody stood out.

No. Someone did. Jazz fixed on a woman who was standing very still, watching luggage bump its way around the segmented track. Her arms were crossed, and she was leaning against a pillar. There was a single black laptop bag over her shoulder and a black ripstop nylon backpack between her feet.

Jazz's cop brain relentlessly photographed her, chronicling long dark hair, glossy and straight; a model's golden, flawless skin. She was tall, long-legged, and dressed in what looked like a designer black pantsuit with a close-fitting white shirt under the coat.

As Jazz watched her, the woman's head turned, and her dark eyes fastened on Jazz. The same merciless evaluation, fast and accurate. Jazz wondered what the final catalog entry had been, but then Lucia pushed off and walked confidently through the crowd.

They both stopped, regarded each other for a few seconds, and then Lucia extended her hand. No rings on her fingers. Short, well-maintained French-manicured fingernails with plain gloss polish. Jazz felt like a clumsy lump of dough next to her, but she held eye contact as she shook, feeling strength in the grip but no challenge.

"Hey," Lucia said simply.

"Hey," she replied. They both stepped back and considered each other for moment, and then Lucia smiled. It was a cop's smile—cynical, secretly amused, as familiar to Jazz as breathing.

"Nice to meet you," Lucia said. "Let's find a place to talk."

They settled in some bright orange battered preformed chairs at the rear of baggage claim, out of the way of the loitering travelers. Lucia crossed her legs, rested an arm on the back of an empty seat and kept scanning the crowd. She looked casual and elegant, and very alert.

"Good flight?" Jazz asked. Lucia made a so-so gesture. "Nice weather?"

"Fair skies."

"Good. Now that we've got the small talk out of the way..." Jazz pulled the envelope from her pocket, handed over the letter and the check, and watched Lucia read them. Lucia, immediately absorbed, dug a similar red envelope from her bag and handed it absently on, as well. Jazz scanned it. Apart from the fact that this one had been mailed from New York, had a different home address, and didn't include a check, it was pretty much the same song and dance.

Lucia's carefully manicured fingernail flicked the check.

"It's genuine," Jazz said. "I called the bank this morning."

"Shit."

"No kidding."

Lucia shuffled the pages to her résumé. Her dark eyes widened, and she shot Jazz a look.

"What?" Jazz asked.

She held up the paper. "This isn't the public résumé. This one's what I give to enforcement agencies. It's got confidential information on it."

"So how did these guys get hold of it?"

Lucia shook her head. "Last place I sent this résumé to was the FBI."

Jazz raised her eyebrows. "They turned you down?"

"Not yet." She shrugged. "But I'm not so sure I want to go back into government service right now. I'd like to do something with a few less rules. So, you said this guy seemed credible to you? How so?"

Jazz thought about Borden, his geeky leathers, his soft, sharply intelligent eyes. Maybe the getup hadn't been clueless, after all. Maybe he'd been deliberately concealing just how smart he was.

"Just a feeling," she said. "But then, I'm not always the best judge of character."

She flung it out there to see if Lucia would react, and she

did, looking up and locking eyes with her for a few deep seconds before turning her attention back to the paper.

"I assume you're referring to your partner," Lucia said quietly. "Yes. I know he was convicted."

Sitting in that airless courtroom, watching the jury shuffle and fidget in their chairs, watching them avoiding McCarthy's eyes, Jazz had known before the forewoman read out the verdict. She'd known, and Ben had known, too. Twenty-five years in prison. He'd be an old man when he got out. If he ever did. Cops were hunted in there, and Ben had always needed somebody to guard his back.

"He's not guilty," Jazz said, mostly just to hear herself say it, to hear how it sounded out loud after all these months.

Lucia didn't look up. "You're sure of that?"

"Yes."

"The evidence looked pretty damning on paper."

"Lots of guys on death row with paper evidence," Jazz shot back, feeling something tighten in her guts. "McCarthy didn't kill anybody. I'd have—"

Known. That was the mantra that rocked her to sleep at night. *I'd have known. All those nights, sitting together, talking, pouring out our lives to each other, I'd have known if he was capable of cold-blooded murder.*

Lucia didn't comment again. She finally looked up and said, "What do you think about all this?"

Jazz shrugged. "I think it's worth a conversation."

"Because?" Those elegantly shaped dark eyebrows rose just a little.

"Because even though you shop at Ann Taylor for your suits, I can't afford to. I need the money. And I need to set up shop with decent resources so I can find out what happened to McCarthy, and maybe keep it from happening to me." Jazz glared at her, daring her to find fault. "I need the money. That's it."

Lucia's lips curved into a smile. "That's it? You're not curious?"

"About?"

"How someone came to learn so much about us. About how they had my home address, which is not something just anyone can learn, believe me. I guard my privacy closely. About how they knew *you* needed the money, and *I* needed the challenge."

Unwillingly, Jazz thought about the tinkle of the bell at Sol's, and James Borden arriving in his un-apropos leather with a message addressed to her. "And how they knew where I'd be," she said. "They know a hell of a lot."

"More than I think either of us is comfortable with," Lucia finished. "At least until we know just how they got their information, and why."

It was like talking to a mirror, Jazz thought. A mirror in which she was better-looking, taller, had better clothes, and knew how to apply lipstick.

Lucia was smiling at her, eyes shining with something that might have been similar feeling, but then her eyes wandered past Jazz, focused on something behind her. Jazz resisted the urge to turn as the woman's smile shut down and left her face blank and watchful.

"Did you bring backup?"

"What? Hell, no. Who would I bring?" She wasn't exactly rolling in allies at the moment.

"Two men have been watching us since we met," Lucia said. "Were you followed?"

"What is this, *I Spy?* I don't know. I don't usually look for tails when I go on perfectly innocent meetings."

"If it was perfectly innocent," Lucia said patiently, "your lawyer friend wouldn't have gone through this cloak-and-dagger routine to put us together, now, would he? Disgraced former detective and a national security risk?"

"Excuse me?" Her hackles came up at the *disgraced* part. She thought about the second part of Lucia's question a second later, with a blink of surprise. "National security *what?*"

"Let's just say that there are things I know that the government would rather I didn't. Being watched is nothing new for me."

"Then maybe these guys are your problem, not mine."

"Except they followed *you* into baggage claim." Lucia's body language hadn't altered at all—still languid and relaxed. "Let's try something. You get up and walk away. Go to the bathroom. Don't look back. I'm going to head outside to the taxi stand. Let's see who they tag."

Jazz frowned. "I thought we were going to talk about this deal."

"And we will. Later." Lucia uncoiled herself from the

chair and held out her hand. Jazz, rising, automatically took it. "Watch your back."

"But—"

Too late. The woman was walking away, parting the crowd with the sheer force of her personality. Jazz shoved her hands in her pockets, rocked back and forth on her heels for a second, and then took off at right angles, heading for the bathroom. Her peripheral vision found the two men—identical buzz cuts, one blond, one brown. Both had the fit look of guys who could run down a suspect without any trouble.

She walked right past them, but they didn't follow. In fact, they didn't follow Lucia, either. They stayed where they were.

She risked a glance back as she pushed open the restroom door. One of them was talking into his sleeve. Hidden microphone, very government-issue.

She fished her cell phone out of the cradle, hit Recall and found the number, then dialed.

"Yes?" Lucia's cool voice.

"They've got radios. There are probably spotters on you out there. Watch yourself."

"Did they follow you?"

"Not into the ladies' room. Hang on." Jazz uncoiled the earpiece and plugged it in, hooked the cell back in its cradle. "I want my hands free."

"Good idea." Lucia sounded amused. "I'm staying in

plain sight. At least it's difficult to start trouble in an airport these days."

"Yeah, let's hope. So. What's the plan?"

"I don't know that I have one, actually."

"We can't hang out here all day. When you think it's safe, hail a cab and take it to my apartment." She gave her the address. As she was telling her cross streets, the door to the restroom banged open; Jazz stopped talking and began washing her hands, staring into the mirror.

"Jazz?" Lucia's voice buzzed in her ear. "Someone with you?"

The woman who walked around the corner looked sleek and businesslike, wearing a tailored black jacket and black jeans, but there was something in her eyes, something...

"Is something wrong?" Lucia asked.

Jazz reached for a towel. As she bent over, the woman angled toward her, moving fast.

"Might be," Jazz said, and ducked.

The punch—intended for the back of her neck—sailed past to crash into glass. Jazz spun, still crouching, and drove the heel of her hand into the woman's solar plexus, sending her flying and gasping for air. She moved for the door—

And it opened to admit the two crew cuts from baggage claim.

"Hey!" Jazz said loudly. "This is the *ladies' room, guys*—"

One of them grabbed for her arm. She danced backward, almost tripped over the woman, who was coming to her feet with a brutal look on her face, and retreated to the empty narrow area between the stalls and the wall. Not a lot to work with, but at least it was defensible, they could only come at her one at a time, and, *Jesus,* how had she gotten into this mess, anyway? She'd been minding her own business, dammit, drinking her whiskey and drowning her sorrows, and now she was about to get the crap beaten out of her in a bathroom for a woman she'd barely met and a check she hadn't even cashed.

Lucia Garza said in her ear, "I'm coming. Don't do anything brave."

"Don't worry," Jazz said out loud, and ducked a punch. "Brave is definitely not my style."

The bathroom was just too narrow for a decent fight, but at least it meant they couldn't use their numbers effectively, either. She backed up into the narrow aisle in front of the stalls until her back was against cold tile and snap-kicked toward the face of the man coming at her. It was a feint. When he flinched, she hooked her foot behind the bend of his left knee and pulled. His head hit the wall with a thick sound, and he went to one knee.

She put him down with a fist to the temple.

She looked up to see a blur coming at her and instinctively put up a parrying arm. The kick caught her on the forearm, and damn, it hurt; she gritted her teeth against the urge to yelp, wrapped her arm around the foot that had just come at her and yanked. Hard.

Girlfriend in the pantsuit slipped and nearly went down,

caught herself and shifted her weight forward, slamming Jazz back against the wall, then breaking free with a twist of her hip.

Nobody had a gun, knife, or even a taser. That was good, Jazz thought. Any kind of weapon would have ended this quick and ugly. At least this way, she'd have a much slower defeat. Time for lots of things to happen, including miracles.

The second man shoved the woman out of the way and lunged to fasten his hands around Jazz's throat. He ran into her fist with his Adam's apple instead and fell back, gagging.

As if they'd gotten some secret signal, all three of her attackers suddenly stopped, backed off—even the one still shaking off her whack to his temple—and just looked at her.

It was weird.

No, it was *creepy*.

"Later," the woman said, and moved to the door. The two men followed her. Single file, straight out into the airport.

Thirty seconds later, the door banged open, and Lucia Garza entered, looking ready for anything—hands up, weight balanced on the balls of her feet, which in those shoes was something of an accomplishment. She looked around in a lightning-fast analysis, then focused on Jazz and raised her eyebrows in an eloquent *what the hell?* motion.

"Party's over," Jazz said breathlessly. She was shaking, buzzing all over. Strangely ecstatic. She swiped the back of her hand across her mouth, looking for blood, and remembered that they hadn't actually laid a hand on her. Well, girlfriend in the pantsuit had kicked like a mule… Jazz skinned up her shirtsleeve and looked at the impact mark. Yep, that was going to bruise like a son of a bitch.

"What the hell happened?" Lucia asked.

"You tell me, you're the superspy. When people attack me, it's usually during the commission of a felony, not just because I took the wrong sink in the ladies' room." Jazz pushed away from the support of the tile wall and walked to the mirror.

Her face was vivid and flushed, her eyes fever-bright. Even her hair looked better.

Damn, she enjoyed this stuff. That was probably sick.

"You," Lucia said, as if she'd read her mind, "need a hobby. Something nonviolent. Maybe macramé." She sounded amused, though. "Let's get out of here."

"Yeah," Jazz agreed. "Probably a good idea."

Walking with Lucia wasn't like walking alone. For one thing, Jazz was used to blending in, slumping, avoiding people's eyes. McCarthy had always laughed about it, called her a chameleon; he'd had the traditional cop presence and radiated an implicit threat even when sitting and reading the newspaper. But then, McCarthy hadn't worked undercover. She had.

Lucia Garza's aura was more like a runway model's. She drew stares as she stalked through the baggage-claim area, lean and elegant in her designer clothes. Jazz still felt invisible, but not in a good way. Next to Lucia Garza, most women would fade into wallpaper.

"Which way?" Lucia asked, sliding on sunglasses as they exited the building. Jazz nodded toward the distant parking lot. She wished she'd thought to pack some shades, but then, hers would have been clunky blue-blockers from a flea market. Lucia's had the sleek, finished look of sculpture and probably cost more than a car. Not that she was comparing or anything.

Lucia's bag went into the trunk, and Jazz scanned the area for signs of her restroom visitors. Nobody in sight. She had a prickling on the back of her neck, though, and wasn't surprised when Lucia, opening the passenger side, said, "They're watching us."

"Where?" Jazz ducked inside. They slammed doors at the same moment. Lucia jerked her chin a bare quarter inch in the direction of a white panel van sitting on the garage roof about five hundred yards away. As Jazz looked at it, it silently backed out of sight. "Son of a bitch. Okay, I give up. What the *hell* is going on?"

"I don't know."

"Well, you know more than I do!"

Lucia brushed long, dark hair back with a distracted air, and frowned. "I picked up a tail at the hotel in Dallas," she said. "Nothing obvious, but it was there. Professionals, like the guys in the airport just now. I don't know who they're working for. Although I have no idea why professionals would try to take you out in such a risky public setting."

"Maybe it isn't about me at all. Maybe it was related to your case. Whatever it is you're working." She didn't ask, but she left the door open in case Lucia wanted to share.

She should have known better. "No. It's not germane," Lucia said. "That was all done when these people showed up. And they arrived within an hour of the letter arriving at my hotel. Those things have to be connected, especially if they're here, following you, as well."

Jazz started the car and backed out of the parking space.

"Where are we going?" Lucia asked.

"I don't know about you," Jazz replied, "but I'm already tired of being the one who doesn't know anything. I intend to change that."

She drove downtown, to the business district, then off into a less Fortune 500, more industrial neighborhood. Office buildings went from sky-piercing steel and glass to squat, square, converted warehouses. She pulled in at the grimy curb next to one and picked up her cell phone. As Lucia watched silently, she paged through numbers until she found the one she wanted and connected.

"Yeah?" A cautious voice on the other end.

"Manny, open up," she said. "It's Jazz. I need an opinion."

"Drive-through's closed."

"Give me a break."

"You didn't pay me for the *last* opinion."

"I thought that was a freebie!"

"Jazz, Jazz…I don't give freebies and you know it."

"Fine, I'll pay you this time. Double."

Silence. He hung up. Jazz waited for a few seconds, and smiled as the grimy garage door a few yards down the street began rattling slowly up.

As soon as her car passed under it, the door reversed course and began jerking and clattering back down again. Manny didn't like open doors. "Who's Manny?" Lucia asked. She didn't sound bothered, for which Jazz had to give her points. If the situation had been reversed, Jazz was pretty sure she'd have been firing off questions every ten seconds and jumping at every noise.

"Old friend," Jazz said, which didn't really answer anything, and killed the engine. She kept the headlights running, bathing the big concrete room in white light. The few spotlights were feeble and far between. Manny also wasn't big on paying electric bills.

She got out of the car, leaned against the cool metal and waited with her arms folded. The car shifted as Lucia got out on the other side.

"What now?"

"We wait," Jazz said. "Oh, and keep your hands where he can see them. He's a little twitchy."

"Twitchy?" Lucia echoed grimly. "Wonderful. I already like your friend."

"Trust me. When someone's out to get you, the best friend you can have is a paranoid nutcase with skills."

"Amen to that," said a dry, raspy voice out of the shadows. "You know the rules, Jazz. Weapons on the ground."

She spread her jacket. "No weapons."

"You've gotta be kidding me."

"Not."

"Then who are you and what have you done with Jazz Callender?" He sounded amused for a second, and then his raspy voice turned serious. "I mean it. Knives, batons, tasers—everything on the ground, or I turn around and walk."

"Manny, I got nothing. We came from the airport, for God's sake. You don't run around armed there, in case you missed the events of the last few years."

Manny edged out of the shadows. He was a big man, not very clean, with a greasy tangle of black hair that he kept cut above too-large ears. Muddy green eyes that with a little polish would have knocked a girl dead, but when combined with his unattractive personal grooming habits, a perpetual slump to his broad shoulders, and a habit of flinching from loud noises…no, Manny wasn't exactly prime date material.

Not that Jazz was in the market.

Manny was watching Lucia. "What about her?" he asked, and pointed. Jazz wasn't exactly a makeover fan, but even she winced from the state of his cuticles. "She armed?"

"She," Lucia said with absolute precision as she took off her sunglasses, "is always armed. So you can just assume that and move on."

Manny was already shaking his head, violently. "No, no, no, Jazz, you know I don't do—I don't let—no, no, no—"

"Hold on." She shot Lucia a look. Lucia tilted her head and gave her one right back, and this one clearly said *I'm not giving it up for your paranoid weirdo friend.* Jazz lowered her voice and walked around to talk to her. "Manny's a little freaky, but he's a good guy. Plus, this building has the best security in the city. He built it himself. He's really good at it. But he's got quirks, okay? You need to cut him a little slack."

"Why do we need him?"

"Because I say we do," Jazz said. Simple. "You can either trust me about this, or we can get in the car, drive out, and go our separate ways. Your choice."

Lucia's dark eyes studied her for several long seconds, and then those elegantly outlined lips curved into a smile. "All right," she said, and reached to her back with one hand.

Gun. *Damn,* Lucia had a gun. It was a small one, a .22 automatic, combat black. "How the *hell* did you get that through airport security?"

"I didn't," she replied, and put the weight of it into Jazz's hand. "I sent it ahead to a courier and had him bring it. I palmed it on the way out of baggage claim from the man with the briefcase."

Jazz hadn't even noticed a man with a briefcase, except as part of the general wallpaper. There must have been a hundred fitting that description. She blinked, the weight of the gun heavy and warm in her palm, and then nodded as if she'd known that all along. Not that Lucia appeared fooled, considering her smile. "Uh-huh. Anything else?"

"Search me," Lucia invited, and spread her arms.

"Oh, this isn't going to be that kind of relationship, believe me." Jazz bent over and put the gun on the ground, then held up both hands in the air and raised her voice for Manny. "Yo! Gun on the ground! We're cool now, right?"

Manny was dithering, half in shadow, half in the white-wash of the car headlights. Clearly spooked. "I don't know, Jazz...you know I don't like it when you bring strangers..."

"She's not a stranger," she lied. "Look, Manny, you do this for me and you get a free lunch. Plus the usual fee."

He stared at her for a long, long moment. "I don't do criminal. You know that."

"It's not a criminal case, Manny."

"No murders. No rapes. No violent crimes."

"It's maybe fraud, and that's a maybe." She was seriously stretching the truth, and saw Lucia watching her with slightly raised eyebrows. "You won't need to do anything but give me results. No depositions. No trials."

He swallowed, wiped his sweaty face with his grimy sleeve and nodded. "Yeah, okay," he agreed. "But only because it's you, all right? Follow me, ladies."

Lucia started to pick up the gun. Jazz kicked it under the car with a skitter of metal on concrete, then reached through the window to shut off the headlights. Darkness closed in around them.

"You don't want to do that," she said. "Really. You don't. Manny may look like some squirrelly little pushover. He isn't."

They followed Manny to the stairs.

Upstairs was a different world. This didn't come as a shock to Jazz, but she saw it register on Lucia as Manny keyed a code into a lock and opened the door at the top of the stairs.

Because beyond was a state-of-the-art science lab, segmented by movable clear glass partitions. Beyond that was a thick leather couch and widescreen HDTV that doubled as Manny's living area. Green hospital curtains hung on suspended rods hid the open-forum bathroom—which, Jazz had cause to know, was an interior designer's wet dream of gleaming marble, Jacuzzi tub and spa shower—and the bedroom, which she'd only glimpsed but looked good enough that if she lived here, she'd never get out of bed. Manny shooed them away from the lab part of the room and toward the living room. He combed fingers through his disordered hair and avoided their eyes.

"Um, yeah, sorry, I don't get a lot of—visitors—sit. Sit down." He moved newspapers and piled them on a glass side table, then picked up the remote control and clicked the TV to some high-definition channel doing a travelogue of China. No sound. "So. Um, tell me what you want. Oh, and hi, by the way. I'm Manny."

That last went to Lucia, who was standing, staring in bemusement. Jazz patted the couch. Lucia sank down gracefully, hands in her lap. Studying Manny like a new and alien life-form.

"This is Lucia," Jazz said. "I've got two documents for you, plus envelopes. I want the full ride. Everything you can give me."

Manny couldn't seem to tear his attention away from

Lucia. Apparently, his hormones weren't dead. "Takes time," Manny said.

"I know it does."

"Also, the full ride doesn't come cheap. And hey, I'm only saying that because, you know, I've got to pay for upkeep around here, supplies, stuff…"

Jazz winced inside, but smiled and nodded. "How much?"

"Two documents? Three grand. That includes my time and materials, by the way. Plus, you get to, um, stay here if you want. Wait on the results."

Hotel Manny. He did have a nice place—scrupulously clean—but she could see Lucia was starting to wish she'd crawled under the car to retrieve the gun. "That's a nice gesture, but how about if we come back later? You call me when you're ready with the results?"

"Um…sure." Manny stared at her with his slightly off-kilter eyes. "Jazz?"

"Yeah?"

"Is this about Mac?"

"No. It's not about Mac."

"'Cause you know I'd do it for free if—"

"It's not about Mac. But I'll tell him." Ben McCarthy, she knew, would shake his head and roll his eyes, but he'd appreciate it somewhere deep down. Manny was a twitch, but he was an honest one. In some ways, he was also the bravest guy she'd ever met.

She took the plastic bag out of her jacket and handed over her letter; Lucia did the same. Manny raised the evidence bags, thick eyebrows going up, and stared at Jazz through the plastic. "You're sure it isn't murder or something? 'Cause I'm getting a weird vibe."

"I'm not a cop anymore, you know that."

"Yeah, well…still. It looks hinky, Jazz. There's blood."

"That falls under the heading of bar mayhem, not murder. Two guys tried to start something with me. They'll live."

"But you want DNA profile on the blood, right?"

"I want every scrap of information you can pull off of either one of those, right? Everything."

Manny nodded. "Okay. Everything."

"Got any idea how long…?"

"Twenty-four hours."

"You're not outsourcing, right?"

"Everything gets done here," he said, and gave her an almost charming grin. "Jeez, grow up. Who would I trust?"

It was a really good point. "Call me."

Chapter 3

Lucia kept silent all the way back down the steps. Without being asked, Jazz got on her hands and knees and fished the gun out from under the car.

"Thanks," Lucia said, and returned it to the pancake holster behind her back.

"Yeah, well, you're wearing a nice suit." Jazz shrugged. "I don't figure my jeans will suffer from a little contact with the concrete."

Once they were in the sedan again, the metal door cranked up like a castle gate, allowing them to exit into the bright morning air.

"So what," Lucia asked with absolutely precision, "the hell was *that?*"

"*That* is Manny Glickman." Jazz pretended to concentrate on the flow of commuter traffic, which wasn't too much of a stretch—K.C., like most semilarge cities, was hell in the morning rush hour. She was trying to decide what to share. "Used to be the go-to guy at Quantico for the big cases after the shakeup of the lab, you remember the scandal over the evidence problems—"

Lucia nodded, eyes fixed on the cars around them. Sweeping the street for surveillance.

"Anyway, he went through a bad patch. Started private practice a couple of years ago, after he got out of the hospital. Most of the P.I.s and lawyers use him, or try to, but he won't do any cases with violent crime elements."

"Sounds like he's limiting his business pretty severely."

"Yeah. But he's got money, and he doesn't want to go back into that world." Jazz shrugged. "Doesn't matter. He'll get us what we need. Manny's hell on wheels when it comes to evidence."

Lucia thought about that for a few seconds, and then turned her head to look straight at her. Sunlight flashed between the buildings and painted her skin in strobing flashes of gold. "What happened to him? Really?"

"Really?" Jazz made up her mind in a split second. There were few people she told about Manny—the real story— out of respect for his privacy, but she couldn't start out with lying, not to Lucia. She'd know. "He was buried for almost forty-two hours in a black box eight feet under the ground, with nothing but some oxygen tanks to keep him alive, and a continuous loop recording playing the sound of the killer's previous victim being tortured. That kind of thing will take all the fizz out of a person."

Lucia understood immediately, it was all over her face. A deep, sad appreciation for everything Jazz didn't say about that ordeal. "Did you find him?"

"No," Jazz said softly. "No, I was across town, interrogating the suspect. My partner found the spot. He and two FBI agents dug Manny up."

"My God," Lucia murmured. "Did you know him?"

"Not then. He was a case file shipped down to us. I met him when he woke up in the hospital." She'd never forget that bloodied, dirt-caked figure. Shaking. Weeping. The FBI agents turning away while Ben McCarthy pulled up a chair and took one of those filthy hands, nodding for her to hold the other. Holding Manny in the world.

"It was related to an investigation." Lucia didn't make it a question. "Something Manny was working on."

"Serial killer," Jazz agreed. "Just our blind luck he decided to dump Manny in Kansas City. He was a coast-to-coast, equal-opportunity son of a bitch. We all got lucky. Me, Manny, Ben..."

Lucia didn't ask about Ben. No doubt she knew everything there was to know on that subject already, had made up her mind as to Ben's guilt or innocence.

"Anyway...now Manny's a friend," Jazz finished awkwardly. "And if he's twitchy, well, hell, you'd be twitchy too after that. But he does his best. He gets by."

"And three thousand dollars? You've got that amount of money lying around to pay him?" Lucia wasn't being insulting, just matter-of-fact. She'd done her research, Jazz knew that. Lucia knew her finances, down to the penny that was breathing its last gasp in Jazz's bank account.

"No," Jazz said. "But I'll get it." She sounded confident.

Lucia threw her an interested look but didn't ask.

If there was a tail on them, it was good enough that neither Jazz nor Lucia spotted it. Just in case, Jazz did some acrobatics on the freeway, taking I-435, then I-70 toward St. Louis through Independence before looping back home. "You know, they have to know where you live," Lucia pointed out. "Don't you think this cloak-and-dagger business is a little over the top?"

"No," Jazz said shortly, and felt a blush high in her cheeks. Dammit. Lucia made her feel like some unschooled hick, which she wasn't. She'd been one of the youngest, most highly decorated detectives ever in KCPD. She'd trained with the FBI at Quantico. She wasn't an idiot. Okay, maybe she wasn't up on international terrorism and proper spy etiquette, but dammit, she was *trying*.

Lucia let it go. "Your gas to burn." She shrugged and tapped her fingernails on the window glass. "If your lawyer was sincere, and if these letters mean what they say, what does that tell us? What are we going to do, in that case?" Lucia's dark eyes turned toward her. Jazz didn't take her attention off the road. "Are you tempted to accept?"

"Hell, yes, I'm tempted. That's a hundred grand you're talking about, not to mention the time and resources to devote to clearing my partner's name. And an actual job would be a good thing, for the sake of my apartment rent, not to mention the gas-burning you're so concerned about." Jazz blew out her breath in an irritated sigh. "But you're probably not into this thing, are you?"

"What makes you say that?"

"Oh, come on. You fly in from some supersecret mission looking like you dressed out of a Bond girl's closet. You're so hooked up that you can score a gun without leaving the *airport,* for God's sake. Why would you tie yourself down with a partner? Particularly one that isn't, you know, all spy-worthy?"

Lucia blinked slowly. "When you put it that way," she murmured, "it's a very good question."

"Yeah. Well." Somehow, this didn't feel like a victory.

"You don't know anything about me," the other woman said. "Yes, I have a job. I have a decent wardrobe. I have resources. That doesn't mean—" She shook her head, frowning. "That doesn't mean I'm not trapped, Jazz. Or that I don't want out of the place I'm in."

She didn't say anything else. Unsure how to take it, Jazz didn't push things.

She rolled up to her apartment building, cruising at a normal speed, and said, "See anything interesting?"

"No."

"Yeah, me neither. Don't you think that's interesting, in itself?"

No sounds or movement, all the way to her apartment. Jazz motioned Lucia away and took the lock-and-handle side

of the door. She slotted the key into the dead bolt at arm's
length, staying well out of range if anybody decided to put
a bullet through the door itself.

Nothing. Lucia watched as the door swung open, then
snapped her gun up into an effortlessly graceful firing position and flowed forward, shouldering the door flat against
the wall with a soft bump. The speed with which she checked
and dismissed blind corners was incredible. Jazz shut the
door and dead-bolted it again, then went to the gun safe in
the corner and keyed it open.

The familiar weight of her H & K nine-millimeter pistol felt cool and heavy, weighing her down, grounding her
against that feeling of having been blown off course by the
day's events.

Lucia stopped appraising the room from a tactical point
of view long enough to say, "I like your taste in colors."

"You'd be the only one, then," Jazz smiled. The rug was
olive green, the furniture a throwback to the worst of the
seventies—dull oranges and duller golds, a truly obnoxious
plaid that somehow captured all three colors plus a muddy
brown for variety. She'd finished it off with a kitschy velvet painting of a matador and a print of one of Dali's lesser
works from his conquistador period.

"I was being polite," Lucia said, and ran her fingers over
the gold armchair's back. "Possibly even sarcastic. Tell me
the place came furnished."

"Nope, it's all mine. However, in self-defense, I did have
to match the carpet. This was the best I could manage."

"Plus," Lucia said thoughtfully, "it makes people think you have no sophistication. Which is all part of your persona, isn't it?"

That came as a shock. Not a pleasant one. "What?"

"You, Jazz, are a lie. A subtle one. It probably works very well for you. Under all that ragged hair and frumpy clothes, you're good-looking. You could make this place look sophisticated—you deliberately choose not to. I think you like having people underestimate you."

Jazz blinked, nonplussed. "That's a load of crap."

"Yeah?" Lucia's carefully shaped eyebrows rose and fell. "My specialty is in controlling perceptions. I do it consciously. I have to take command in a psychological way when I enter a situation. I have to make people believe that I'm capable of anything and everything to avoid a fight."

"You don't strike me as the kind to avoid a fight."

"My point exactly," Lucia said, and smiled. "I'm not nearly as strong as you are, Jazz. It's better for me if I can avoid the fight instead of taking things head-on. Not that I can't win if I'm pushed, but I can't do it fairly, like you can. I fight dirty, and I try not to fight at all. Like most women, actually."

Jazz cocked her head, trying to get all that through her head; she knew, intellectually, what Lucia was saying, but she'd grown up fighting just as hard as her brother, and the idea that most women weren't wired that way...it had always thrown her off. She'd blamed it on wussy girl attitudes about not mussing their hair or breaking a nail, but she had to admit, there was nothing wussy about Lucia. And she didn't strike Jazz as somebody who admitted to shortcomings just for the hell of it, either.

"Okay." Jazz shrugged. "So maybe I like to sucker people in. You like to intimidate them into avoiding a fight. We can agree to disagree."

"Actually," Lucia said, and picked up a particularly hideous ceramic bull getting ready to gore a gaudily gilded matador, "looking at this, for the first time, I believe we have something we can use to form a solid partnership."

"Because of my amazingly bad taste?"

"Strengths and weaknesses," Lucia said, and put the bull back in its place. "We complement each other. Also, I like your sense of humor."

"How do you know I have one?"

"The bull." Lucia smiled. "It's anatomically correct."

"You should see the matador in the bedroom."

"It'll be twenty-four hours before Manny gets back to us," Jazz said about a half hour later. "You want to stay?"

Lucia, who was sipping coffee from a plain black mug and watching low-playing CNN on the TV, said, "Why?"

"Why not? I'd say you might have cats to feed back home, but women like you don't have cats," Jazz said, and made kissy noises at Mooch, who was peeking around the corner of the bedroom door. He froze, slitted green eyes wide in his smushed-in fluffy face, and darted back out of sight. "Women like you have, oh, fish. Colorful ones."

"I might be a dog person."

"The only animal you'd keep on a leash is a boyfriend."

Lucia laughed. It had a nice sound, easy and unselfconscious, and Jazz found herself smiling in return. "*Mira,* have you been through my closet? I thought I'd put all the leather away where nobody else could find it."

"Am I right?"

"About the boyfriend?" Lucia still sounded on the verge of laughter.

"About the pets."

She nodded. "Too much trouble. I travel."

"So, you can stay another day."

"Actually, I was thinking that the two of us might want to use the waiting time productively," Lucia said, and finished her coffee in three gulps. "How do you feel about taking a flight this afternoon to New York?"

"To see Borden."

"Yes."

She had to admit, she felt a little tug in her guts at the thought. Good tug? Bad? Not sure. But then she felt a wave of frustration roll over her. "Not possible."

"Why not?"

God, she was going to hate admitting this. "I'm tapped. I've got no cash, and I'm already on the hook with Manny for three grand. I'd better not. You can go on, if you want to, and let me know what you think of the setup."

"I have half a million frequent-flyer miles in my account," Lucia said.

Jazz, openmouthed, just stared at her for so long that she was sure she was starting to look like the hick Lucia made her feel. "Oh," she finally said. "Right. And you'd buy me a ticket with—"

"Yes."

"You're sure?"

Lucia rolled her eyes in exasperation. "I wouldn't have mentioned it if I didn't mean it. Of course I'm sure. Also, the three thousand for Manny? If this works out, you can pay it from the hundred thousand. If not, I'll cover it. Call it an investigative expense. Believe me, I won't miss it."

Mooch abruptly left the shelter of the doorway and stalked over the carpet to stand directly in front of Lucia, tail high, back arched. Staring.

She stared back.

Mooch let out a velvet-soft purr and rubbed his head against her black pant leg, leaving a trail of gray.

"I think he likes you," Jazz said, and grinned at Lucia's expression. "All right. I'll go with you to New York."

Lucia sighed. "First, find me a lint brush."

Lucia left her .22 in the gun safe, along with Jazz's nine-millimeter, and Jazz took about ten minutes to pack. She spent three minutes of that in the bathroom, staring at her reflection, frowning. Maybe Lucia was right. Maybe she'd been deliberately cultivating this unkempt look instead of just failing to spend time and money on something she'd always considered frivolous. And maybe Lucia was right, that it would serve the two of them well to be mismatched.

Maybe.

But she had a sudden impulse to clean herself up a little, for Lawyer Borden. *Stupid. He's not a date, he's a…*a what? A witness? A suspect? Suspected of what, exactly?

It was too complicated and cloudy to work through. She shoved essentials into a ditty bag, hesitated, and fumbled in the surplus-stuff drawer for perfume. People were always giving her perfume, most of it sickly sweet and horrible, and she'd always made a point of keeping herself fragrance-free on assignments. Bad guys had noses, too. You couldn't exactly get away with playing a homeless woman if you reeked of Obsession.

She compromised with two tiny dabs of some red variant of Poison given to her two Christmases ago by Ben… it had a warm feeling to it. Made her feel, well, feminine. She tossed the bottle into the ditty bag and zipped it closed, then added that to the small carry-on bag that held exactly two changes of clothes, both casual. One more than she'd need, but she liked being prepared.

Lucia was examining her CD collection when she came back, ready to depart. She held up one for inspection and said, "I never would have thought you liked Beethoven."

"Hey, I'm down with Metallica, too," Jazz said. "I've got layers. Let's move. We've got two hours before the flight."

Nobody followed them. Nobody Jazz could spot, anyway. Without discussion, Lucia kept scanning crowds once they'd reached the airport, even while giving rote answers to the security questions and submitting to a wand scan and bag search. Jazz was passed through without a second glance. She waited, checking her watch, as Lucia patiently underwent the security process and finally ducked through the crowd to join her. They took off at a jog for the far end of the terminal.

"What was that about?" Jazz asked. Lucia looked at her, unsmiling. There was a glitter in her dark eyes.

"Think about it," she said. "You're blond and pink. I'm not."

"Racial profiling's—"

"Illegal, yes, but you'd be amazed how many random searches I turn up on," Lucia replied. Her voice sounded tight. "I'm lucky I've got federal credentials. As much as I travel, this could get to be a real problem."

The flight was full. The vast majority of travelers were sour-faced businesspeople with more bags under their eyes than in the overhead compartments. She and Lucia had wing seats, midcabin, next to an emergency exit. Jazz didn't think it was luck. Lucia seemed to think about these kinds of things.

They chatted about light stuff during the inevitable delay and the bumpy takeoff...family, to start. Lucia had none to speak of beyond an aunt in Spain who didn't approve of her. They moved on to favorite movies and bad dates. Jazz didn't have a lot to offer on the dating story front, although she was hell on wheels with the movies. She was content to listen to Lucia spinning stories, after a while.

"Chefs are the worst," Lucia was saying, as the plane leveled out its climb for the relatively short arc to New York City. "Never marry a chef."

This was a novel sort of idea. "You're kidding, right? Don't marry a guy who can actually cook?"

"That's their day job. Sure, they *can* cook. And while they're trying to impress you and charm you into bed, it's crème anglaise and shrimp soufflé, but after that, it's all too much work for them. You'll never get anything right, and you can't go out to dinner with them, either. Everything's a review. The soup's too thin, the meat's too tough, the dessert's not served hot enough." She shook her head and flipped pages in the *Cosmo* she'd retrieved from the magazine rack. "And God forbid you shouldn't ever care for something they create. There's less drama on HBO."

"Did you marry him?" Jazz asked.

"Hmm?" Lucia lifted her eyes from contemplation of the Fall Fashion Lineup. "Michel? Oh, no. He would have been a disaster as a husband. He never met a hostess he didn't greet, if you know what I mean." Those dark eyes appraised her for a cop's hard second. "How about you?"

"Hey, I can promise you I never greeted Michel. Hell, I don't even know any man French enough to be named Michel."

"I mean—"

"I'm clear on your meaning," Jazz said. "You're trying to find out if I'm gay."

Lucia blinked. "No… I was actually wondering if you and Ben McCarthy…?"

Sore subject. Jazz swallowed and fixed her gaze on the beverage cart slowly trundling its way down the narrow aisle toward them. She felt like a drink, early morning or not. Maybe she could get away with something disguised as healthy, like a mimosa. "None of your business," she said. It sounded hard and cold.

Lucia stared at her for a long second, then went back to her magazine.

Sex, and Ben McCarthy. Jazz sighed, leaned her head against the backrest and closed her eyes.

Maybe, with the help of the mimosa, she could sleep the rest of the way to the city, without dreams.

JFK felt crowded, breathless and a little grubby. Lucia led Jazz past baggage claim and toward the outside, where New York was having a fabulously—probably unexpectedly—golden day.

She slowed in her stride before they reached the doors.

"What?" Jazz asked. She was already alert, but Lucia's change in body language elevated it a sharp notch to outright paranoia.

Lucia jerked her chin sharply. "Look."

A uniformed chauffeur, cap under his arm, was holding up an erasable board on which were written in block letters the names MS. GARZA/MS. CALLENDER. He was a tall guy, long in the torso and wide in the shoulders, probably pumped under the well-tailored coat. A burr haircut, light blond heading toward gray. Eyes to match. Ex-Marine, Jazz would have said, straight out of Central Casting.

"My ID," he said, and produced a picture ID card with watermarking and some kind of fancy holography on it, with the bold logo of Gabriel, Pike & Laskins, LLP under the lamination. "Can't be too careful these days. May I see yours, please?" He held out his hand. Lucia wordlessly produced her ID. Jazz fumbled hers out a second later, watched him scrutinize the postage-stamp picture and then turn those laser-beam eyes on her. She revised her estimate of his rank upward to drill sergeant. "Nice flight?"

"Fabulous," Lucia said. "I didn't arrange for ground transportation."

The Marine settled the cap back on his head, adjusted it to his exacting specifications and nodded. "No, ma'am. The firm arranged for it." He reached out and took their bags with the proprietary air of a man who never expected to be refused. Jazz let him do it, though her impulse was to stiff-arm him and snarl *Back off* in her most intimidating voice. She restrained it mainly because she knew picking a fight with this man wasn't just stupid, it was damn near suicidal, and besides, he hadn't done anything.

Yet.

She looked over at Lucia, who had a rueful half smile on

her face. "I made an appointment," she said, "with Borden. Apparently, he's a thoughtful guy."

"Apparently," Jazz agreed. They fell in behind the Marine, who marched them through the doors and to a black Town Car idling at the curb with a cop standing guard. The Marine nodded to him as he stowed the bags in the copious trunk, and the cop nodded back, and then they were on the way.

The Marine drove along a scenic route, but Jazz couldn't follow it; she'd never been to New York City before, and the scale of it overwhelmed her. Pictures didn't do it justice, really. Buildings loomed impossibly tall, not just one or two, but dozens, all jammed together. The patch of sky overhead looked pale and on the verge of disappearing altogether.

Lucia had out some kind of computerized personal organizer and was making notes, ignoring the scenery. Jazz doubted it was *her* first trip to the city. She could probably give the Marine helpful tips on shortcuts.

Three traffic jams and one near-crash later, they pulled in at the curb, and the Marine unpacked their gear onto the sidewalk. He touched the brim of his cap and refused Lucia's offer of a tip. "The firm pays me very well," he said, and handed them each a bag. "Forty-fifth floor. Mr. Borden is expecting you."

Jazz craned her head back as the car whispered away from the curb, back into traffic. The building soared in stacked tiers, each one smaller than the last, like some very angular wedding cake. The polished brass number over the revolving doors read 6716, but she had no idea what street they were on.

Lucia was already on the move, shouldering through the rotating glass. Jazz followed.

Beyond, the lobby was small and chilly, with some leather armchairs and throw rugs near one corner and a reception desk all in marble at the other, near a massive elevator bank. Three people were behind the desk. The woman gave them a warm smile. The two security men gave them blank, appraising stares.

"Here to see James Borden at Gabriel, Pike & Laskins," Lucia said. "We have an appointment."

They had to produce ID again, but it was fairly painless, and one of the security guys detailed himself to escort them up. Floor forty-five required a key card. He used his and stood in silence, hands at his sides, watching as the floor count moved in red dots on the readout. Around the thirtieth floor Jazz had to pop her ears. That was the only excitement.

The elevator doors opened onto what surely must have been a lawyerly version of Shangri-la. They stepped out onto a massive marble deck facing a huge bank of floor-to-ceiling windows with a spectacular view of the Manhattan skyline.

"May I help you?"

The voice was, somewhat to Jazz's surprise, a honeyed Southern drawl. Once her eyes got past the shock of the view outside, she focused on the reception desk located over to the side, next to a black wall of stone with a near-silent curtain of water wavering over it. Another perfectly made-

Rachel Caine

up woman, this one deserving the cover of *Elle* at the very least. Brunette, brown eyes, a smile that looked collagen enhanced even if it wasn't.

If Lucia was intimidated by the competition for the I'm-the-Most-Beautiful-Girl-in-the-Room award, she didn't show it; she gave Reception Goddess a warm smile and produced ID for the third time in an hour. Jazz followed suit. "James Borden's expecting us," Jazz added, before Lucia could blurt it out. It felt good to take charge, even in this petty little area.

"Ah," the woman said, and touched buttons on some hidden console behind the marble counter. "He's on his way. Please have a seat."

Jazz eyed the chairs, which looked modern, uncomfortable to sit in and impossible to get out of, and decided to disobey. She paced restlessly, examining bromeliads and exotic flowers. This was the kind of place that had fresh arrangements delivered every day, just for the effect. Lucia settled on a hard-looking couch, looking poised and deadly.

"Jazz?"

She turned at the familiar sound of James Borden's voice, and paused, blinking. If it hadn't been for the voice, and the warmth he put into the sound of her name, she wouldn't have even known him. He was wearing a flawlessly tailored double-breasted blue suit, something with just enough of a sheen to the fabric to make it look rich instead of cheap. A turquoise-blue tie with subtle dark gold flecks. A crisp, blindly white shirt. A single gold stud in his ear, which these days she supposed qualified as corporately daring.

His dark hair was combed down, no longer gelled into spikes, and looked...conservative. A little too long, maybe, but good.

She focused on his dark brown eyes and got a flash of deep-seated warmth, then remembered her manners and stepped forward to take his hand in a firm shake. "Counselor," she said. "Nice suit."

He grimaced. "Yeah, the judges seem to like it. You all right?" He was looking at her too closely, holding her hand a little too long. She didn't know whether it was flattering or insulting.

"Fine," she said, and pulled away. "This is—"

"Lucia Garza," he finished, and did the handshake thing again. Lucia was tall enough to look him in the eye, and her smile was at least twice as winsome as it needed to be. But maybe she was just overpowered by the suit, which Jazz had to admit was pretty damn fine. "I'm glad to meet you."

"We have questions," Lucia said, still with that winsome smile, and no softness at all in her eyes.

"Yes," Borden said, and glanced from her to Jazz. "I figured you might. Please, follow me."

He led them down a shallow flight of stairs through what looked like a meditation garden, with stone benches and mannered vegetation and a Zen sand pool in the center.

They walked along a dark wood corridor, with spotlit portraits of old men and a few old women who must have been former partners of the firm. At about the halfway point, Borden opened up a door with one of those sliding nameplates that read James Borden, Esq. Inside, a perky young woman in a short red suit was bustling around a hissing espresso machine. She had pixie-cut dark hair and a gap in her two front teeth, which made her look like a cheerful urchin for all her polish and gloss.

"Pansy..."

"Coffee, boss, yeah, I'm all over it," she said, and waved a hand at the machine. He gave her a thumbs-up and opened the inner office door.

Standard lawyer office, straight off of a movie set. A massive dark desk, a green-shaded banker's lamp, executive pen-and-pencil set, framed diplomas on the wall. Law books, ranked according to color and size. Two visitor chairs, big and leather in a manly dark green. Jazz sat at Borden's gesture and noted that Lucia settled comfortably, legs crossed, chin down as she watched Borden move around the room. Jazz, as usual, was antsy. She wanted to pace, but she controlled the impulse to a light tap of her fingers against her leg.

Borden perched on the corner of the desk, not behind it. "Sorry you came all this way," he said. "There's nothing I couldn't tell you over the phone just as easily."

"I like to do my deals face-to-face. Less chance of... misunderstandings," Lucia said pleasantly, as if she hadn't just implied, oh, a world of things. "Nice offices. Criminal practice?"

"Not really. We have two criminal attorneys on staff, and one's a full partner, but we specialize in tax and corporate law," Borden said. "I've never taken on a criminal case in my life." He made it sound like a failing. "Not really cut out for it."

"No?" Lucia let her head fall to one side, watching him. "Why not?"

"If you want to practice criminal law, you end up spending a lot of time with criminals," Borden said, and shrugged. "Not really my thing."

"I'm sure associating with corporate polluters and tax dodgers is much better," Lucia agreed. "How did you get my résumé, Mr. Borden?"

"James," he said, and flicked his eyes toward the door as it opened. "Coffee?"

The assistant—Pansy? Did anybody really name girls Pansy anymore?—entered burdened by a black lacquer tray, and passed out delicate little cups of espresso. Jazz sipped and thought her veins would explode. The stuff was like black oil. She knew she was making bitter-coffee face and set the saucer and cup aside on a small octagonal table. Borden didn't even try to drink his.

"I repeat the question," Lucia said once Pansy had withdrawn. "My résumé. How did you get it?"

"It was provided to me," Borden said, and held up a hand to stop her from going on. "I can't tell you, Ms. Garza. I'm sorry. If I had to guess, I'd say that it was passed along from within the FBI, but that's just a guess."

"You use information without knowing its source?"

Borden sent Jazz a look. Not quite a plea, more of an assessment, trying to see where she stood in all this. "I trust the source. He's very reliable."

Lucia's eyebrows indicated sarcastic doubt. Jazz drummed her fingers on leather, and said, "Yeah, okay, fine. You got the résumé from a file clerk at Quantico. Let's talk about this deal you're offering."

Borden straightened up and met her eyes again. "It's simple enough. The initial funding, plus we pay five thousand per case you take for us. Do you want to review the partnership agreement?"

"No, I want you to explain to me whose money is funding this," she said. "Or there's no deal."

Borden let several dry ticks of his mantel clock go by, then slid off the edge of his desk and went behind it to open a drawer. "You know the check is valid," he said. "You verified that with the bank."

"Yeah, I did. I know it's drawn on your corporate account. I also know that no law firm in the world fronts money for its clients without a damn good reason. You specialize in tax cases, right? Trying to hide some money the feds want to confiscate? This is all some bullshit designed to get the two of us to take the heat as accessories. Somebody wants us brought down."

Lucia flicked her an unreadable look. Borden let out a slow, aggrieved breath. "Look, I'm not saying nobody's out to get you. I'm sure that between the two of you, you might have charmed your way into a few…trouble spots. But this is a legitimate deal, offered legitimately. I'm an attorney. Believe it or not, I take my fiduciary responsibilities seriously."

Lucia's mock surprise was really too funny. "An honest lawyer? Now you really *are* making me suspicious, Mr. Borden."

He looked from one of them to the other, brown eyes bright. "You two really were separated at birth, did you know that?" Borden reached into the drawer, pulled out a thick manila folder and slid it across the highly polished surface. He had lovely long fingers, Jazz noticed against her will. Well manicured. No wedding ring, and no sign there'd ever been one.

"I'll leave you to look it over," he said. "I've got a meeting down the hall. Back in about thirty minutes. Oh, don't try to walk out with any loose change or files or anything, Pansy's tougher than she looks."

He left them without a backward glance. Jazz knew her eyebrows were soaring, and her lips compressed against a laugh. She caught the same glitter in Lucia's eyes.

"Well," Lucia said in the silence after the door had clicked shut, "he's not what I expected."

"Taller?"

"Smarter." She edged her chair closer to the desk and reached for the folder. "Oddly, that does not make me feel better about this."

The folder contained loads of legal paperwork about the

partnership. Jazz blurred out after a couple of pages, but she was pretty expert in shaking wheat from chaff, when it came to legal papers, and flipped through the thick sheaf until she found what she was looking for.

"Looks like the money's coming from a nonprofit organization called the Cross Society," she said, and scooted over to give Lucia a lean-in on it.

"A religious thing?" Lucia hooked silky black hair back over her ear.

"Um...no idea, actually. Why. Are you a zealot?"

"I'm religious, I'm not actually militant." Lucia shrugged. "You?"

"Define religious."

Lucia gave her a warm, quick smile. "And that answers my question. So, what do we know about them?"

"Not a damn thing." Jazz flipped through the rest of the paperwork. "Address is care of the law firm. I don't see anything else to go on."

"Ah." Lucia nodded, and went around Borden's desk to test the drawers. Locked. She reached into her neat little designer purse, came out with lock picks in a zippered leather case, and set to work. It took her about ten seconds flat to open up the file drawer and start flipping through. "Hmm, he works for some interesting people—do you want to know about Donald Trump?—never mind, here it is. The Cross Society."

She pulled out a fairly massive-looking folder and spread it open on the blotter, on top of the partnership paperwork.

Jazz came around to take a look as Lucia's elegant fingers fluttered pages.

"Here. Not religious, apparently. The Cross Society is a nonprofit organization established seven years ago with a mandate to research time, physics and causality."

"What the hell is causality?" Jazz asked.

"I was hoping you'd tell me. They seem to have given out quite a load of grants and loans over the past couple of years. Take a look at the list. Anything look familiar to you?"

"Nope, but I'll bet if we did an Internet search, we'd turn up with science stuff."

"Not all of them," Lucia murmured, and ran her finger down the list to stop on one name. Gregory Valentin Ivanovich. "I know this one. Definitely not a scientist."

"Who is he?"

"Spy," she said absently. "Once upon a time. He's in security these days. Or that's the euphemism for it. Actually, I think he more or less works for the highest bidder.... What would you say, there must be a few thousand names listed here, right?"

Jazz felt her eyebrows quirk again. "Seems to be a lot. This Ivanovich guy...you know him from business or pleasure?"

"Both," Lucia said, and ran her fingertip over the name again, as if it was a bar code she could scan. "Although you mix those together often enough you get something that doesn't fit the definition of either. Anyway, Gregory isn't a scientist by any stretch of the imagination."

"Neither are we," Jazz pointed out, and pointed at the footnote on the page.

Offers extended to Jasmine Evelyn Callender and Lucia Imelda Losano Garza on March 23...

"Interesting."

"Yeah, no kidding. I'd call it more like shocking. *Imelda?*"

"Shut up, *Evelyn.*"

"If they're researching egghead stuff, why do they need spies, cops and whatever the hell you are, anyway?" Jazz asked, and tapped the paper nervously.

Lucia said, "Let's find out," and flipped through the files again.

"What are you looking for?"

"I don't know. Anything out of the ordinary, I suppose." She flicked the tabs, reading names. "Active cases. Mr. Borden's a busy young man. He's defending an insurance company against a class-action suit on denial of claims... a tobacco company...some rich billionaire with tax problems—*not* The Donald..."

She paused, backed up, and eased a file out of the middle of the drawer.

"What?" Jazz asked.

"Eidolon Corporation."

"Never heard of it."

"I have." Lucia kept staring at the file folder. She pulled it out and opened it on the desk, flipping pages.

"Well?" Jazz prodded.

"I know the name. I just can't remember—" Lucia shook

her head and looped silky dark hair behind her ear as she bent over the folder. "This is nothing. Tax accounting on assets, standard corporate stuff. But I know this name, I know I do."

They were interrupted by the sound of the door opening. In retrospect, Jazz supposed it would have been a good idea to keep an eye out, even though Borden had said he wouldn't be back for thirty minutes. Rookie mistake. She controlled the impulse to sweep the folders off the desk and looked at Lucia, who was looking utterly cool and composed and not at all tempted to try to hide what she was doing.

Must have been a spy thing.

"Ah. Eidolon Corporation." The voice had a hoarse edge that came from a lifetime of close acquaintance with cigarettes or, Jazz amended, maybe Havana cigars. The old man standing framed in the doorway—short, neat, white-haired, with electric blue eyes—looked as if he'd never stoop to anything so pedestrian as cigarettes. Old money. Polish and style and sophistication. His immaculate tailoring made Lucia look dowdy. "I thought you might recognize it. You have an excellent memory, Agent Garza. That's one of the reasons you came so highly recommended to us."

Lucia said nothing. She met the newcomer's stare squarely, chin firm, eyes bright. He came forward and put his hand on the back of Jazz's chair, and turned his attention to her for a few seconds. "Miss Callender," he said, and nodded down at her. His eyes were Paul Newman blue, and they looked as if they might require a separate power source. Maybe he recharged them at night, along with his cell phone. "My name is Milo Laskins. I am a senior partner with the firm, and Mr. Borden's immediate superior. You may address any questions you have about the agreement to me, as Mr. Borden has been temporarily detained." He nodded toward the file still sitting on the desk under Lucia's hand. "Although I see your research is going quite well without me."

"Are you expecting me to apologize?" she asked.

"Hardly. But I do expect you to abandon the attempt to rifle through the firm's confidential records, if for nothing else than simple courtesy." Laskins took the desk chair and looked at Lucia expectantly. She shrugged, slotted the files back in place and closed the drawer. "And if you wouldn't mind locking it...?"

She took out the lock picks again and turned tumblers, then came over and sat in the visitor chair again, legs crossed. Jazz met her eyes for a brief second, and was surprised at the strength of communication between them. *Careful,* Lucia was warning her, which was the same that she was broadcasting.

"Tell me about Eidolon and how it connects to this Cross Society," Lucia said. "You know that if I have five minutes and an Internet connection, I'll find out everything I need to know anyway."

"True," Laskins said, and shot his cuffs and inspected his cuff links, which were gold and looked expensive. Like the suit. "Eidolon Corporation," he said. "I'm sure what you're remembering is the scandal some years ago in which the company's chief executive officer was convicted of murder."

Jazz felt an unexpected jolt, and connections fired in her brain. "Wait, I remember. Max Simms," she said. "Serial killer."

"Alleged," Laskins said, and those Paul Newman eyes laser-beamed her.

"Convicted," Jazz shot back.

"Not everyone believes he was guilty."

"Sure, conspiracy theorists who also believe that OJ was framed and Elvis is running a bed-and-breakfast in the Blue Ridge Mountains. And those bodies in Max Simms's basement…? Wait, let me guess—people broke into his mansion, tumbled down the stairs and buried themselves in the mud. Oh, and then mixed concrete and covered themselves. I've heard of guests not wanting to leave, but that's pretty ridiculous." Jazz remembered the case vividly. She remembered the forensic investigators and detectives climbing out of the crawl space wearing gas masks, looking sick and exhausted. It had made quite an impression.

Laskins was silent a moment, then turned back to Lucia. "You asked about Eidolon. That's the only event worthy of note. Apart from that event, Eidolon has been a solid corporate citizen, employing thousands of people in dozens of locations around the country."

"You haven't answered the question," Lucia said coolly. "How does Eidolon relate to the Cross Society?"

Laskins's white eyebrows notched upward a bare degree. "It contains some board members who are, shall we say, alumni of that firm. However, you needn't worry. Max Simms no longer has the legal standing to associate himself with any organization, nonprofit or otherwise." He had a self-satisfied smile. Jazz wasn't sure she approved of it. "Apart from seeing a complete roster of our clients, what can I do to set your mind at ease about the offer we've extended? I understand it's unusual—"

"Unusual?" Jazz interrupted. "Try crazy. You want to give us money for no good reason? You don't even know us. And how exactly do we fit in with a bunch of scientists and spies, anyway? What makes us a good investment for their money?"

The door opened again. She expected Pansy, but instead, it was Lawyer Borden, strolling in with a chunky-looking coffee mug in his hand. He passed it over to Laskins, who accepted it with a nod. Casual. It almost hid the tension in his shoulders and back.

"Everything okay?" Borden asked without looking at Laskins. He was watching Jazz. She felt a touch of heat in her cheeks. "Enjoying the guided tour of my drawers?"

They'd been monitored. No getting around it. She couldn't believe Lucia hadn't picked it up…and then she wondered if Lucia had, and simply hadn't cared. She wasn't sure which one was more unsettling.

"It's not been very enlightening," she said. "Okay, give. What's the catch? You give us money, we open a detective firm. Presuming we're willing to do that, I'm supposing that the Cross Society isn't in this to perform a public service or they'd give it to the homeless shelter down the block, right? So what's their angle?"

Laskins and Borden exchanged a look. Laskins sipped coffee.

"I cannot answer for the society," Laskins said. "It would be a conflict of interest."

"Right. Whatever." Jazz rolled her eyes. "I'm thinking you have about ten seconds to start making sense, or the two of us walk out of here, tear up your check and go about our lives. Poorer and sadder, maybe, but—"

"We'd send you cases," Borden said. "Not many, maybe one a month, if that. Nothing big, for the most part. Escort duty, stakeouts, surveillance."

"I knew it," Lucia said, and stood up. "You're trying to set us up for something illegal."

"No, I promise, it's nothing like that. We're not in that business, and neither is the Cross Society." Borden spread his hands. Jazz's eyes followed the sweep of those long, elegant fingers, then snapped back to his face. "You'd be paid for each case. Regular billing rates. The only thing is that we'd expect our designated cases to take priority."

It sounded reasonable. Surprisingly reasonable. Jazz glanced at Lucia and experienced that surge of communication again.

"In writing," Lucia said. "No offense, but your word of honor is meaningless if we don't know you. Also, we'd need to talk to these people at the Society."

"That won't be possible," Borden said. "Before you get upset about it, there's nothing mysterious going on, it's just that most of the members travel extensively. Our word is binding to them. We have their power of attorney."

"How do we know they even exist?" Jazz asked. "Maybe you guys are the Cross Society. Maybe this is just a way for you to funnel drug money through the system."

"If so, it's an extraordinarily stupid way to go about it," Laskins said waspishly, and frowned at Borden. "Can you handle this on your own? I really should be attending the meeting with Richmond and Fieles. God only knows what they'll bargain away if they're not supervised."

"Yes, sir." Borden nodded. "I can handle it."

Laskins gave him a cynical twist of his lips that was not exactly a smile. "I'll hold you to that, my boy." He put the mug of coffee aside and left without another word.

Borden opened up the folder—the one containing the partnership paperwork—and handed Jazz and Lucia each a bound copy of what must have been a hundred pages of legalese.

"Let's go through it step-by-step," he said.

Jazz looked at the pound of paperwork and sighed.

"Maybe I'll have that espresso after all," she said.

Chapter 4

Two hours later, they had a catered lunch in a quiet, cave-like boardroom, with indirect lighting and a silently playing plasma-screen TV showing the latest disaster footage on one of the news channels. Just her, Lucia and Borden; Counselor Laskins hadn't returned from his other meeting, thank God, so they were able to order sandwiches instead of some impress-the-boss spread. Jazz stuck to tuna fish and low-fat chips. Lucia did her one better with a salad, dry, which Jazz guessed was what it took to maintain that statuesque perfect shape.

She had a cookie in retaliation.

Borden sat next to her, still thumbing through the paper-work as he gobbled down a roast beef on wheat, dripping with mayo. "Not that I want to rush you," he said, "but my boss is bound to bring up the fact that I'm burning billable hours waiting for you to make up your minds. Any decision yet?"

Lucia had her copy of the partnership agreement in front of her, and she flipped pages and scratched notes on a legal pad as she speared lettuce. "No."

"Afraid not," Jazz said. She had another mouthful of tuna salad, which was excellent, packed with walnuts and celery and some kind of lemon spice. "We're going to need time."

"How much?"

"We're not signing anything today," Lucia said. "We have to get back later this afternoon, we'll be in touch. You understand, we have to be sure about this."

"I'd never advise you to sign anything you weren't sure about. Still, we do have some cases coming up, and we'd like to have you on them."

"Very flattering," Jazz said, "but I'm not sure you're going to get us. Yet."

She got a full-on stare from his brown eyes, and remembered how he'd been in the bar—off base, off balance, awkward. Out of his element but determined enough to tough it out. She'd liked that Borden. This one—slick, sophisticated and in control—was less easy to trust.

"Your choice," he said neutrally. "But just remember, I picked out the cookies personally."

Lucia snorted.

Jazz took a second one and ate it contemplatively, watching him.

He suddenly rolled his leather chair back and said, "Jazz, can I have a minute? Just one minute."

She looked at Lucia, who raised her eyebrows in an eloquent *whatever*. Jazz stood up and fisted her hands in her jacket pockets. "Sure, Counselor."

He led her out into the hallway. Instead of turning toward his office, which was two doors down, he took her to the right, to the big indoor garden with its quietly tinkling fountain and elaborately raked Zen sand. He walked her down the path to a blind corner shielded by a broad-leafed palm. There was a stone bench, but he made no move to sit down. He was staring at the tops of his shoes.

"Well?" she asked finally. "Nice plants. What else?"

"I know you don't trust us," he said. He didn't seem to know what to do with his hands, and the awkwardness made her remember how he'd been back in K.C., at the bar. Standing up to two men when it was a foregone conclusion he was in for an ass-kicking. For a lawyer, he sure didn't lack spine. "But…please believe me when I say that you need to try to believe me. Things are coming. Bad things. And I don't want you to get hurt."

She felt a sudden chill and stepped closer, trying to get his eyes. He avoided her. "Borden?"

"Look, I can't tell you anything. But things are going to happen, and I'd rather you were inside than out. Right? For your sake as well as ours."

"Are you trying to threaten me?"

That got her a stare, a big wide one, shocked. "No! Of course not. Besides…hell, I've seen you kick ass, Jazz. Threatening you is the last thing on my mind, believe me. I'm just…worried."

"What have you heard?"

"That there were men after you in the airport," he said. "Jazz, you were in danger from the minute I walked into that bar and handed you that envelope, just like Lucia was in danger the moment hers was delivered. I wish I could make this easy for you. I can't. It isn't just…money and opportunity. This is about something else."

The Cross Society. And Eidolon Corporation?

"About what?" she asked, instinctively. Keeping her voice down. He was almost whispering. "Borden? About what?"

"Time," he said. "We're almost out of it."

He was wearing the same aftershave as he had at the bar, she realized suddenly. It radiated off him in warm waves, and she had to fight an impulse to breathe in deeply. She'd stepped closer again without realizing it. Inches from him. He was stooped, looking down into her eyes. She'd always considered herself pretty stocky, but he made her feel delicate, somehow.

She felt his fingers brush hers, then slowly enfold her hand in warmth.

"Watch yourself," he said softly. "Even if you don't do this thing, you need to be careful. You're on their radar now."

"They, who?"

He shook his head but never looked away from her face. The gaze was getting deeper. More intense. She felt her breath coming faster and struggled to slow it down. Warmth was creeping up her arm, and her hand felt unnaturally sensitized, as if she could feel every whorl in his fingerprints on her skin.

"Counselor," she said slowly, "are you trying to come on to me?"

That got a sudden, brilliant grin. "Why, would it work?"

"I don't do lawyers."

"We're even. I don't do cops."

"Ex-cop."

"Too bad I'm a current lawyer."

"So where does that leave us?"

He didn't answer. Silence fell, deep as the Zen pool. Mist drifted through the garden and brushed the back of her neck with damp fingers, and she shivered.

"Nowhere," she finally murmured, and pulled away. He let her do it without a fight. "Also? One more thing. If I find out you're behind those assholes at the airport, your ass is mine."

She was executing a perfect Hollywood exit when he murmured plaintively, "But that was my *plan!* The ass thing, not the other part."

She didn't give him the satisfaction of turning around. She walked away down the stone path, back to the conference room. Lucia was finishing her salad.

Jazz picked up her purse and the partnership agreement, and said, "I need some air."

Lucia neatly speared the last cherry tomato, forked it into her mouth, and nodded. "Time to go, anyway. I expect we've worn out our welcome."

Borden, still standing in the garden, nodded to them as they left, but never said another word. Jazz wasn't sure whether to be angry or hurt by that, but really, when it came down to it, there was only one logical choice.

Anger at least kept you sharp.

"Well?"

They were somewhere over Illinois, heading toward Missouri, when Lucia asked the single-word question. Jazz, who'd been drifting steadily toward nap land, came awake with a hard jolt. The drone of the airplane filled her ears, and she glanced out the window to make sure they were still flying, not falling. So far, so good.

Lucia was nursing a drink. It fizzed, so it was probably sparkling water, something suave and European. Jazz flagged down the flight attendant and got a Sprite, which she figured was the Americanized version.

"Am I in favor?" Jazz asked. Lucia inclined her head. "Honestly? I don't know. But, presuming it checks out..."

"And if your friend Manny doesn't turn up anything unusual..."

"Then I'd say maybe we should seriously consider it." The money. The thought of that crisp, cashable check in her wallet made Jazz's mouth go dry.

Lucia closed the partnership agreement and stared down at the cover, which was embossed with the logo of Gabriel, Pike & Laskins, LLP. She rubbed a finger over it, silently, and then nodded. Just a bare inch of agreement. "Maybe," she said. "Where would we have the office?"

"What?"

"The office," Lucia repeated. "Garza & Callender Investigations. Where do we hang the shingle?"

Against all reason, Jazz found herself grinning. "K.C.'s a nice town," she said.

"Yeah, it's not bad."

"But it'd be Callender & Garza. Alphabetical order."

"Age before beauty."

"Pearls before—"

"Oh, I wouldn't if I were you." Lucia took a sip of her water. The flight attendant arrived with a small plastic cup of fizzing Sprite on the rocks, and passed it across to Jazz.

They looked at each other mutely for a few seconds, and then Jazz held up the Sprite. Lucia held up the sparkling water.

They clinked plastic.

"Deal," Lucia said.

"*If* there's nothing hinky that turns up."

"Obviously. Goes without saying."

The Sprite tasted cool and refreshing, like champagne. *That's it,* Jazz thought with a sudden surge of mingled dread and euphoria, as the plane started its descent for Kansas City. *Something just changed.*

She hoped it was for the better.

Two independent attorneys had reviewed and signed off on the partnership agreement—and one of them called it a "work of art"—by the time Manny got back to them with the forensic results. "I was thorough," he explained to Jazz on the cell phone. "I got nothing off the letter."

"Nothing?" she repeated, startled. She was standing in the lobby of the second law firm, one selected at random from the phone book, and Lucia was in the restroom. The partnership agreement, well thumbed, was lying in front of her on the coffee table, decorated with grubby yellow sticky notes. "What do you mean, nothing?"

"Well, I mean that the paper's consistent with the official letterhead of Gabriel, Pike & Laskins—I had their nice receptionist courier me some pieces—and the fingerprints on the paper are yours, one James R. Borden, and a woman named Pansy Taylor, who is his—"

"Assistant, yeah, I've met her."

"She's really named Pansy?"

"Apparently. What else?"

Manny shuffled papers noisily on the other end of the phone. She checked the number he was calling from, and saw a caller-ID-blocked message. He was probably phoning from the lab, but with Manny, you could never tell. Even with all of the delicate equipment and lush lifestyle, he'd been known to pull up stakes and move in less than a day. *All it takes is money,* he'd told her once, with a shrug. She supposed that was true.

"The blood on the note? A positive. Not your type."

I don't know about that, she thought, and suppressed it. "Borden's," she said. "Did you do a DNA test?"

"You said the full ride, Jazz. Yes. DNA profile. I don't

know what good it will do you, but it's here. You'll be pleased to know he's not your long-lost brother or anything."

She was, actually. "So there's nothing you can tell me about this letter? Nothing hinky?"

"Hinky?" Manny was silent for a few seconds. "No. Not about the letter."

"But…?"

"It's the envelope."

The big red Valentine's Day envelope. "What about it?"

"Two sets of fingerprints on the envelope, besides yours and Borden's. Not Pansy Taylor's."

Jazz tried to remember if either of the truckers had touched it. No, she was pretty sure they hadn't. "Get any hits?"

"Actually, yeah," he said. "One of the sets belongs to a guy named Bernard Lozano, he was sent up for assault ten years ago, but he's been out a couple of years now. I didn't get anything off of the other set."

Maybe the trucker twins had touched the envelope, after all. The name Lozano wasn't ringing any bells with her. "Okay. Anything else?"

"Ink, paper, blood. That's all you gave me, Jazz. Not a lot to work with here."

"I get it, Manny. Thanks."

He grunted. "You'll get the bill. Oh, and don't come by for a while. I don't like the company."

"Manny!"

"Not you, Jazz. The other guys."

She felt a sudden chill and clutched the phone tighter. "What other guys?"

"The ones who pulled up in a van and sat surveillance outside my building for two hours after you left," Manny said. "I had to move. New address is in the usual place."

He dead-dropped his address and phone numbers into a post office box when he got paranoid. Jazz had been through it before. "I'll pick them up once I'm sure I'm not being tailed."

"I thought you were sure the last time."

I was. She didn't tell him that. "Sorry, Manny."

"Yeah, well, there's a bump in your bill for it." He hesitated. Static crackled the phone. "The other woman? The one you brought here?"

"Lucia?" Who was, as it happened, coming out of the bathroom and heading her way.

"I liked her," Manny said. "She can come around if she wants."

He hung up before she could say another word. She blurted, "You're kidding me!" but it was lost to the ether.

"What?" Lucia asked, sinking down to the couch beside her.

"Manny likes you," Jazz said. "You have no idea how deeply weird that is."

Lucia smiled and shrugged. "People like me. It's a gift."

"Manny's got nothing hinky, except two sets of prints, one belonging to one Bernard Lozano, ex-con, on the outside of the envelope."

"And the letter?"

"Clean. I've also asked him to look into the Cross Society, but it'll take time."

Lucia hitched her shoulders wordlessly. She tapped the partnership agreement with one high-gloss fingernail. For someone who'd been living out of a very small suitcase for two days, she looked fresh from the showroom. Jazz, who'd had access to everything in her own apartment, hadn't managed to achieve much more than comfortable and awake. *I need a haircut,* she thought, swiping the shag out of her eyes again. Lucia's hair always stayed where it was told. But then it was that glossy, silky black, and Jazz's was coarse and blond and not very damn cooperative, in general.

She was thinking of these things to avoid the next step, she realized. Lucia was watching her.

"Look," Jazz said, "I'm not going to lie to you. I need the money. I need it to pay for Ben's appeal. I want to sign this thing."

"Jazz, I'm not judging you. But these people know you need the money. It's a lever."

"And you don't need it, do you?"

Lucia shook her head. "That's not what they're offering me."

"Then what?"

"Independence."

Jazz had had a bellyful of that. "It's not all it's cracked up to be."

"It is when you've spent half your life trusting your life

to pinheads who have no idea how to plan their way out of their offices," Lucia replied, grim lines around her eyes and mouth. "I don't mind fighting for the right things. I mind being wasted. I want to set my own priorities for a change."

There was a passion behind the words that surprised Jazz. A frustration carefully hidden behind Lucia's glossy, composed surface. She met the other woman's dark eyes and saw an absolute fury there, quickly damped down.

"Lucia, we either do this thing or we don't. I don't have a lot of time to burn." She was thinking about Ben, sitting in a cell, waiting. When she'd seen him last, he'd been quiet and guarded, but she'd seen the bruises. A cop in general population. He was a target, and there was no question that his enemies would get him. Ben was tough, but he wasn't a superman, and even the tough had to sleep. "I need this."

Lucia took a breath deep enough to stretch the pin-striped tailored jacket she was wearing. "I'm sorry." There was a cold, hard light in her eyes. "I know you do. But I've been thinking about it, and it just doesn't feel right. I did some checking on the Cross Society. You know who first established it? Max Simms."

"Simms? The serial killer?"

"When he was the head of Eidolon Corporation, he formed the Cross Society as a nonprofit. He was head of it for a year before they started digging up bodies in his basement. The only thing that saved the society from going down the toilet was that he kept his involvement with them strictly low-profile, and somebody else stepped in to run it when he was shipped off to prison. Although my informant says that Simms was mostly a figurehead, anyway. The Cross Society was just a way to funnel money out of Eidolon. Apparently, Simms wasn't getting along with his board of directors."

Jazz looked her right in the eyes. "Then this isn't going to happen," she said.

"No," Lucia agreed. "It isn't going to happen. I'm sorry. I know you wanted it. I wanted it, too. But not if it tangles us up with people like Max Simms."

Jazz felt it all turn to ash, all the hope she hadn't even realized she'd been nursing. She'd schooled herself not to feel, not to care, and she'd been suckered in this time, and it damn well *hurt*. She stared mutely at Lucia, who stood up, retrieved her designer purse, and said, "Can you take me to the airport?"

Jazz nodded silently. She gathered up the partnership agreement, rolled it up and stuffed it into her coat pocket.

That was it. Game over.

Borden was going to be very disappointed.

Jazz kept her head down, thinking, all the way down in the elevator to the parking level. Lucia didn't speak, either. There was an awkward silence between them, and they couldn't meet each other's eyes.

It was a relief when the bell dinged to announce Parking Level 2, and they could escape from being too close. Jazz put several feet between them as they headed for her car, two rows down.

"I'm sorry, Jazz. I like you. I'd like to work with you someday," Lucia said. It was quiet, almost lost in the squeal of tires of a car pulling out of its space down the row. Headlights washed over them, turning Lucia's rich golden skin pale, pulling diamond glints from her earrings, and since Jazz was watching her, she saw the other woman's eyes suddenly shift to focus behind her.

She knew that look. She felt it in a swift, hot prickle down her spine, and she was diving forward even before Lucia yelled "Gun!" and lunged for the cover of a pillar. Jazz hit the ground hard and rolled, feeling the bite of rough concrete on exposed skin; she banged up hard against the massive tire of an oversize SUV and rolled on her side, fumbling for her gun.

A spray of noise, and sparks off the concrete next to her. She yelped, twisted and aimed for muzzle flashes. They were coming from the window of a slow-moving car, a black Lincoln with tinted windows. Everything was moving in snapshots, freeze-frames divided by the rapid gasps of her breath. More muzzle flashes, and bullets peppered the ground and the cars and the pillar behind which Lucia had taken shelter. Four rapid sharp *pops,* and she saw gray-rimmed holes appear in the passenger-side door. Lucia was firing. Jazz steadied her hand and squeezed off six shots. Every one of them went through the open window. She couldn't tell if she hit anyone.

The gun—a Mac 10—disappeared back inside the window, and the car became a blur as it accelerated away. She focused on the license plate, but it was smeared, too, oddly indistinct. Tape? Some kind of disguise. They'd probably stop and peel it off later.

And then it rounded the corner with a screech, struck sparks as it hit the ramp going up, and was gone.

Smoke hung heavy in the air, acrid, burning Jazz's eyes as she blinked and coughed. *Well, it's certainly one of the fastest firefights I've ever been in.*

She focused on the glittering cascade of castoff on the ground. There must have been fifty shells, maybe more. Some were still rolling. The whole garage reverberated with the sounds of war.

"Shit!" Lucia was suddenly beside her, pale and furious, black eyes wide. She was staring at the ramp, and the gun was still in her hand. Tiny little thing. Ladylike.

"You need a bigger gun," Jazz said, and laughed. It didn't sound right. Lucia looked down at her, and stopped breathing. "What?"

Lucia went down on one knee, never mind the expensive pantsuit, and put the gun on the ground to flip Jazz over on her back. "Hey!" Jazz protested, but everything felt odd, didn't it? Strange and liquid and...

Lucia pressed both hands to her side, pushing so hard Jazz couldn't breathe.

"You're going to be all right," Lucia said. "Jazz. You're going to be all right."

Oh, shit, Jazz thought numbly, and saw the blood flooding over Lucia's hands.

She fumbled in her coat pocket, got her cell phone, and dialed 911 to report her own shooting.

Lucia was right, although Jazz didn't think it had been an actual diagnosis. Sometimes optimism worked out. The bullet had passed through her side and caught a few minor blood vessels, missed her liver and kidneys, and come out the other side. The doctor—way too young to be a surgeon, in Jazz's painkiller-altered opinion—was cheerful about it. "Seen lots worse," he told her, patting her hand. "I have three guys downstairs who had an argument in a bar who wish they were you, I promise."

"How long am I going to be stuck here?" she asked. She hated hospitals. Hated the stiff, starchy sheets, the smell of disinfectant, the clean doctors. Hated the idea that she was lying in a bed that had probably seen more dead people than that kid in *The Sixth Sense*. Emergency rooms always smelled like blood and vomit, no matter how carefully they were scrubbed. "If I'm all stitched up…" She eased a leg over the side of the bed. And almost passed out. *Ow.* He grabbed it and moved it back.

"You're here overnight," he said. "And there are some police who want to talk to you. They're already talking to your friend."

Jazz had figured that. She could safely guess that what Lucia was saying was the truth, just not the whole truth. The two of them had been to the lawyers' offices to consult about a partnership agreement. They'd been jumped by persons unknown. Case closed. Jazz figured she could leverage being shot to keep her statement short and sweet. If she had any luck at all, maybe she wouldn't know the cops, and this would be…

Behind the doctor, the big wood door eased open, and a slightly built guy in a cheap suit looked in. He had rough-cut spiked hair and cold dark blue eyes and a rubbery mouth that looked as if it might smile or smirk or scream at a moment's notice.

He looked at her as if she might be a corpse ready for autopsy, nothing but clinical interest.

Apparently, luck was not on her side. God, she really didn't feel well enough for this.

"Stewart," she said with a noticeable lack of warmth. He blinked at her. "You going to skulk or come in?"

"Skulk," he said. "How you doin', Jazz?" He had a Bronx accent, usually stressed for effect, and she felt a familiar weary surge of dislike. *Poser.* She'd known him for nearly five years, and she'd never liked him one minute of that time.

"Shot," she replied shortly.

"Yeah, so I hear. Doc, can I…?" He gestured from himself to Jazz. The doctor shrugged, stuck his hands in his lab-coat pockets and sauntered out. Stewart—Kenneth Stewart, not that she'd ever called him by his first name or ever intended to—pulled up a chrome-and-plastic chair next to her bed and sat down. He poked the IV bag with a fingertip and didn't look at her as he said, "So. Long time no see."

"Yeah." She didn't want small talk. Her head hurt, and her side was starting to really ache. She suspected the painkillers were more Motrin than morphine. "You already talked to my friend?" She didn't give him the name. If Lucia wanted to go undercover, she wasn't about to blow it for her.

"Friend?" he repeated blankly. Poked the IV bag again, then rang a fingernail off the screen of the heart monitor. "Oh, yeah. Luz something. Hermann's talking to her. Pretty girl. I think I got the short straw."

"Me, too." Not that Stewart's partner Hermann was any great prize, either. "I want another detective. I'm not talking to you."

"Fuck you, Callender." It wasn't a casual, off-the-cuff insult between friends. This was a gut-deep venting of feelings, and she felt the menace behind it.

"Same to you, Stewart." A hot pulse of fury along her spine. Her hand curled into a tight fist, and relaxed. Much as she wanted to kick his punk ass, there was no way she could do it dressed in a backless gown with a through-and-through bullet hole in her side.

"So, did anything happen to you I need to know about?" Stewart asked in a bored tone.

"This is how you conduct an investigation?"

"It is when I know the witness is a lying bitch who wouldn't know the truth if it bit her in the—where were you shot exactly?"

"See my previous *fuck you* comment. Fine, if we're done,

get the hell out. I don't want to look at your ugly face any-more."

Without looking at her, he reached over and put his hand on her side. Over the bandages. "Does it hurt?"

She didn't move. Those twilight-blue eyes—on anybody else they might have been pretty—focused on her face, and his mouth stretched into a vindictive grin. He patted her bullet wound. Not gently. She bit the inside of her mouth to keep from wincing.

"Want to hear my theory?" Stewart wasn't moving his hand. "I think some of McCarthy's drug-dealing asshole buddies decided to send him a message by putting a few caps in his ex-partner. It was a classic drive-by hit, you know. Big dark pimp car, full auto spray. You're just lucky, is all. But then, you get lucky a lot, don't you? I've never seen anybody as lucky as you."

He pressed harder. Jazz knew she was going pale, but she didn't look away from his stare.

"Maybe if you'd tell the truth," Stewart said, "you'd quit being a target. This isn't the first trouble you've gotten into, since you turned in your shield. Is it?"

One attempted firebombing of her apartment, which had failed when the glass bottle full of gasoline hadn't shattered on impact, and she'd been able to scramble over and drag the burning rag out of the mouth of it. She could still smell the bitter tang of the gas, the smoky, oily cloth. No prints on the bottle, according to police forensics. She still wished she'd taken it to Manny. She was pretty sure he'd have come up with something to trace it back to Stewart.

She'd also been jumped coming out of a bar downtown. Two guys with knives. If she hadn't been drunk, she'd have had them, but even so, she'd managed to put them on the run. No good description, though. She'd always wondered if the small one had been Stewart himself.

"I hear that you were just minding your own business and this car rolled up on you. You fired six shots back, your friend fired four, and the car took off. That correct?"

"Don't know. Count the shells."

"Oh, we will." He nodded. "And Jazz? If I catch you in a lie, you're mine."

He squeezed this time. Hard. Fingers digging into her stitched-up side.

She couldn't keep from gasping, but she didn't just lie there for it, which was what he must have expected. She came straight up in bed and stiff-armed the heel of her hand into his nose.

Pop.

Stewart's head snapped back, and he fell off his chair, rolled to his knees and staggered back to his feet. He caught himself with a hand on an IV stand, which rolled, and for a happy second she thought he might go down again. No such luck. He felt his nose with his other hand, sniffed, and glared at her.

No blood. Too bad. She'd been hoping for a broken nose, at least.

"Sorry," she said. "Reflex."

He didn't say anything, just stared at her for a burning second, then turned and walked out of the room. The door slammed hard behind him.

Jazz let out a long breath and closed her eyes. Her forehead felt damp, and now that the crisis was over, she was shaking. And sick to her stomach. She pushed the button for on-demand morophine.

Just what she didn't need. A bullet in her side, no partnership agreement, and a closer acquaintance with Kenneth Stewart.

Lucia came back twenty minutes later, looking not exactly grim but definitely tense. She took the chair that Stewart had dragged close, gave Jazz a long look, and said, "I don't like this."

"Hospitals? Hey, I'm not a fan of them, either. And I think I have more reason to bitch about it."

"No, I don't like that they knew where to find us." She wasn't talking about the hospitals, or even Stewart. "I've been watching for tails. So have you."

"So we missed one. Or they've got some high-tech tracking bug on us." She remembered Borden, walking into Sol's Bar without any reason to be there. That still bothered her.

"No, I've swept us and the car for bugs," Lucia said, and combed sleek silky hair back from her face in a distracted motion. "Nothing. There's no way they've retasked a satellite just to follow us around, so if they're not doing line-of-sight surveillance, then they shouldn't know where we are. And if they were doing line-of-sight, we should have spotted them."

"Unless they're good."

"More than just good. *I'm* good." Lucia definitely looked stressed, as if she felt responsible for Jazz lying here, leaking fluids. "Those cops—I take it not friends of yours?—aren't investigating, they're filling out paperwork."

"It's Stewart," Jazz said, and stared up at the ceiling. It was blank, white, and noninspirational. "He helped put McCarthy away. He's been gunning for me ever since. No, actually, I take that back. He's never liked me. He's just actively started hating me since the whole thing with Ben."

Lucia paused in the act of tying her hair back with a businesslike black elastic band. No scrunchies or decorations for her. She looked different with her hair back. Harder. Jazz approved. "About McCarthy..." Lucia began.

"No."

"You don't think we should discuss that?"

"No, we're not talking about Ben, or his case, or whether or not he's guilty, or what he has to do with this because I guarantee you, he's got *nothing* to do with it. He's in prison, Lucia. Let's leave him out of this."

Lucia didn't answer that, just finished wrapping her hair in the elastic with a snap. "I called your sister, told her you'd been in an accident."

"Oh, no." Jazz sighed. "What did Molly say?"

Lucia avoided her eyes. "She was concerned. She said she'd tell your dad."

"I bet. I'll expect a cheap floral arrangement delivered to the wrong address next week."

"She's not that bad."

"Bullshit."

"Manny wanted to visit, but—"

"He's got a thing about hospitals. Manny has a thing about everything."

"He did some good work for us, looking into the Cross Society."

"And?"

Lucia shrugged. "On paper, it's legit. He came up with a few flags—not so much red lights as yellow. Max Simms, for one. He may be in prison, but it's likely he's still got some influence." She fell silent. The moment stretched, long and awkward.

Jazz though longingly of on-demand morphine.

"You should go," Jazz said. "I'm sorry to have kept you hanging around. You've got a life to get back to."

"Planes leave all the time." Lucia shrugged. "I'm not going if it means you end up lying unprotected in a hospital bed and the cops aren't going to put out any effort to find out who shot you. And shot at me, by the way. I take that kind of thing personally."

The look in her eyes was usually accompanied by shooting back, Jazz figured. Or, at the very least, grievous bodily harm.

"So you're sticking around," Jazz said. A tight knot in the area of her chest eased a little.

"For a while. Until you get back on your feet, anyway. Also, I'm going to wake up some sources and see what they can find out for me. I don't like the way any of this is playing out."

She started to get up. Jazz stopped her with an outstretched hand. "Wait. Listen, you need to be careful, all right? You're not from around here. If you disappear…"

Lucia gave her an uncomplicated smile. "If I disappear, *chica,* your cop friends are going to have a lot more trouble than they ever bargained for, because the kind of people who'll come looking for me won't take a shrug for an answer. And they don't ask nicely." She stood up, gazing down at her. "Also…I'm not that easy to make vanish."

"I get that." Jazz found herself smiling back. "Hey. Thank you."

"That's what partners are for," Lucia said, and reached down to retrieve her sleek black oversize purse. She pulled out a large flat envelope and placed it gently on Jazz's stomach. There was a pen clipped to it. "I signed," she said. "It's up to you whether or not you want to."

Jazz stared at the envelope, frowning. "Why'd you change your mind?"

"Because I don't think it matters anymore whether I sign it or not. We're in this together. Whoever these guys are, they're not going to back off because we go our separate ways, and I don't know about you, but I'd like to have somebody I trust at my back." Lucia's dark eyes were level and clear. "And if somebody's going to shoot at me, I'd rather get paid for it."

Jazz laughed. It hurt. She caught her breath, slid the paperwork out and thumbed through it to the last page.

Lucia's signature was flowing and bold over her typed name. Jazz set pen to paper, hesitated a second, and then scratched out her own messy, jerky autograph.

The check was attached to the partnership agreement with a clip. Jazz took it off, turned it over and endorsed it, then handed it all back to Lucia. "Maybe you'd better handle the bank stuff," she said.

"Yeah," Lucia agreed quietly. "I will."

In the silence after she was gone, Jazz went over all the ways that she'd just totally screwed up her life. There were dozens. Hundreds. Disaster stretched out in the distance, as certain as the Titanic and the iceberg.

What if it works? That was the scariest thought of all, strangely. *What if it works out, and I don't need to be a cop anymore?* Because that was secretly what she'd always thought would happen. McCarthy would be vindicated. They're return in triumph, conquering heroes. Life would pick up where it left off.

What if nothing's the same?

That filled her with a kind of fear that had nothing to do with bullet wounds and drive-by shooters and people attacking her in bathrooms. Those things she could deal with. External threats.

But this…this was different. She'd just done something that would change her future.

She fell asleep still thinking about that, and reaching no conclusions as to whether or not it was a good thing.

Chapter 5

When she woke up, it was morning, and she had a visitor. For a cold second she thought it was Stewart sitting in the shadows watching her, and how creepy would *that* have been, to have that vulture staring at her in her sleep, but no, this was a tall shadow, kind of lanky.

"Hey, you're awake," said a low, warm voice, and the shadow scooted forward into the soft dawn light.

Lawyer Borden. He looked tired, and a damn sight more informal than at the office; she got a quick impression of blue jeans and a black V-necked knit shirt before she focused on his smile. Luminous, that smile. Like morning.

"You're not allowed to get shot," he continued. "It's against the rules, you know."

"Rules?" she asked, and blinked. She was feeling slow and had a ridiculously strong desire to run into the bathroom, take a shower and brush her teeth before continuing this conversation. Not that she was going to be running anywhere right now. Her side felt as if she'd been sucker-punched by a giant. Bullet holes were no laughing matter, even if no organs got perforated.

"Yeah, rules," he said. He stood up and loomed over her, and for some reason, that felt good. Safe. She let her gaze slide down him, and had an instant appreciation for the way the black knit shirt hugged him. She had a sense-memory of soft skin, hard abdominal muscles fluttering under her touch as she'd checked him for broken ribs. *Okay, that's enough. Back off, Callender.* Must be the drugs.

She dragged her focus back up to his face. "Why didn't you tell us about Max Simms?"

Borden blinked. "Simms?"

"Founder of your little society. Serial killer."

"Laskins told me to." He paused. "I just—I knew you'd walk away. And I didn't want you to walk away."

Her breath caught, but it wasn't pain this time. "Who says I don't walk away now?"

"I don't think you can. Walk." He held up a hand to stop her response. "You might, but at least you've had time to look into things, think about it. If you go now—there's nothing I can do."

"We signed the agreement," she said, apropos of exactly zero. But Borden just nodded, unsurprised. "Lucia gave you the papers?"

"Yeah, they should be filed tomorrow."

"Shouldn't you be doing that, instead of flying off into

the buckle of the Bible Belt to loom over me?" Not that she minded the looming. But she wasn't about to let him know it.

As if she'd reprimanded him, he sank back into the chair, but he reached out and captured her IV-punctured hand in his. "I did everything I needed to do and sent it on to Pansy. Special courier. It'll be in her hands in about—" he checked his watch "—two hours, give or take. By the way, I've been asked to say that Mr. Laskins sends his regards, and your hospital bills are being taken care of."

"What?"

"The firm's picking up the tab."

"Bullshit, they are!"

"He feels responsible," Borden said, and his warm thumb rubbed gently up and down her palm. "Not a big deal. It's part of the partnership agreement, you know. The firm pays up any medical bills you incur in the line of duty for us. Technically, we aren't liable because this happened before you signed, but..."

She yanked her hand back. "I pay my own bills."

"With what?" he asked calmly. "The signing fee wasn't that generous. Apply that toward leasing the office, getting the utilities set up, furniture, maybe hiring someone to run the place for you, and what do you have left? Enough to live on. Not enough for extravagances like painkillers and surgery."

Not to mention she already owed Manny three grand. She opened her mouth to tell Borden to go to hell, then closed it again.

This was already starting to feel like a spiderweb, wrapping tightly around her. Holding her in place for a good sucking-dry. *I should have talked to Ben first. Ben would have known what to do.*

Oh, yes, that sarcastic part of her brain replied. *Go running to the murderer for advice. Don't you ever learn?*

She swallowed and tasted dust. Her tongue felt as if it had grown fur. "Water?" she asked. Borden, eager to please, nearly fumbled pouring from the little pitcher on the nightstand, but got a cool glass of K.C.'s best, straight out of the tap. She gulped it down in long, breathless spasms until the cup ran dry, then held it out for a refill. The second dose she took slow, in sips. She could already feel the heavy weight of the water in her stomach, and the last thing she needed was nausea with a hole in her side.

"Okay," she said at last, "let's say I let you guys pay for the medical stuff. This time."

"There's going to be a next time?" Borden said, as he replaced the pitcher.

"Could be." She smiled wolfishly. "I tend to get into trouble, in case you haven't noticed."

"Hasn't escaped me," he agreed. "Jazz…" He leaned forward, and clearly didn't know what to do with his hands. He ended up dangling them between his knees, looking lost. "You baffle me. You're all edges and angles and whup-ass, but…"

"But?"

"I don't know," he said. "I hate seeing you like this. I feel like I got you into it, and I don't like it."

"Counselor, don't strain a muscle shouldering the blame. Besides, wasn't this the point? Didn't you want us in this thing, me and Lucia? Well, you got your wish. We're in."

He looked briefly grim, tired, and older than his age in the soft morning light. This time, he knew what to do with his hands. He ran them through his hair. "That's not what I wanted," he said. "It's what the firm wanted. I'm not the firm."

"Are you telling me—"

"No. I'm telling you that objectively, it's good you took the deal. But personally, I'd rather not see you laid up with tubes in you. That's all." He sucked in a deep breath. "Not that I know you. I just—think you're kind of cool."

"Really." She kept any hint of encouragement out of her voice, although her pulse jumped and the monitor beeped out a betrayal. "Cool." Her dismissive tone painted a slight flush along his sharp cheekbones. "Thanks. Don't let me keep you."

He stood up, and looking down at her, there was no sense of protectiveness this time. Just height and distance.

"I just wanted to make sure that my client stayed alive long enough for the ink to dry on the legal agreements. I'll catch the noon flight back."

"Hope you have a use for all these frequent-flyer miles."

"Vacation," he said shortly. "With my girlfriend."

He left. Jazz waited long enough to make sure he was

gone for good, then buzzed the nurse and told her to get the tubes out, because she was leaving.

Lucia was, predictably, not happy with her, what with the checking out against medical advice, the bleeding into the bandages, and the shortness of breath, but Jazz wasn't one to worry about things like that. She dry-swallowed some of the painkillers the doctor had pressed on her, fed Mooch the Cat and listened to Lucia's cool, unemotional account of the day.

"I suppose it won't do any good to tell you to go to bed, so I won't bother," Lucia said, and that was the end of the lecture, to Jazz's satisfaction. Lucia dug in her purse and came up with a folder crammed with papers. She began laying them methodically on the kitchen table. Bank stuff. Jazz signed until it was done and then sat back, watching Lucia stuff it all into her bag.

This was moving too fast. Jazz felt massively tired. She swigged orange juice and focused on the cat happily chowing down in the corner of the kitchen. "It's real, isn't it?"

"Real enough," Lucia agreed. "By next week, we're going to have an office, a phone, Internet access…and hopefully, we'll both still be alive to enjoy it."

"We'll also have our first case," Jazz said. She picked up her orange juice, limped out of the kitchen into the living room and, with her toe, nudged the four file cartons stacked in the corner. "You may want to start reading up."

Every box was labeled McCarthy, Benjamin, with the

case number and box ID. Wasn't legal for her to have them, either, but since they were all duplicates she didn't figure anybody but Stewart and his crowd would care much. An ex-boyfriend in Records had done her the favor—and it had been a big one, but then she'd been *real* grateful—and she'd been poring over them obsessively for months now. The answer was in there. She just knew it was in there.

Lucia, who was carrying some kind of odd-looking sports drink, took a sip and raised her eyebrows. "Who's paying us to work on your partner's case?" she asked bluntly. Jazz just looked at her. "Ah. That's what I thought. I don't suppose we can count on friendly local cops sending business our way, either, can we?"

Jazz shrugged. "I've got a few buddies left."

It didn't sound convincing, even to her own ears. She wondered if Borden had gotten on his noon flight. She wondered if he really had a girlfriend, and if he did, if he was really going to fly her off to Jamaica soon and spend a week making love on white beaches with surf foaming over their feet. Probably. She'd been an idiot to think—

The doorbell rang.

Lucia, in the act of flipping open the first McCarthy carton, paused and looked at Jazz, then set down her drink. "No, I'll get it," she said when Jazz turned toward the door. "Sit."

Jazz sank down in the straight-backed desk chair with a tiny sigh of relief, and watched Lucia move toward the door. Not, she noticed, coming at it in a straight line; Lucia hugged the hinge side of the door and slid a gun out of the holster at her back. She held it down at her side, leaned over and covered the peephole with one finger for a few seconds.

Nothing happened. No bullets came flying through the door.

"Who is it?" Lucia asked.

"Borden." Definitely his voice. Jazz nodded. Lucia holstered the gun and undid the two dead bolts with sharp clicks.

Borden still looked casual and rumpled and tired, but he'd thrown on a leather jacket over the black knit shirt. Not the aggressively biker-wannabe thing he'd worn the first time Jazz had seen him; this one was cut straight, hung down to mid-thigh, and had lapels. Nice. It looked soft enough to cuddle, well-worn and conforming to his angles.

"Hey," he said, and came in. Lucia shut the door behind him, locks and all. "I went by the hospital."

"She's out," Lucia said simply.

"So I heard. The words *against medical advice* came up—" He spotted Jazz sitting at the table, and stopped dead in his conversational tracks.

"Counselor," she said. "Nice of you to drop by. What, no flowers?"

"No, I brought a card," he said. He reached into his jacket and came out with a red envelope, exactly the size and shape of a holiday card. Maybe not Valentine's Day after all. Maybe something left over from Christmas instead.

He handed it to Lucia.

"What's this?" she asked. She knew, though. She'd gotten a red envelope before.

"Your first case," he said. "Nothing too demanding, considering Jazz has a thirty-two-caliber disability. But something to start you off. Listen, I'd stay to chat, but my flight's leaving soon. Try not to get yourselves killed before we can get your paperwork finished, okay?"

He moved to the door, threw back the dead bolts, and didn't look at Jazz directly at all.

"Borden," Jazz said. He froze but didn't turn to look at her. "Sorry. Listen, you're being careful, right?"

"Always," he said neutrally. "You should try it sometime. Might cut down on the scarring."

He opened the door and left. Lucia relocked the bolts before saying, eyebrows raised, "Forgive me for noticing, but we've barely started and you're already having a problem with our benefactors."

"No," Jazz sighed. "I'm having a problem with lawyers. Specifically, that one."

Lucia sounded amused. "Are you really? Because that's not how it looks from over here."

"Shut up, will you? And open that thing, if you're going to do it."

Lucia took an elegant-looking pocketknife out and zipped it through paper with a hiss to open the envelope. She shook out two things: a Polaroid photograph and a folded sheet of paper. She looked at the picture for a few seconds, then passed it over to Jazz.

It was a photo of a young woman, maybe twenty-five. Blond, tall, walking with a load of books in her arms. Mod-looking glasses and a blunt haircut. Rounded shoulders. That, and the fluffy pink cardigan, screamed *librarian*. The camera had caught her frowning, looking three-quarters toward the lens, as if a sound had startled her. It had been taken on the street, in full sunlight. Going to work, maybe? The outfit didn't look like casual wear, although it wasn't a business suit, either.

No ring on her finger. Not a lot of jewelry, period, although there was a diamond glint in her ear.

Lucia was studying the piece of paper.

"What?" Jazz asked.

"We're supposed to go to this address, sit in a car and watch her load up her van," Lucia said. "Take some pictures. That's it."

"That's it?" Jazz examined the picture again. "Does she look like a criminal to you?"

"How do criminals look? I've busted seventy-year-old grandmothers running counterfeit operations out of their garages," Lucia said. "Sure, she looks like a grade-school teacher. Doesn't mean anything. Maybe she's hiding an Uzi under the cardigan."

Which was an odd enough image to make Jazz laugh. She reached for the paper. Lucia passed it over. She hadn't misstated; that was all it said. It gave an address, a time, no names or other information. Just directions on what to do and how long to do it.

Watch her load the van. Document with still and video photography. Forward all records and reports to James D. Borden at Gabriel, Pike & Laskins.

Okay. No problem. At least it would be easy work. The notation at the bottom—in Borden's handwriting, Jazz felt sure—said that the fee would be two thousand dollars, but that both of them were required to be there, since Jazz was, quote, "impaired." *Get your leather-jacket ass back here, I'll show you impaired,* she thought, smoldering, and handed it back. Lucia folded it and stuck it back in the envelope, along with the photograph, which they'd both handled carefully, without getting their prints on it. Jazz felt warm and fuzzy over the fact that they hadn't even had to talk about it.

"Manny?" Lucia asked.

"Just the photo," Jazz said. "Have him run the prints and do an image recognition search through his databases. See what turns up."

It was a little amazing, really, that they were thinking along the same lines. Lucia seemed to think so, too. They exchanged a slow smile, broken by Jazz clapping a hand to her forehead and then wincing at the hot pull along her side at the movement.

"Shit, I forgot," she said. "Manny was being watched, too. I have to get his new address from a dead drop."

"Well, you're not driving," Lucia said, and picked up the keys as Jazz reached for them.

"They won't let you open up the mailbox. I'm the only one with access, and even then, they card me for it."

"I won't go in. Taxi service only."

Not much choice, really. Jazz nodded and levered herself out of her chair with only a small wince. She limped to her gun safe and got out her backup piece—a snub-nosed .38—and attached the clip-on holster to her belt. The cops had confiscated her main gun, of course, along with Lucia's. She hadn't asked where Lucia's backup piece had come from. Probably wouldn't be wise to ask too many questions.

The cloak-and-dagger show proceeded slowly; Jazz retrieved the new phone number from the dead drop and spent thirty minutes convincing Manny to let her leave the photo in the same spot. He wanted to switch locations, too, all the way across town. She was more than a little out of the mood to coddle his paranoia. She was the one who'd been shot, after all.

Which did nothing to calm him down, of course. But she got him to agree to send a courier for the photo. He could dead-drop it all over town if he wanted. She had a job to do.

That was a nice change, she decided. And if she hadn't been, well, shot, she'd have probably proposed a drink in celebration.

Just as well, all things considered, that the bars weren't open, and painkillers didn't go down well with alcohol.

And that having Lucia along lessened the desire to screw up her life any further.

* * *

An hour later, they were parked on a suburban street, eating food from a paper bag marked with a logo, and sipping diet drinks. Jazz hurt all over but didn't complain about it. Lucia kept the radio on, tuned to a classic rock station, and they sat in comfortable silence watching the nondescript tract home with its pale brick and black shutters and closed garage door.

"What if she loads it in the garage?" Jazz asked. Lucia shrugged. "Do we still get paid?"

"I think we'd better take pictures anyway," Lucia said, and proceeded to click the shutter. The camera was sleek, digital, and right out of the box. The battery was charging off a car adapter. Lucia checked the time code on the photo and said, "We're right on time, according to the letter."

Jazz nodded and took a bite of her hamburger. "Hey, if I fall asleep from the adrenaline, scream if there's anything interesting."

The day was still bright, although sunset would be coming on within the next hour; Jazz chewed mostly tasteless food and wondered if the silver plane threading the clear blue sky was carrying Borden back to New York. Lucia snapped pictures at some military interval known only to her own internal stopwatch. Cars drove by, some slow, some faster. None of them seemed interested in the house they were focusing on.

"We look suspicious," Jazz said.

"Stakeouts do," Lucia agreed. "And I'd suggest we get

out and jog around, but neither of us is dressed for it and I don't think that was what the doctor had in mind for you when he said light exercise. If you think sitting in a car looks suspicious, keeling over and bleeding profusely attracts even more attention."

Jazz grunted around a mouthful of French fries. "Probably," she agreed.

"I know it's not necessary to say this, but if something goes wrong, you're going to let me handle it, right? You're not going to decide to kickbox a dozen ninjas and die on me?"

"Ninjas? Let me see the file."

"Funny." The light tone left Lucia's voice. "I mean it. Don't do anything to jeopardize yourself. You shouldn't even be here, much less be exerting yourself."

"Listen, at this rate, I'm more likely to die of cholesterol overload than a bullet."

"Let's keep it that way…heads up."

A black van—cargo, not mini—turned the corner behind them and proceeded slowly up the block. Jazz felt a sudden flicker of something. Instinct, maybe. She dropped the rest of the fries into the bag, tossed it into the backseat, and made sure she could get to her gun.

Lucia snapped some pictures and watched the van glide up the street. Most of the houses were vacant of cars or people—it was a working-class neighborhood, largely deserted during the day—but there were kids out playing three yards down.

No sign of life from the house they'd been assigned to watch.

The van slowed, turned and bumped up into the driveway.

"I think we're officially on duty," Lucia said unnecessarily. "Think she's going to load it up?"

The front door of the house swung open, and Pink Cardigan came out. It probably wasn't fair to call her that, as the pink cardigan wasn't in evidence today—there was a brown pullover sweater and khaki slacks, instead. Lucia snapped off a photo as the woman walked toward the driver's side of the van. From their perspective, the driver was hidden.

"We should have parked up there for a decent shot of the driver," Jazz noted, nodding about twenty feet ahead. Lucia didn't respond. She was focused on the van, the woman. Snapping multiple photos of the license plate. Jazz left her to it and checked the side mirrors again. The kids were still galumping around in the yard a few doors down, spraying each other with water hoses. Nothing seemed to have changed.

Pink Cardigan went back into the house, and after a few minutes, the garage door rattled up.

"Uh-oh," Jazz said. "That's it. They're going to pull it inside."

But there wasn't any room. The garage was packed full of boxes, and a small silver Nissan was squeezed into the remaining space.

Lucia took a picture.

Pink Cardigan grabbed a box—it appeared to be fairly heavy—and went around to the back of the black van. She opened the rear doors and slid the box inside.

Click.

Box number two. Same drill.

"Why isn't the driver helping?" Jazz wondered. "They'd be done in half the time. He's a little obvious sitting there idling the engine."

"Maybe he doesn't want to be seen," Lucia said. Which was logical, and Jazz wished she hadn't opened her mouth. She sucked on diet cola and glanced at the side mirrors again. Nothing sinister going on anywhere that she could see.

Pink Cardigan went back for the third box. *Click*. "Watch out for lens flash," Jazz said.

Lucia threw her an irritated look. "I'm not a novice," she said. "Relax."

That really wasn't possible, because this was feeling really *wrong*. Not that there was anything obviously strange going on…another bright shiny day in suburbia…but Jazz felt tension creeping up her spine and into her shoulders.

Pink Cardigan was getting red in the face, hauling boxes. She was working on the fifth one now, looking harassed. If what she was doing was illegal, she was pretty unconcerned about it. Of course, that was the secret to getting away with it, not being furtive. Still, this was a little *too* blatant, wasn't it? Out in the open, at her own house, personally loading up the shiny black obvious van?

Didn't make sense.

Click. Lucia ran off another photo. Jazz was willing to bet they all looked pretty much the same.

"What are we looking at?" Jazz asked.

"Good question," Lucia answered. "I have no idea. She's a neat person, conservative dresser—I'd put the outfit she's got on at high-end department store—and there aren't any markings on the boxes. Plain brown cardboard and tape. Everything sealed up, like for shipping. I don't know."

"Drugs?"

"Not like any drug shipment I've ever seen. Way too obvious. And look at the number of boxes stacked in there. She'd be a Colombian drug lord, with that inventory. And the lack of security…"

Jazz's cell phone rang, caller unknown. When she answered, it was Manny.

"Jazz," he blurted before she could say a word. "That picture? Her name's Sally Collins. She's a single mother, one daughter, Julia, fourteen. No criminal record, not even a speeding ticket in the last ten years. Normal debts. She co-owns a ceramics shop."

"Thanks, Manny…." He'd already hung up.

She relayed the information to Lucia.

"Ceramics," Lucia said. "Could be what's in the boxes."

"Ceramics with drugs?"

"It's a stretch," Lucia admitted.

"Yeah." Jazz chewed her lip. "So what do we do?"

"Take pictures," Lucia answered. "Until it's done."

Pragmatic, but not satisfying. Jazz sipped cola and scanned the mirrors again. Still, all quiet on the neighborhood front. It was positively Mayberry out there.

Pink Cardigan carried a total of ten boxes out. When she had the tenth one stacked in the van to her satisfaction, she closed the rear doors and walked around to the driver's side again. A short conversation ensued.

"Parabolic mike," Lucia said softly.

"On the shopping list," Jazz agreed. "We definitely need more toys."

The black van reversed out onto the street. Lucia leaned over, angling for a driver's side shot, but the windows were tinted and rolled up tight.

It pulled away and made a left turn out of sight.

Jazz turned back to the house. Pink Cardigan was standing there, arms folded, staring down at her shoes. Frowning.

Lucia took another picture.

In between one breath and another, everything changed.

An engine growled behind them, and Jazz's eyes flew to the side mirror. An electric blue car was turning the corner—a big thing, probably dating back to the seventies, square and solid and shining with chrome.

Pink Cardigan looked up, alarmed, saw the car and backed up.

Lucia swore, and dropped the camera to reach for her gun. Jazz was already going for hers, as well. The car glided nearly silently down the street, casual as a shark heading for a plump baby seal.

The car slowed even more. The kids in the yard played on, oblivious…and then, suddenly, it lurched into motion with a squeal of tires. Accelerating fast.

"Down!" Lucia yelled at Jazz and aimed across her. Jazz grabbed the handle that controlled the car seat and yanked it up, gasping as her seat slammed into full recline and she dropped hard with it. Gut-shot abdominal muscles complained with a hot, dizzying flash. She was staring up at Lucia, who was leaning over her, gun extended in firing position and braced with her left hand. Steady as a rock.

She didn't fire. The muzzle of the gun tracked smoothly in an arc.

Jazz heard a world-shaking rumble, saw a shadow flash over Lucia's face, and then the blue car was past them and still accelerating. No gunfire.

Jazz grabbed the dashboard and pulled herself back upright, ratcheting the seat to a straight position. Lucia slowly relaxed, both hands still on the gun, staring at Pink Cardigan.

The blue car swerved left at the corner, taking the same route as the black van.

"What the hell was that?" Jazz blurted, and turned to look at Pink Cardigan, who was staring at the car intently, but not as if she recognized it. She turned and went back into her house, slamming the door shut behind her with such violence that it echoed like the gunshots that hadn't been fired. After a few minutes, the garage door cranked down, as well, and rattled shut with a hollow *boom*.

"I don't know," Lucia admitted. She still looked pale, breathing fast. Jazz related. She was about to pass out from the rush of adrenaline. "I thought they were going to kill her."

"What stopped them?"

"Us," Lucia said. "They saw us and kept driving. I think we just saved her life."

"Without firing a shot? Excellent. I really don't want to talk to Stewart twice in one day." Jazz sounded steady and cheerful; she didn't feel that way. Sweat dripped down the back of her neck, soaked her shirt. She needed to pee. Badly. Straight-up fighting she could take. This battle-of-nerves thing, not so much. "Man. That was..."

"Weird?" Lucia supplied. "Yeah." She finally realized she was still holding the gun and put it away. "Sorry. I should have gotten the plate number."

"One-six-four *HCX*," Jazz said automatically. "That's not the weird thing."

She had Lucia's full attention.

"The weird thing is that the license plate was black with yellow letters," she continued. "Missouri plates, all right, but Missouri hasn't issued that style since 1978."

Lucia was outright staring at her. Big eyed. "You know the state license-plate colors by year?"

"Yeah." Jazz shrugged. "Useful knowledge."

"Just for Missouri, right?"

"If I say no, will you think I'm weird?"

That got an outright blink. Lucia, the calm and unsurprised, was finally thrown for a loop.

Jazz smiled, reached into the glove compartment, and pulled out a steno pad. She wrote down the plate number and details about the plate itself.

"So what does that mean? About the plate?" Lucia asked finally.

"Means they probably pulled it off a junker at an auto graveyard," she said. "Although it fits the age of that car."

She flipped open her cell phone and hit the fourth speed dial on the list. She got an answer on the second ring, as always.

"Hey, Gaz," she said. "Run a plate for an old friend?"

"Don't think so," he replied. Gary Gailbraith was an old friend, and he'd never answered that way before. He sounded guarded. "Things are kind of busy right now. Can't really talk."

Oh, crap. "Has Stewart been on your ass?"

"Positively up it," Gaz said. He was an older cop, white haired, with a broad face and a whiskey-drinker's blush across his nose and cheeks. He always seemed vacant to most of the other detectives, but that was a deliberate cultivation on his part. He was sharp as a tack, was Gaz, just not in any obvious ways. He never competed. And he didn't play politics, more than he had to in order to get the job done. "I think I need a proctologist."

She grinned. "Okay. Call me when the heat's off, right?"

"Right," he replied. "Take care."

"You, too." She hung up. Lucia raised eyebrows at her. "You got any local contacts to do a plate check?"

"Local? No. The sources I have work at, ah, higher levels. And using them might raise a red flag."

"Kind of what I figured," Jazz nodded. "Okay, we do it the hard way."

"Meaning?"

Lucia started the car. She reached down, retrieved the fallen digital camera and handed it to Jazz, who thumbed quickly through the pictures. Too bad they hadn't gotten a shot of the blue car, but Jazz had a pretty vivid mental image, and she was sure Lucia did, too.

"Meaning," Jazz said, staring at Pink Cardigan's picture, "we go see Manny again."

Lucia groaned softly, and put the car in gear.

Convincing Manny to track a plate for her was just about the toughest thing Jazz had ever done, considering she was doing it with a leaking bullet wound in her side, a massive throbbing headache, and an adrenaline-rush aftermath that made her feel like roadkill. Manny eventually figured out that she wasn't operating at her usual levels and decided to take it easy on her, having exacted only a few dozen promises that he wouldn't be put on any hit lists or have shape-changing aliens showing up at his door.

"I swear," Jazz groaned as she flipped the cell phone closed, "I'm personally going over there to set up parental controls to keep him from ever watching *The X-Files* again."

"Probably wouldn't do any good," Lucia said, poker-faced. "I think I spotted DVD collections."

"Crap."

Lucia pulled the car into a space near the apartment stairs, killed the low beams, and reached up to flip the overhead dome light off. When Jazz reached for the door handle, Lucia stopped her. "Wait," she said.

"For?"

"My eyes to adjust," Lucia said calmly. "I want to be able to see the shadows before you decide to present another target."

"You know, I think you and Manny might be a match made in heaven."

"Another crack like that, and I catch the next puddle jumper out of here."

Still, Lucia was right; Jazz would have thought of it herself, been more cautious if she hadn't been so tired and hurting. She sat in silence, watching the shadows as her eyes adjusted; nothing she could see waiting out there. Parked cars were always a worry, but there wasn't much she could do about them.

"Okay." Lucia finally nodded. "No deviations. Straight up the stairs, fast as you can. I'll be behind you."

Jazz didn't waste breath on agreeing, just ducked out, kept her head down and took the steps as quickly as possible. Which was agonizingly slowly, actually, given the crappy state of her body. She was gasping and feeling a little sick by the time she achieved the top landing. Behind her,

Lucia, lingering down at the bottom, watching the parking lot, turned and soundlessly came up, three steps at a bound.

Jazz felt tired just watching her.

She slipped her key into the first dead bolt, then the second, and reached for the doorknob.

It didn't turn in her hands.

Jazz backed up, fast, breath short again. She planted her back squarely against the wall, eyes wide, and nodded Lucia silently back to the far side, out of the line of fire.

What? Lucia mouthed. Her gun was out, fast as a magic trick. Jazz fumbled her own out, but didn't like the way her hand was shaking. *I'll probably shoot myself. Again.*

Jazz pointed at the doorknob. *Locked,* she mouthed. *Shouldn't be.*

Lucia nodded in understanding. Jazz habitually shot dead bolts, but never bothered with the relatively nuisance-value lock on the knob. They could be overcome by a bright ten-year-old with a hairpin, much less anybody serious about breaking and entering. Lucia held out her free hand. Jazz tossed the keys underhand to her, watched as she neatly—and nearly silently—fielded them, and then stepped up to slot the key neatly into the last lock.

No hail of gunfire. Jazz held her breath as the door swung wider onto darkness. Something moved inside, and her heart lurched, but it was only a bushy gray ghost of a cat stepping cautiously over the threshold. *Mooch.* She resisted the urge to dive over and grab him, and let him prance his slow way past her and down the stairs. He gave her a curious look and a rumble of a purr as he passed, but he was embarked on serious business.

Lucia moved fast and low, and entered the apartment. Jazz waited. She'd be crap as backup right now, and she knew it. Plus, crouching was pretty much out of the question.

Silent moments passed, and then lights blazed on in the hallway and spilled out in a golden syrupy glow over the concrete and Jazz's shoes. Lucia appeared at the door as she reholstered her gun at her back.

"Come on," she said, and checked the outside again one more time before she locked the door. "You've had company, all right, but they're gone now."

"Crap," Jazz sighed. She stared mournfully at the mess left behind. Mounds of crumpled papers. Drawers pulled open and contents strewn all over the place. Pictures askew on the wall, although truthfully none of that would matter even if they'd slashed every one of them to bits.

The boxes of files, the ones she'd wanted Lucia to look through...they were gone.

She froze, staring at the empty corner. There was an impression in the cheap, ugly carpet where the weight of the stack had rested, but unless the damn boxes had turned invisible, they were gone.

She kicked disconsolately at the papers on the floor, trying to see if they'd left anything behind, but what was abandoned looked like her regular household stuff, correspondence, bills, nothing important.

"What?" Lucia asked, and followed her stare to the empty corner. "Oh, God. They took your case files, right?"

"Right," Jazz murmured. "All the work I did since Ben's arrest. All the notes, all the leads. Everything."

"Anyone in particular come to mind?"

"Besides that asshole Stewart?" She shook her head. Too sick, too tired, too numbed. She sank into a chair and heard papers crackle under her ass, but she didn't care. "I don't know. Ask me in the morning."

Lucia stared at her for a few seconds, then turned and walked into the kitchen. Whatever disaster was there, she returned with a glass of water and a handful of pills. "Take them," she said. "I mean it."

And for once, Jasmine Callender did as she was told. She meekly swallowed the pills and sat watching Lucia straighten up papers, making stacks, clearing the floor. Then straightening up fallen chairs, putting drawers back in place, closing open cabinet doors.

Rehanging those god-awful pictures.

Jazz's eyelids got heavy without warning. She woke up with a start when she felt a hand on her shoulder, and somehow made it on numbed feet back to the bedroom.

Lights out.

She didn't even have time to worry about why somebody who'd broken in and trashed her house had taken the trouble to lock all of her dead bolts.

Or how.

* * *

She'd had better mornings after four-day benders.

Jazz woke up sick, aching, slightly feverish, and wishing she were dead for the first full minute before remembering that it was good to be alive. Mostly. Part of the reason that kicked in was the smell of fresh-brewed coffee wafting through the apartment. Unless Mooch had learned how to program the coffeemaker, she still had company.

Jazz groaned, tried to sit up and stayed flat for a few more minutes, gathering strength. Yep, it hurt. A lot. It hurt like the morning after indulging in some insane exercise orgy and doing a thousand sit-ups. Only worse. She wasn't sure she could force her abdominal muscles to do even the simple work of getting her out of bed.

Suck it up, Callender, she ordered herself, and somehow managed to get up. After she'd swung her legs over the bed, she discovered that Lucia had taken off her shoes but left her wearing the loose sweatpants and T-shirt. Beneath, the bandages felt stiff. She tried not to think of what that might mean.

Getting to her feet was an adventure, but she managed. She ran fingers through her hair, felt unruly tangles and shuffled, on athletic-sock feet, into the living room.

Which looked like someone else's apartment.

She blinked, cocked her head and tried to remember if she'd suffered a head injury, in and around the general insanity of yesterday. No, she was pretty sure not.

Maybe it was the same room, it just looked...better. Cleaner, at least. And neater. Weirdly *not* her home.

Everything was neat, squared up, polished. The carpet had been vacuumed to the point that it looked as if it might have been new, if anyone was unwise enough to make carpet that color in this day and age.

No sign of the chaos of the night before.

Lucia came out of the kitchen, looking glossily perfect, as usual. Sleek and shining. Her hair was still back in the action ponytail, and she had on some tight spandex-type workout pants and a jogging bra.

"Morning," she said, and looked Jazz comprehensively up and down. "You look like hell."

"Thanks. Very comforting." Jazz found the coffeemaker and a mug and poured. She tasted bitter oily heaven, swallowed, and kept going until the cup was empty. Then refilled. Lucia watched her, leaning against the door frame and frowning.

"Wow," she finally said. "That's...frightening. Do you always drink that much caffeine?"

"Any messages?" Jazz asked. Her brain fog was starting to clear, at least a little.

"Borden called. He wanted to check on you. I don't think he was very happy to hear you weren't in bed."

"I *was* in bed."

"I mean, were planning on staying there. As in, recovering."

"Borden's not the boss of me," Jazz said, and then wondered. Maybe he was. Not a pretty thought. "Did you tell him about yesterday? The assignment?"

"Yes, I told him. I typed up reports and faxed them in. I included the plate number and description of the car, too. I'd have waited for you, but…"

"No, that's okay." Jazz sank down at the kitchen table. Her abdominal muscles gave a sob of relief. "What'd he say?"

"Good job?" Lucia lifted a shoulder in a fatalistic shrug. "I tried to get some kind of idea from him about what it was we were supposed to have accomplished, but he's a brick wall. I think he responds better to you. Maybe you can give him a call."

Jazz shot her a look. "I don't think so. Last thing I need is a lawyer going all sweet on me. No sign of the files, I guess?"

"No, no sign. I did a little canvassing up and down the hall. Nobody saw anything, apparently."

Jazz reflected that if her neighbors were going to talk to anyone, they'd talk to gorgeous Lucia; no leads, then. She felt unreasonably depressed.

"I swept the apartment for bugs, by the way. Nothing. It still looks clean."

"Cleaner than it did when I went to bed," Jazz observed. Lucia looked away and studied the polish on her fingernail. "Never mind. Thanks."

"I'm going out for a run," Lucia said. "You going to be okay here?"

"Yep. Fine and dandy." Jazz filled her coffee cup again and shuffled over to the gun safe. She dimly recalled having stowed her .38 in there, and sure enough, there it was, fully loaded and ready. She got it out and clipped the holster to her waistband. "You're strapped, right?"

"In this outfit?" Lucia shook her head. "I'll be all right."

"No, you won't." Jazz limped to her bedroom, found a reasonably clean floppy sweatshirt and tossed it to Lucia, who pulled it on. It made her look adorably lumpy. Lucia added the pancake holster to the small of her back and nodded.

"Lock it behind me," she said. "And if you have time and energy, you might want to read some things I found on the Internet."

She indicated a small, neat pile of papers on the kitchen table and went out the front door. Jazz followed instructions with the dead bolts, then carried coffee and gun back to the table.

Max Simms had been arrested in the winter of 2000, claiming innocence. Nothing unusual in that, and of course he retained high-powered counsel. What was interesting was whom he'd retained.

Jazz cocked her head and studied the grainy black-and-white AP photo of white-haired, distinguished-looking Max Simms in handcuffs, with the lawyer striding next to him, head bent to confer.

James Borden. What had he said, in the office? *I've never tried a criminal case in my life.* Next to him was Milo

Laskins, stone-faced, extending a hand to block photographers and reporters.

She stroked the printed side of Borden's face with one blunt finger and whispered, "Liar." It felt as if the whole world had shifted to the left, creating a slope, and she couldn't get her balance. From the beginning, from the first time she'd seen him, she'd believed Borden. She'd felt that on some very deep level he was just plain honest.

And if she was wrong about that, what else was she wrong about? Lucia Garza? The partnership? Ben McCarthy's innocence?

She swallowed hard and forced herself to keep reading. Lots of background on Simms, who had all the usual quiet sins that could be dug up on any adult. Gossip from his peers, mostly. Nasty comments about his work habits, ogling his female subordinates, having harsh words for people... the kind of stuff that came to the forefront when someone was down and probably not getting up again.

Simms had taken a plea agreement. Twenty-five to life. Or just life, for someone of his age. He'd been lucky to escape the needle.

The kitschy gold sunburst clock on the wall said that morning was rolling on. She washed up the mug and coffeepot, shuffled off to the bathroom and attempted a sponge bath, with limited results. Her hair was a disaster, and she wasn't up to washing it. Bending over wasn't really in the cards. She settled for giving it a punky spiked look with gel—thank you, Liar Borden—and climbed into fresh underwear and sweatpants and T-shirt.

Then she collapsed back on the bed, spots dancing in front of her eyes. Painkillers beckoned seductively from her bedside table, but no way was she doing that, not today. Too much to do. Too much at stake.

She got out her cell phone and dialed.

"Gabriel, Pike & Laskins," said a crisp female voice, all business. "How may I direct your call?"

"James Borden," she said, and eased herself to a sitting position against the headboard. She didn't want to be lying down for this.

"One moment, I'll see if he's available."

Thirty seconds, a fluttering click, and Pansy's cheerful voice said, "James Borden's office, how may I—"

"Let me speak to the lying rat," Jazz interrupted. "Tell him it's Jasmine Callender."

There was a second's puzzled pause, and then Pansy said, "Ms. Callender, I'm sorry, but the lying rat isn't here. He flew out yesterday. I understood he was coming to see you. Incidentally, how are you feeling?"

"Good enough to kick his legal briefs," Jazz snapped, and heard Pansy choke on what might have been a laugh. "He flew back last night. He's not there?"

"Not at the office. He called to say that he'd be out of town a couple of days at least. Do you want me to try his cell phone?"

"No, I'll do it." Jazz was suddenly struck by an evil inspiration. "Do you like your job, Pansy?"

"Sure."

"Like New York?"

"It's okay," Pansy said. Jazz could almost see the shrug. "I'm from Kansas, originally. New York takes some getting used to."

"If you're homesick, do you want to come to work in K.C. for me?"

"I couldn't do that," Pansy said cheerfully. "But thanks for the offer."

"Suit yourself. But I can promise you that I'll never, ever make you get coffee."

There was a long, long pause, and then Pansy said, "Kansas City, huh?"

Jazz grinned. *Take that, Lawyer Borden.*

Chapter 6

Upon returning from her run, Lucia informed Jazz of two things. One, she'd be camping out on Jazz's couch until her leasing agent found her a local apartment. Two, they had an appointment to shop for office space.

"We're *shopping?*"

"Shopping is a necessary part of life, Jazz, you should reconcile yourself to it. Unless you want me to make all the decisions." Lucia didn't sound averse to it. Jazz eyed her distrustfully.

"Fine," she said. "I'll take a look."

Lucia drove. All the way, Jazz kept an eye on the street, but traffic patterns looked random and safe, and she saw nobody following—either from in front or behind—for more than a couple of blocks. It was possible the faceless bad guys had enough manpower to do fast-rotating teams, but if so, they were screwed anyway, and all the eagle-eye vigilance in the world wouldn't help.

No white vans, no black cars with tinted windows, no electric blue sedans with out-of-date plates.

But when they pulled up in the parking lot of a five-story office building, she spotted someone she knew waiting, leaning against the granite-faced entrance with his long arms folded. Borden was back in casual mode, long leather jacket and blue jeans and an oatmeal-colored long-sleeved Henley underneath. Gelled hair again. He looked up as Jazz's car rattled to a stop, and straightened.

Jazz took her time getting out, partly so as not to run over and bash his head against the wall, partly because she didn't want to show any awkwardness or hesitation from the pain. Smooth and controlled. She was going to out-Lucia Lucia.

"Hey," Borden said, and took a couple of steps toward her. She shut the car door, put her hands in her jacket pockets and looked at him with what was probably not a polite smile.

He stopped.

"Let me guess, Counselor," she said, "you're in the real estate business, too."

"More or less. How are you—"

"Feeling?" She forced herself not to limp as she walked toward, then past him. "Great. You?"

In the shiny tinted glass of the building's double doors, she saw Borden toss Lucia a look. Lucia shook her head.

"You should have stayed in the hospital," he said, coming up next to her with a thick set of keys in his hand. He unlocked the door and pulled the right one open with a sigh of cool air. "And for the record? I'm not the landlord. I just helped Lucia find the place. Third floor. Take the elevator. You don't have to prove how tough you are by tackling the stairs."

She glared at him but walked inside the building. It was dark, except for some indirect spots illuminating empty alcoves and an equally empty reception desk. Still had that new-building smell, equal parts paint, drywall and fresh carpeting.

"Ready to move in?" Lucia asked.

Borden nodded. "If you sign the lease, you could be operational in a few days."

Lucia nodded and tucked her hair back behind her ear, sneaking a look at Jazz as she did so. Jazz watched the numbers flash on the floor counter overhead. When the right one arrived, she pushed through the still-opening doors...

Into a dream.

Déjà vu, she thought, and fought the disorientation. She knew this place. *Knew* it. She knew what she'd see before she looked left, or right. She knew that there would be a big-ass boardroom behind the reception-desk half wall directly in front of her, and that the table in there would be a long black lacquer thing, and she could see someone sitting there, looking up at her.

Ben. Ben McCarthy. I remember Ben McCarthy being here, in these offices.

She told herself it was just a dream, but she couldn't make

herself move. Her heart was hammering, her skin suddenly coated in sweat.

I know this place.

Borden went to the reception desk and did something behind the counter. Lights flipped on and marched left and right in fluorescent banks. The place took on light and color. It was champagne-and-blond woods and dull silver, very chic.

"It's fully furnished," he said. "The management fitted it out for an Internet firm that went belly-up before move-in. They've been trying to lease it out for months."

"Other tenants in the building?" Lucia asked.

"They've got a law firm moving in on five, and an investment firm coming in on the ground floor," Borden said. "It's pretty safe. Very corporate."

Jazz walked over to the reception desk and looked at the half wall behind the empty chair. It was begging for a name. She blinked and imagined the silvery lettering on it: *Callender & Garza*. She wasn't sure if that made her feel better or even more disoriented.

She went around the wall. Behind it sat a black lacquer table that seated at least a dozen, with black leather chairs pulled around it. A Zen-appropriate arrangement of dried flowers in the center of the table. Beyond it, tinted glass had a view of the K.C. skyline.

The sense of déjà vu was fading. Maybe it had just been one of those things, a weird-ass chemical imbalance of a brain that had suffered too many shocks recently.

She heard Lucia say something about taking a look at the offices. She turned and followed.

There were two large offices to the right, sharing an administrative station. Jazz entered the one on the left, moving by instinct, and noticed Lucia moved to the right. She stood in the doorway and looked at the expanse of carpet, the empty bookshelves, the desk and chair.

Borden had moved behind her. She could feel him there, even though he was staying a prudent few steps away.

"You did a good job," he said, "with the assignment. The client was pleased."

"We didn't do anything." Jazz turned to face him. The indirect lighting did things to his face, made him look like a stranger. But then, he was a stranger, wasn't he? And she didn't really know a thing about him, except that he wasn't telling the truth.

"You did exactly what you were supposed to do," he said, and suddenly put out a hand to grab her by the forearm. "Jazz?"

She'd faltered, lost her balance, and only realized it after the fact. She leaned against a wall and sucked down deep breaths, clearing her head. "Paint fumes," she mumbled. She felt light-headed and more than a little sick. "You lied to me, Borden."

He could have moved his hand. He didn't. She felt his strong hold slacken a little, but he kept touching her.

"I didn't," he said, and moved closer. Too close. She felt smothered. "I wouldn't."

"You told us you don't do criminal cases." *Like Manny,* she thought. *Manny won't do them, either.*

Borden's sharp face went blank for a few seconds, then settled into an expression of resignation. "Yeah. I don't."

"I saw the pictures. You and Max Simms."

The name rocked him back, and she saw a startled flash in those big brown eyes, quickly concealed. "That's what I get for generalizing to a cop," he said. "I didn't try that case, I was second chair. Laskins was principal. It was my first, last and only criminal trial with the firm."

"Because of Simms?" she asked.

He smiled sadly. "My firm doesn't like losing."

The office's waiting silence closed around them. He still hadn't taken his hand off her, and she hadn't insisted, by word or motion, that he do it. Her eyes met his, and she felt a jolt deep inside, something warm and frighteningly real.

"I wish you'd stayed in the hospital," he said, his voice low and hoarse. "You have a hole in your side, you know. Not a hangnail."

"Believe me, Counselor, I know."

He studied her for a long moment, and then suddenly let go of her arm and stepped back. Two feet back. Hands in his pockets, as if he didn't trust himself not to touch her again.

Lucia was coming out of the right-hand office, arms folded, looking at her shoes as if deciding whether or not the new fall line would be out soon. She glanced from Borden to Jazz and back, dark eyes glittering, and said, "Reached any conclusions?"

"Looks good to me," Borden said. He didn't take his eyes off Jazz.

"It seems like it will work," Lucia replied. "I want wireless broadband installed, and we're going to need lots of storage space. But yes, I like it. Jazz?"

Callender & Garza.

Ben McCarthy, sitting at that black table, looking up at her with a tiny little smile.

Jazz sucked in a deep breath and surprised herself by saying, "Yeah. I can live with this."

That, apparently, was all it took to change the course of a life.

The cases came slowly at first. Welton Brown, who'd always been a friend, directed a couple of noncriminal cases Jazz's way, and as the weeks passed, as office supplies got delivered and put away and lights turned on and Internet connections tested—as the lettering turned from dream to permanence on the reception-area wall and the building officially opened—things slowly began to change.

Jazz healed.

It was more than the bullet wound, although that closed up nicely without complications. It was more about something inside that had been broken and bleeding for much longer than that. Since she'd seen Stewart throw McCarthy up against a wall and snap handcuffs around his wrist and sneer out words she still heard in her nightmares. *Under arrest for murder...*

She'd been lost for a while, since then, and as she began to learn the routine of driving to the office, checking her perimeters before leaving the car, walking into the offices and being greeted by Christine Sparrow, Lucia's choice for receptionist...it began to feel real.

Lucia had moved without fanfare. She'd just stopped commuting from D.C. about a week into things and handed Jazz a slip of paper with an address on it. Her new home was in one of the nicer, secured apartment buildings.

Every day, they met in the elevator, or in the coffee room, or in the administrative area—still empty—between their two offices. And every day, there was something more to talk about. Something *important*.

Lucia brought cases with her from Washington. One of them required travel, which Jazz wasn't up for, given her physical limitations, and she found she missed Lucia's light conversation while she was gone, the quiet competence she brought into the office, like the scent of her perfume. Jazz took a job doing background checks on a prospective executive for Hudson Industrials out of Boston—another Welton Brown referral, however oblique—and turned up drug-possession charges and proof of current cocaine purchases, provided via a subcontractor in Boston proper. The company liked their thoroughness so much that they sent over their corporate business.

Jazz discovered she really did need an assistant. Badly. She made another phone call.

Turned out that Pansy was tired of getting coffee after all.

Three weeks later, their office staff had doubled its size, the business was running at a steady, if unexceptional, clip, and Jazz was starting to feel that little bull's-eye on her back flicker and fade. Neither she nor Lucia had seen anything like a tail or a suspicious vehicle in weeks.

She was just starting to feel really good and pretty well healed when Chris Sparrow rang the intercom in the middle of her transcription of the notes for the latest executive background review to announce a visitor.

James Borden.

Jazz hesitated for a second, staring at her lit computer screen, fingers poised on the keys, and then wheeled her chair back. Lucia was gone, still, on one of her nonlocal cases. There really wasn't much of an alternative, except to tell Chris to send him on back.

Through the open door, she witnessed the priceless moment when Pansy, coming out of the coffee room, encountered her ex-boss on his way in. They blinked at each other, and then Pansy, without a tremor, offered Borden the cup of coffee in her hand.

And he, without a tremor, accepted it, toasted her with it, and continued into Jazz's office, where he took a seat on the couch, sipped coffee and sprawled as if he was sitting in his own living room.

"Make yourself at home," she said, and got up to close the door on Pansy's curious smile. "I'd ask what brings you here, but I'm thinking I already know."

Without comment, Borden—who had just had a haircut,

and it suited him—reached inside his trenchcoat and took out a red envelope. She walked over, took it from his hand and sat down next to him to rip it open.

"Why red?" she asked absently.

He finished sipping his coffee before saying, "What?"

"Red envelopes. Seems like a pretty obvious way of delivering a message. Why red?"

"You wouldn't believe me if I told you."

"Okay, that goes without saying, but humor me." She unfolded the paper inside. More Gabriel, Pike & Laskins letterhead, the same businesslike printing.

Proceed at 11:00 p.m. local time tonight to the 1400 block of Legacy Drive. Park on the left side of the street and wait for a black Toyota Celica to arrive and park on the opposite side of the street. Follow the woman in the Celica from her car until she enters the building at 1428 Legacy Drive.

"That's it?" Jazz checked the back of the letter. Apparently, it was. "No pictures, no video, no nothing? Just park, follow, leave?"

"Yes," Borden said. "I told you, they wouldn't all be exciting stuff."

She flapped the envelope. "Why red?"

"Are we back to that again?" He'd not only cut his hair, he was freshly shaved. And if she wasn't mistaken, that was a fresh application of cologne, too. She scooted a little closer, just to confirm her suspicions. "It's so we won't get them mixed up with other correspondence. There's a lot of it in our offices, in case you haven't noticed. Lawyers. We do paperwork."

"Bullshit."

"Excuse me?" He put the coffee cup aside on the side table and turned toward her, resting an elbow on the back of the tufted leather couch. "By the way, I like your hair."

She blushed. She didn't mean to, and she was furious at herself for doing it, but she instantly felt the burn climb from her neck into her cheeks, and saw the immediate lazy amusement in his eyes. She'd let Lucia talk her into a new hairdresser, and as a result, she barely recognized herself in the mirror. Her hair was still in a shag, but no longer reminded her of sheepdogs or thatched roofs; it looked cute, perky and fluffable. It even felt soft, thanks to some expensive conditioners she wasn't sure she could afford, or had enough training to use. But it seemed to work. Lucia had pronounced her fit for boardroom meetings, anyway.

"Thanks," she mumbled. "Yours, too."

He shrugged. No blush, damn him. "How's the side?"

"Fixed."

"But you're taking it easy."

"No, I'm going to sign up for the Ultimate Fighting Championship cage match later today. Yes, of course I'm taking it easy. The toughest thing I've had to do so far is walk fast." She smiled, just a bit, as the blush started to fade to a distant prickle. "Bet I can still kick your ass, though, Counselor."

"No bets," he said. She wondered if he was humoring her.

"Regular rates on this?" She waved the envelope between them, which should have formed some kind of barrier and instead just wafted more of his warm cologne toward her.

"Regular rates," he agreed. Was he leaning closer? She thought he was.

"Are you going to keep doing this? Being the GPL Postal Service?"

"GPL?"

"Gabriel, Pike...?"

"Oh." He raised one shoulder in a very tiny shrug. "Lead time's usually not long enough to trust this stuff to the mail. Even overnight. Though sometimes I might not be available, and you might have to check FedEx, but I'll give you a heads-up first."

"Why?"

"Why would I give you a heads-up?" He sounded mystified by that. She had to admit, it would have been a stupid question.

"No, why is there not enough lead time? Don't you know this stuff a couple of days ahead of time? Surely you don't do this all at the last minute."

He looked at her for such a long, unblinking moment that she actually felt she'd said something wrong, but then he smiled and said, "I never said we were the most organized bunch of lawyers in the world."

She remembered getting off the plane in New York and finding a crisply pressed ex-Marine holding up a sign with names on it. His ability to organize was, so far as she'd been able to tell, pretty damn close to perfect. Like the explanation about the envelopes themselves, it didn't sound right, but she could tell that she wasn't going to get anything more from him. Not yet.

Not now.

"So you're just here to deliver a letter and get back on a plane," she said.

"No. I'm here to deliver a letter, take you out to dinner, and get back on a plane," he said. "You eat, right?"

"Dinner," she repeated, frowning. "You want to go to dinner."

"Early dinner, yeah. Say, six o'clock? That way we'll be finished up before you have to get to work." He nodded slightly at the envelope in her hand, and then looked a little disconcerted. "Unless you have plans."

"As if I have an actual life, you mean?" She snorted. "No. If Lucia was here, we might have a working dinner here, but no. No plans."

"Ah. Right. Lucia's working?" He looked guilty, as if he had forgotten about Lucia. Which Jazz had a hard time imagining, because, well, *Lucia.* If there was going to be a Swimsuit Edition for *Private Investigator Monthly,* Lucia would be the centerfold.

"She's in Washington," Jazz said. "Back tomorrow. But not to worry, Counselor, I can handle sitting in a car and following somebody all by myself. And dinner. I can handle dinner without backup."

He yawned hugely, traded looking guilty for looking shocked and embarrassed, and mumbled something about early-morning flights. She cocked an eyebrow at him, got off the couch and went back to her desk. He watched her go, mouth slightly open on a question that wasn't able to quite fight its way free.

"Stretch out," she said. "You won't bother me."

She went back to typing. She didn't watch him, but after a while her peripheral vision reported that he'd followed her advice. By the time she thought it was safe to focus on him again, his eyes were shut, his limbs loose and relaxed, and he was breathing evenly and quietly.

She stared at the rise and fall of his chest, then let her eyes wander over the rest of him. Long, sleek lines, especially in the blue jeans and boots. Did he wear cowboy boots because he was coming to Kansas City? Were they some kind of special costume, like the leathers? She hoped not. She liked the idea that he wore them because he enjoyed them, not because he needed them to fit in.

Without any transition at all, she wondered how he'd look without the clothes and had to shock herself out of the vision to focus on the dry, quiet text of her report again. In her experience, the better she was able to visualize that kind of thing, the deeper she was in trouble, and that had been, well, vivid.

Really, really vivid.

She grimly tapped keys and forced herself to keep working as the hours slid past toward evening.

For an out-of-towner, dinner in Kansas City required barbecue. Barbecue, in Jazz's opinion, required Arthur Bryant's, and by the time they were tucked into a booth around a Formica table, she was feeling pretty good about the choice. Not too romantic, barbecue. Not an inducement to imagine the other person naked. She didn't even order beer, which was quite a sacrifice, and stuck to soft drinks with her ribs. After an initial reluctance, Borden dove into his dinner with abandon, smearing himself with sauce and grease and mumbling praises about the taste.

She only imagined licking him clean a few times. *I really need to get out more,* she thought sternly, but she was only a little bit embarrassed. He had that kind of mouth. It just…begged to be licked, especially when there were beads of Arthur Bryant sauce clinging to it.

She was feeling relaxed and confident and happy— *happy!*—when her cell phone rang.

"Sorry," she said, and wiped her sticky fingers clean enough to scramble for the call. She didn't immediately recognize the number. "Hello, Jazz Callender." She had to stop her other ear to hear over the dull roar of the restaurant.

"Yeah, Callender?" An unfamiliar male voice, brisk and businesslike. "You're listed on the notify sheet. There's been an incident at Ellsworth. Inmate Benjamin McCarthy's been the victim of a beating, and he's going to be in the hospital wing for a couple of days. No immediate life-threatening injuries."

She felt all of the happiness drain out of her, as if a plug had been pulled from the bottom of her soul. "What happened?" Her tone had changed, and her body language; she saw Borden straighten up and watch her, leaning forward.

"Unclear at the present time, ma'am." In other words, they didn't want to say. "We're looking into it."

She shut her eyes tight enough to see white stars. "Injuries?" She sounded just as businesslike as he did. "Be straight with me, sir. I'm his ex-partner. You know he used to be a cop."

"Yes, ma'am, I know." No emotion in his voice. "He has some busted ribs, a broken arm and a cracked collarbone."

"Anything else?"

A long hesitation. "Not to my knowledge, ma'am."

She shivered all over. She felt sick, hot, disoriented, and the smell of good food and the sound of casual conversation was too much. "Visitation?" she asked.

"I've been instructed to tell you that he can have visitors for one hour tomorrow, from noon until one o'clock."

"Fine. I'll be there."

She hung up and dropped the phone back in her coat pocket. When she opened her eyes again, she saw that Borden was leaning back in his chair, motioning for the waitress.

"What are you doing?" she asked.

"Getting the check," he said. "Doesn't look like you're in the mood for this right now."

She felt a hot, hard surge of gratitude that made her eyes sting with tears. He was careful not to look at her, and she was grateful for that, too.

"Your partner? McCarthy?" he asked. She nodded. "He okay?"

"No." She pulled in a damp, shaking breath. "It was just a matter of time. Could have been worse, I guess. They'll let me see him tomorrow."

Borden finally focused on her face, then turned to smile at the waitress and do the mechanical duty of paying the check and boxing up the rest of the food to go. "You're crazy if you think I'm leaving any of this on the table," he said. "Besides, I'll need something for breakfast in the morning."

"Breakfast?" she blinked.

"I'm interested," Borden said. "I'd like to meet the guy you're so sure is innocent. If you don't mind having a lawyer escort you to the prison."

Her throat closed up. She wasn't sure what it was she was feeling—a dizzying, hot, disorienting mix of fear, anger, pain, guilt, relief…just that it nearly undid her.

Borden reached over and took her hand. Sticky fingers. She gripped them with desperate intensity.

"Thanks," she whispered. "But I thought you had to fly back."

"Vacation day," he said.

She offered her couch for the night, but Borden, with

impeccable instincts, took a cab to a four-star hotel instead. No kiss, nothing like a romantic goodbye unless you counted a skimming touch of his fresh-washed fingers over the back of her neck and a reminder to be careful.

She put her hands in her pockets, watching the cab pull away, and felt the crackle of paper. She checked her watch and found she still had an hour to get to the address on the envelope.

She'd never wanted to do anything less in her life, but driving to Ellsworth right now wouldn't do her any good. They wouldn't let her see him, and Ben wouldn't thank her for any female hysteria anyway. No, she needed to focus on something else. Get calm. Get cold.

She went to work.

Legacy Drive was near a lot of clubs, and the late hour made parking tough. She circled the block for several minutes before she caught a break with a Cadillac pulling away from the curb on the left-hand side of the street of the correct block. Quickly she parallel parked between an SUV and a dusty pickup. A muffled rhythmic bass thump from the country bar down the block shivered through metal and skin as she killed the engine, slightly out of tempo with the headache throbbing in her temples. *Focus.* She checked the car's clock and found that she had fifteen minutes to spare before eleven. She turned off the dome light and made sure everything she needed was ready, including the digital camera, though Borden had told her she wouldn't need it.

Then, because she had nothing else to occupy her head, she thought about what might have happened to land Ben McCarthy in the prison hospital, and what that significant pause on the other end of the phone had meant when she'd asked about any other injuries.

This was her fault. Her fault for letting him down, for not pushing his case to the top of the list. For not turning down these crazy assignments. *Watch a woman park and walk to her building?* What the hell was that about? They could've gotten anyone for that. They didn't need her. And she'd let other things get in the way, too. What right did she have to be out talking and laughing and eating Arthur Bryant's barbecue when her best friend, her *partner,* was getting the hell beat out of him and...

She shut her eyes, sucked in a hard, hurting breath, and deliberately let it go.

At just before eleven—minutes before—she saw a couple walk out of the cowboy bar down the block and stagger to a truck parked across from her on the right side of the street. They managed to get doors unlocked with a minimum of giggling and groping, and wove off down the road, hopefully to a destiny that involved flashing lights and DUI citations. She was considering phoning in a tip when headlights turned the corner behind her, and she saw a car coming, moving slowly.

It slowed even further as the driver spotted the empty space and executed a smooth parallel-parking maneuver.

Black Toyota Celica, furred with a light coating of road

dust. As Jazz watched, the driver opened up a vanity mirror, and as the light bathed her face, Jazz saw an attractive middle-aged woman with dark, shoulder-length hair checking her lipstick. That didn't take long. The driver opened her door and stepped out of the car.

Jazz let her get a few steps away before noiselessly opening her own car door and crossing the street, keeping out of the harsh pools of light near the corner. The woman was wearing a dress, and her high heels tapped concrete as she walked up the street. She had a notebook in her hand, and a penlight, evidently consulting an address. As Jazz hung back in the shadow of a large truck, the woman scanned building numbers, spotted the one she was looking for, and headed decisively in that direction.

Jazz checked for anyone watching or following, but the night was quiet and the street was clear. She was the only tail in sight.

She moved carefully as the woman jogged up the steps to 1428 Legacy Drive and pressed buttons. Jazz got close enough to see which one was pressed—bottom left.

The access gate buzzed. The woman entered.

Well, that's it, Jazz thought, and watched the door snap shut again behind her. *Whatever they thought would happen, didn't. Obviously.*

She watched for a while longer, waiting to see if anything interesting would come along, but apart from a few more amorous couples exiting the dance club, nothing popped.

She went back to her car and checked the time.

Eleven-fifteen.

"Five thousand dollars," she said aloud as she backed out of the parking space and headed home. "You people are totally insane."

She stopped off at a bar on the way back, and after a few shots, she no longer felt the raw ripping edges of fear over what she was going to see at Ellsworth in the morning.

It was worse than she'd thought, and better than she'd hoped. Ben looked different, lying in a hospital bed with tubes in his arms and splints and bandages all over him, but not that much different. His smile was the same, even through puffy, bruised lips. Cool blue eyes, brush-cut medium-brown hair that looked longer than she remembered. Some gray in it, maybe a bit more than the last time she'd been by.

"Jazz," he said. His voice sounded muffled and indistinct. She could hear him breathing. "Sorry about the mess. Slipped in the shower."

She sat down in the chair next to his bed, suddenly unable to find anything to say. McCarthy didn't give her much of a chance. He skipped his attention away from her to lock on to Borden, who was standing behind her.

"You're new," he said. "Let me guess. Lawyer?"

She looked back at him. Borden's smile remained cool and tightly controlled. "I'm a friend," he said. "Why? Do you need a lawyer?"

"Lawyers got me where I am today," McCarthy said.

"Pull up a chair. I hate people looking down at me. Then again, you're so tall you'll probably look down on me any-way...so. Jazz. What's up?"

She was speechless, again. He looked at her, clearly wait-ing, and she felt an insane urge to laugh. This was pure McCarthy. Lying here hooked up to tubes, bubbling blood in a punctured lung, with broken bones and a morphine drip, demanding to know how her life was going.

"Who was it?" she heard herself ask him. McCarthy's blue eyes suddenly went shadowed, twilight cold, half-hid-den by lowered lids.

"Not your problem," he said. "It's like Vegas inside Ellsworth, sweetheart. What happens here stays here."

She had things to ask him, but there was no way she could put it into words, no way that she could imagine him let-ting down his guard in any way. Especially not with Borden here. She'd seen the shields go all the way to full strength the second he'd seen Borden at her back.

"I want to know," she said. "I want to know what hap-pened."

His smile flashed again, but it didn't reach the rest of his face. "No, you don't," he said. "No reason for that. Look, it happened, it wasn't fun, it's over. I'll take care of what needs to be taken care of, yeah? But I need you to do some-thing for me."

She nodded wordlessly, watching him. His hand sud-denly shot out and wrapped around hers, tight and warm. McCarthy had always been the kind to touch, to put a hand on her shoulder, an arm around her shoulders. A celebratory kiss on her temple when things went well. Nothing sexual about it, just…family. As close as could ever matter.

His blue eyes were intense and dark with emotion.

"I need you to stop coming here," he said. "I need to forget what it's like out there if you want me to survive in here."

"No!" She held on to his hand when he tried to pull it away. "No, dammit, Ben, I'm not giving up. I'll find a way to get you out."

"Drop it, Jazz. I mean it. Stewart's trying to bury you, too, and if you give him an excuse he'll do it. Forget me. Move on." His eyes flicked suddenly from her to Borden, then back. "I hear you're working freelance these days."

"Who told you that?"

"You don't think Stewart comes to see me? Keeps me up-to-date on all the gossip? I hear you've got a P.I. license. He can get it pulled, he hears you doing anything you shouldn't be into. Be careful." He studied her through those bruised, wary eyes. "What are you handling? Routine stuff?"

"Yeah," she said. It was partially true, anyway. "I have—" She was about to tell him, *I have a partner,* but the words stuck in her throat. She wasn't sure if saying it would be a reassurance, or a betrayal. "Lighten up, Ben, it's not like I can't take care of myself."

"Yeah," he agreed. His thumb skimmed gently over her bruised, abraded knuckles. He had big, square hands, disfigured now with bruises and cuts where he'd defended himself. They looked like they'd been in the same fight. "Wild woman."

She found herself grinning, suddenly. "Saved your ass a few times."

"More than a few, yeah. But you need to pick your battles. Can't make war against the world." He looked somber, as if what he was saying applied to himself as much as her. "You do what I said last time?"

She didn't answer, because she didn't want to out-and-out lie to him. The last time she'd been to Ellsworth—the day she'd met James Borden, she realized with a shock, had it really been that long ago?—Ben had told her in no uncertain terms to box up the files she was keeping on his case and send them to his attorney. Not that his attorney had ever done him a damn bit of good that she remembered. Skinny little kid, looked more like an actor than a real lawyer...

She found herself glancing over her shoulder at Borden. He was chatting with a nurse, head bent, smiling.

He didn't look like a real lawyer, either.

"I'm going to get you out of here," she said aloud, not quite looking at Ben because it was easier than facing those eyes, that silent whisper of things done and endured she didn't want to know. "Swear to God, I will."

"God put me here," McCarthy said, and shrugged. He put on a false Irish comic-opera lilt. "It'll take the devil himself to get me out."

She jerked her attention back to his face. "Then I'll deal with the devil."

McCarthy sent that unreadable look again, to Borden, who was still talking to the nurse and well out of earshot. "Believe it or not, sweetheart, I think you already did."

By the time she left the prison, Jazz felt exhausted, shaky and desperately in need of a nap. She let Borden have the wheel heading back, and fell asleep to the rhythmic hiss of tires on asphalt and the soft wail of the radio. If she dreamed, it was probably unpleasant, but she didn't remember.

They rolled back into Kansas City in time for rush hour, which Borden negotiated with ease—he would, she supposed, being from the Big Apple—and she realized by the time they'd pulled into her apartment parking lot that she had barely said a word to him since entering the prison.

As he pulled the brake, she looked over at him and said, "Thanks."

"For what?"

"For…not trying to make me believe he's guilty."

Borden shrugged. "I don't know if he's guilty. And what I think doesn't matter, it's what *you* think. You took on the job to have the resources to find out, right? You should use them."

"I intend to."

"Even though he told you not to try?"

She smiled slightly, and tasted bitterness. "Especially since he said that."

Borden finished the business of unbuckling himself from

the seat, turning off the engine, and handing her the keys before he asked, "Are you going to see him again? Even though he told you not to go back?"

"I don't do everything I'm told," she shot back, and got out of the car.

She could have sworn he muttered, "I think you mean *anything*," but when she checked, his face was polite and bland, and he had the good sense not to smirk about having the last word.

Out of habit, she grabbed a paper from the dispenser near the mailboxes, then collected the daily mail carrier's allotment of bills and circulars. Took the stairs. She had started taking the stairs again as soon as she was sure the sutures wouldn't tear loose, and now she was nearly back up to strength, able to trot up the six flights at a good clip without elevating her heart rate more than a few beats a minute. Borden loped next to her without breathing hard, too. Like Lucia, he was a runner. She wondered if he was a swimmer, too.

She put the vision of Borden in a Speedo out of her head with a heroic effort.

Inside the apartment she dumped the mail on the kitchen table as she poured herself a tall glass of orange juice, then another for Borden when she remembered her manners. She sorted through things one-handed, absentmindedly, thinking over how McCarthy had looked, how he'd acted...

She stopped in the act of shoving the newspaper aside and pulled it slowly toward her, then unfolded the front page.

"What?" Borden asked.

She held up a finger for silence, reading, and then turned the front page toward him and pointed to the black-and-white photo of a woman on the front. "Her," she said. "I recognize her."

"What?"

"I followed her last night."

She went back to the article.

Wendy Blankenship, 42, was found dead in an alley near the bar where she worked. She was last seen yesterday evening at six o'clock by co-workers, who described it as a "normal day." "She didn't seem different or anything," said Janelle Vincent, who covers alternate night shifts at Jaye's Tavern. "She just clocked out and went home like usual. It's terrible, you know? She was just getting her life back together. She was like a den mother around here, we're going to miss her so much."

Police have not released the details, but have confirmed that they believe Blankenship's death is a homicide, and are searching for witnesses to put together a timeline of events leading up to her death.

There was no mention of time of death, but Jazz had a sick feeling that she would have been one of the last people to see Wendy Blankenship alive. She remembered Wendy checking her lipstick and walking down the street to the building. Buzzing the intercom.

Last one on the bottom left.

"You knew," she said, and looked up at Borden. He paused in the act of raising his orange juice to his lips. "You *knew.*"

"Knew what?"

"Don't give me that crap! Why else would you send me?"

He put the glass down carefully and extended his hand for the paper. She watched him read the entire article, face composed and emotions hidden, and when he was done he folded the paper again and set it on the table between them without meeting her eyes.

"I don't know," he said hoarsely. "I don't know why we sent you there."

"Bullshit. Why didn't you have me stop her? Save her? I was *right there!*"

He looked up, then, and she saw the suffering in his eyes. "I don't know, Jazz."

She stared at him for a few long seconds, then reached over and picked up the cordless phone and dialed a number from memory. "Yeah," she said to the woman who answered. "I need to speak to Detective Stewart. I have some information about a murder."

"Don't," Borden said.

"It's worse if I wait," she said to him. "They'll have surveillance footage, security-camera video, something. If Stewart thinks I'm hiding something…"

"You can't do this."

"Why didn't you save her?" she screamed at him.

He looked back at her, stark and pale, and shook his head. "Because we can't save everybody," he said, and he sounded just as sick as she felt. "Because it isn't possible. You know that, Jazz."

"Where the hell does this stuff come from?" she demanded. "All this…this…*bullshit!* Go here, watch this, videotape this—? Who tells you where to send me? Who tells you *why?*"

She was so intent on his answer that the appearance of Lucia in the kitchen doorway made her flinch. Lucia, looking sleek and dark and dangerous, put down her black nylon bag and backpack, crossed her arms, and said, "I knocked. I guess you were too busy screaming at the top of your lungs to hear." She transferred that fierce black look to Borden. "She asked you a question, Counselor."

"You, too?" he murmured.

"Yes. Me, too. I'm just as tired as she is of the cloak-and-dagger, and I'd be willing to bet I'm just all-around more tired, period. Tell us, or get out and take your red envelopes with you." Lucia couldn't possibly have a clue what they were arguing about, but you'd never have known it from the self-possession she displayed—then again, hell, for all Jazz knew, *Lucia* had the apartment wired for sound and vision. Maybe she knew everything.

Maybe she always did.

Borden looked from one of them to the other, wordlessly,

and Jazz didn't blink. Neither, so far as she could tell, did Lucia.

"I need to make a phone call," he said.

"Then dial," Lucia said softly. "Before we pick up the phone and tell Detective Stewart everything we know about Gabriel, Pike & Laskins. You put my partner in a compromising position, Mr. Borden. I don't think I like that very much. Make amends."

He visibly swallowed. Jazz might have felt sorry for him, except the fierce gratitude and pride she was feeling for Lucia crowded all of that out.

He reached in his pocket and retrieved his cell phone, and dialed. "Yeah," he said slowly. "It's Borden. I need to take Callender and Garza to the next level."

Silence. His eyes fixed on the newspaper lying folded on the table. The picture of Wendy Blankenship, who hadn't survived the night that Jazz Callender barely remembered after the blur of drinks.

"Yes," he said. "I understand." He hung up and looked at each of them in turn, Jazz last. His eyes were asking her for something, but she couldn't understand what it was, and she wasn't in the mood to grant him any favors anyway. "We need to go downstairs," he said. "Right now."

"I just got off a plane," Lucia said. "Mind if I change clothes first?"

"Actually, I do," he said. "There's a car waiting."

"What?" For the first time, Jazz actually saw Lucia thrown off her stride. "What the hell are you talking about?"

Borden didn't answer. Jazz, after a few unmoving seconds, answered for him.

"They knew," she said. "They had to know all of this
before it happened. Why else would they have a car here,
now?"

"That's insane," Lucia said flatly.

"Yes," she agreed. "Like hiring two people who don't
know each other. Like paying them to set up a detective
agency and carry out assignments that don't have any pur-
pose. That's insane, too. Remember?"

Lucia stared at her, a frown grooved over her eyebrows,
a light in her eyes that Jazz hadn't seen before. Wary.
Mistrustful.

"It's crazy," she repeated slowly.

"Yeah," Jazz agreed. "My point exactly." She turned to
Borden. "Let's go see the wizard, Tin Man."

It wasn't just a car downstairs, it was a limousine. A big,
black stretch limo, with tinted windows and a uniformed
chauffeur who looked vaguely familiar. Jazz blinked at the
sight of him—it was odd, seeing a stretch limo and a liver-
ied driver on the streets of Kansas City—but it was Lucia
who said, "We've met you before."

The driver doffed his cap and nodded with military precision. "Yes, ma'am," he said, and Jazz remembered. Same
driver from New York City, from the visit to the Gabriel,
Pike & Laskins offices, only more formally dressed and
captaining a bigger land yacht. He opened the back door

and handed Lucia inside, then reached for Jazz, who avoided him and climbed in on her own.

Milo Laskins, Borden's boss, was the sole occupant of the car. He was dressed in another natty suit, this one charcoal-gray, with a navy tie and a diamond stickpin.

"Ms. Garza. Ms. Callender." Laskins offered them a gentlemanly nod. "I understand you have questions. That's perfectly reasonable. I'm authorized to answer them."

Jazz had been prepared to argue, but his easy, courteous manner threw her off stride. Not so Lucia, who stepped in to say, "Fine. Who are you?"

"That's simpler than you might think," Laskins said, and raised thick eyebrows. "I'm just like you. I'm an Actor."

Jazz heard the capital *A*. Didn't understand what it meant, but she heard the emphasis.

He tapped the thick, tinted divider behind him. The limo pulled into traffic, smooth as silk. Jazz fisted her hands. She felt helpless, moving out of control.

"Which means what, exactly?" Lucia asked. "Conspiracy theory dinner theater on the weekends?"

"I will give you a very simple overview of what we—or, more properly, the Cross Society—now know about the world, Ms. Garza. There are two kinds of people in it."

"Only two?" Lucia murmured, sounding amused.

"For our purposes, yes. There are Actors and Chorus. At any given time on this planet, out of the billions of human lives being lived, only a handful—about ten thousand, all together—are doing anything that really matters on a larger scale. These are people we term Actors. Everyone else…" Laskins made a languid, elegant motion with one hand. "Chorus. Extras, if you will. It isn't the *same* ten thousand from moment to moment, understand. Almost every life on Earth will experience at least one decision, one event in their life that has large ripples of consequence—almost everyone moves from Chorus to Actor once in their lives. But it turns out, rather unexpectedly, that once you begin to analyze the world in this manner you find that it doesn't look as random as you would expect."

"I don't understand," Lucia said. She did sound interested, though Jazz had ceased to have any investment somewhere around the Actor/Chorus explanation, which was a load of horseshit; she was waiting for Laskins to stop spinning fairy tales and get to the point.

Unexpectedly, Laskins focused his gaze on her.

"Do you?"

"Afraid not," she said, and shrugged. He sighed.

"Have you ever heard the old adage, nothing succeeds like success? Or, it takes money to make money? They share a common theme. The more you have of one thing, the natural tendency is that similar things attract."

"I have no idea what the hell you're saying," Jazz said. "Can we move on to the part where you tell me why you had me let a woman *die* last night? Because that's the part I'm really fascinated about."

Laskins's smile vanished. He looked tired and old and,

suddenly, unhappy. "I wish I could explain it to you in a way that made sense. I can't, not really, but I'll try.

"Certain people are never Chorus in this life, Jasmine. They are, quite simply, always Actors. Everything they do ripples and has consequences, even the smallest thing. They are rare, these...Leads. We have identified perhaps a hundred of them. The woman that you were asked to follow was a Lead, and you were there to counter a move by the opposition. It was the right move, but it simply failed."

"What the *hell* are you talking about?"

"We put you in place to save her life."

The limo made a right turn. Jazz glanced out the windows, half-claustrophobic, and saw that they were on the back side of the office building.

Circling the block.

She took a deep breath. "Hate to break it to you, but it didn't work."

"Yes," Laskins said quietly. "I'd like to tell you that it was a foolproof system. It doesn't always work out."

"Doesn't always work out?" Jazz repeated hotly. "She's *dead!* If she's so damn important and you knew she was in danger, why didn't you use one of those—those *Actors* or *Leads* or whatever to protect her?"

Laskins leaned forward, fixed her with a look, and said, very softly, "We did."

Borden sucked in a breath. Jazz looked sharply at him, but he didn't say anything. He avoided her eyes.

"Are you telling me that I'm a—whatever?"

"Yes. A Lead. Both of you are. That's why we chose you. That's why we've financed you, and we've put you in a position to do things on our behalf. Because you can. Because you must."

"Then I guess the fact that Wendy's dead in the morgue is proof that you're all insane," Jazz said grimly. Lucia, next to her, was oddly quiet, watching Laskins. "If we're so important, why the hell haven't we made any difference? You know what? This is useless. You're all crazy, and I'm out of here."

She shoved on Borden, trying to get him to move, but he was more solid than he looked, and she was hampered by the close confines of the car. He didn't look at her.

"You have made a difference," Borden said. "Jazz, listen to me. I know what we're saying sounds crazy—"

"Let me out!" Jazz was half-standing now, furious, reaching over Borden for the door handle. He grabbed her hand and held it, trying to get her to look at him; she flatly refused. She was shaking all over. "Dammit, I'm *done,* do you hear me? Let me the hell out *now!*"

But it wasn't Borden who stopped her from getting out, it was Lucia. Lucia's quiet voice, unnaturally calm. "The woman loading boxes in the van," she said. "The first job we did for you. She was going to be killed?"

"If you hadn't been there, yes. At least, we think so."

"So we put the chaos in chaos theory," Lucia said, leaning forward, hands clasped between her knees. "It's like chess, isn't it. You move us like pieces on a board. We're pawns, protecting your bishops and knights and castles."

"Don't sell yourself short," Laskins grunted in reply. "Pawns don't rate this explanation. And although Wendy Blankenship had the potential to become important, she wasn't a castle."

"If you're any good at chess," Lucia continued, "then you know there are a limited number of outcomes when you have three pieces interacting—especially if the point is to take one of the pieces off the board. Why didn't you warn Jazz and let her save Wendy?"

"None of this is an exact science, Ms. Garza. Every action, by any of the Actors at the moment, can turn events. We can't warn against specifics, because we only are sure of generalities. We knew Ms. Blankenship was marked for death, and indeed, we couldn't find an outcome in which she didn't die. But we chose the moment most likely to make a difference. If events had gone a bit differently, if their Actor had made an error, Jazz *would* have saved her. But sometimes it isn't possible." To his credit, Laskins sounded almost as if he gave a damn. "Chess is my specialty. And the focus is not upon pieces that will inevitably be lost, but on making that sacrifice meaningful."

"You used Jazz to take out the killer, after the fact."

"We put her in a position where she could provide the police with a vital lead, yes, without placing her in danger. She's already taken far too many risks."

Jazz parted her lips to fire off a response, but nothing came to mind.

"As I said," Laskins continued, "chess is my specialty. And while this isn't the outcome we'd hoped for, it's far from a lost cause. Jazz can safely come forward with her information, and we achieve our goal in a different way. We stopped a serial killer, who will shortly leave the chessboard himself, and we did it with only inevitable losses. It isn't always about bullets and bombs, you know, Ms. Garza. Or lying."

There must have been a hidden message in that. Jazz saw a flicker in Lucia's eyes, a downright flinch in her body language. "If you're playing chess," Lucia asked, "who do you play against? And don't tell me God. I don't believe you're quite that good."

The privacy screen between them and the driver suddenly eased down with a whir, and their ex-Marine chauffeur turned to look back at them. "Excuse me," he said, "but you wanted to know when the other car left. It's leaving now."

"Thank you, Charles," Laskins said, and checked his expensive watch. "Right on time. I'm sorry, Ms. Garza, but we'll have to cut this meeting short. Some things simply won't be postponed, as I'm sure you can appreciate."

"Answer my question first," she said.

"No." Laskins nodded toward the door. "Charles, if you please—"

Lucia, without seeming to be in a big hurry or doing anything important, reached around and pulled out her gun. She pointed it directly at Laskins. "Nothing personal," she said, with a hint of a smile, "but I'd *really* like an answer to my question first. And Charles, don't do anything foolish, please, because two of us shooting in here really won't help the situation."

Laskins threw out a warning hand to the Marine. "Interesting. There was only a very small chance that you would do that, you know."

"Unless you're wearing bulletproof armor under that Hugo Boss suit, I don't think that means much," Lucia replied. They exchanged cool little smiles. "How is it done?"

"How is what done?"

Jazz jumped in. "The fortune-telling. What do you have? Tarot cards? A crystal ball? Twelve thousand monkeys with calculators?" She knew she sounded sarcastic, and didn't give a damn. This was scary. The fact that Lucia was buying it downright terrified her.

Laskins gave her a narrow, sour smile. "No. We have a few people who do these things—freaks of nature, if you will. But the rest of us apply science, not superstition. It might surprise you to know there are solid, scientific methods that can be applied to the problem of alternative realities. String theory, for instance."

"You have a psychic," Lucia cut in. "Right?"

"Yes. You could say that."

"Then why all the chess?"

"This is what happens," Laskins said irritably, "when you have *two* psychics who both want to win."

Lucia glanced aside at Jazz, who hadn't quite figured out

a move, either. At least, nothing that wouldn't compromise Lucia's. "You believing anything he's told us?" she asked.

"I believe that I'm going to report seeing Wendy Blankenship buzz herself into that apartment," Jazz said. "I would have done that, anyway."

"You'll need a cover story. Some reason you were on the street and saw her," Lucia replied. "I can handle that part, back-engineer an assignment you were on. It'll check out." She transferred attention back to the two facing them— not, Jazz suspected, that it had ever really wandered. "Mr. Laskins, you have ten seconds to answer me before my partner and I exit this vehicle and your plans, forever. If you know anything at all about me, you know that I mean what I'm saying."

"Yes," Laskins said sourly. "I know you mean it, Garza. But use your common sense. The Cross Society is giving you information, and you're acting upon it. Do you really think you can just walk away?"

"Oh, yes, I think I can. And should."

"From the moment our psychic—"

"Max Simms?" Jazz asked. Laskins cut his steely Paul Newman stare her way.

"Yes, fine, Max Simms. From the moment you appeared in his visions, you became important. We got to you first. That made you targets—low-priority, at present—for the opposition. You will be targets for as long as you continue to be Actors."

"How do we quit?"

It was a perfectly good question, but Laskins's smile got wider. "You can't, Ms. Callender. Not of your own accord. For as long as the greater forces of the universe—God, the devil, or chance—deem you an Actor, you will remain one. But don't worry. Eventually, it will be over."

"Yeah," Jazz snapped. "Eventually we all die."

Laskins didn't bother to deny it.

Laskins said, "We've reached a hard stop, Ms. Garza. You can either shoot me, which would have a less than pleasant outcome for both you and your partner, or you can exit the limousine and refuse to take any further support or information from us. But if you do that, you cut yourselves off. You've been marked as Leads, both of you. What you do matters. *Everything* you do matters, one way or another. You're targets, as surely as Wendy Blankenship, and you'll end up just the same if we don't help you."

"I don't like threats." Lucia almost purred it.

"That isn't a threat," he said. "It doesn't need to be. You've become part of what we are. Our enemies know that."

Lucia smiled and looked at Jazz. It was crazy, weird, *exhilarating,* the way the two of them communicated. The way things hummed at moments like this.

"Well," Jazz said, "I suck at chess, but I *love* contact sports."

On some unseen signal, Charles pulled the limo in at the curb again. Lucia reached over and opened her door. "The thing about hiring what you call Leads? We aren't going to always do what you tell us."

"If you don't, people will die," Laskins said.

"I did what you asked. Blankenship's still dead," Jazz said. Lucia slid smoothly out of the limousine. She scooted over to follow. "Don't call us. Oh, and those red letters? Stuff them."

She looked back, one last time, at James Borden. He was staring at her as if he was trying to memorize everything about her in the last second.

"See you, Counselor," she said, and shut the door.

The limo pulled away, accelerating fast.

She and Lucia stood on the empty street in front of the apartment building, staring after it. Lucia absently holstered her gun.

"Well," she said. "That was...unusual."

"Which is so unusual for us, these days," Jazz agreed blandly. She didn't feel bland. She felt wired, juiced, jittery, more alive than she had in months. As if she'd finally found...

What?

Something.

Lucia turned toward her. "Do you want to stop?"

"Stop?"

"Quit. Dissolve the partnership. Go separate ways." Lucia nodded after the limo's taillights. "Clearly, these people are insane. It's probably far better that we get out now, before the damage is permanent."

"Yeah," Jazz agreed softly. "They're crazy."

"Then you want to quit?"

Silence. There were cars coming. Jazz glanced at the distant oncoming headlights, then met Lucia's eyes and held them. "No," she said. "I don't want to quit. Not the partnership, anyway."

Lucia's smile was warm, wicked and utterly crazy. "Neither do I. This is just about to get…interesting."

Chapter 7

Four months later

"Pansy, where the *hell* is the DeMontis file?"

"Under *D*."

"It's not under—oh. There it is." Jazz grabbed it and slammed the lateral filing cabinet shut, then used a corner of her assistant's desk to support the folder as she flipped the massive thing open. "Dammit. Has Lucia not filed her latest surveillance report yet?"

Pansy, for answer, clicked keys on her computer and a sheet of paper was spit out of her printer. She chunked a couple of holes in the top and handed it to Jazz. "E-mailed ten minutes ago."

Jazz read the text, frowning, pacing, and reached across Pansy for the desk phone. Pansy glided her chair out of the way and sorted mail. No suits for Pansy these days; she had on a flower-patterned top, black pants, cat-eye glasses, and red streaks through her dark hair. The real Pansy, Jazz was sure. She'd told her to wear whatever she liked, but it had taken a good two weeks, in the beginning, for Pansy to slowly give up the formal wear.

Jazz continued to set a bad example by modeling the latest in fleece pullovers, blue jeans, and—on special occasions—loose-fitting shirts over colored T-shirts. And by failing to practice political correctness in the workplace.

The past few months had been tense at first. They'd kept waiting for the other shoe to drop, for the attack, for…something. But the Cross Society had been mysteriously quiet. And despite Laskins's scare tactics, the world hadn't come to an end. Evil psychic ninjas hadn't shown up to kill them, and the Cross Society hadn't even demanded their hundred thousand dollars back. And so, they'd settled into business as usual.

Jazz read as Pansy sorted mail, flipping junk into the trash, catalogs into a to-be-reviewed pile, personal mail for Jazz and Lucia into a third. Pansy hesitated over one envelope and ripped it open with a sharp little steel opener and pulled out a check. The printing was familiar. Their favorite client, DeMontis, had come through with another payment. Pansy waved it at Jazz, who nodded as she dialed the phone.

Lucia picked it up on the second ring. "*Holá,*" she said.

"Can you talk?"

"For now. I'm busy cleaning toilets."

"I hope you're using hands-free on the cell, because, you know, ugh."

"Very funny. What?"

"The report," Jazz said. "You still haven't seen them make the drop?"

"I think that's what it says in my last report, why, yes. And let me ask again why I'm the one wearing a sloppy green apron and emptying trash cans and scrubbing toilets? Is this a commentary on my national heritage?"

"It's a commentary on the fact that you agreed to take this crappy industrial espionage case, not me," Jazz replied. "I like the background checks."

"You like the divorce cases," Lucia said gloomily.

"I like easy work where I don't get shot. So, are these guys just smarter than you, or what?"

"You know, if you're trying to piss me off, that's not very difficult when my eyes are burning from cleaning products, and I'm contemplating how men always miss the urinals."

"I like you better pissed off."

"Love you, too," Lucia said. "Two more days and I'm out of here, and then *you* can come and show them how to scrub a bathroom while I call you and make taunting remarks about your detective skills."

Jazz hung up without a response.

"We're losing money on that one, boss," Pansy said. "Two weeks of her time? Unless she brings in the whole pig, not just the bacon—"

"I know." Jazz nodded at the check in Pansy's hand. "Covers expenses, right?"

"Yeah, but I've got a bonus coming. Oh, and boss?" Pansy hesitated, then blurted out, "He called again."

"He?" Like Jazz didn't know.

"Ex-boss."

Ex-boss meant James Borden, of course. "Did you hang up on him? Insult him using lots of short Anglo-Saxon words?"

"I *like* him," Pansy said mournfully. "Do you, you know, have to—"

"Make him suffer? Yes, Pansy, I do. It's my job. And it gives me such a nice, warm glow of satisfaction, too." Jazz piled mail on top of the heavy DeMontis folder and headed toward her office. "If he calls again, tell him—"

"He's coming."

She stopped dead in her tracks and turned to look at Pansy, who had the grace to seem embarrassed. "Repeat that."

"He's on a plane," Pansy explained. "He's going to be here in a couple of hours, tops."

"You told him I wouldn't talk to him?"

"Boss, I've told him a thousand times. Which is, you know, how many times he's actually called, and you'd think somebody at GPL would start tracking those phone charges, wouldn't you?"

"If he shows up, call Security," Jazz said grimly, and walked into her office.

Pansy called, "Want me to make reservations? Someplace nice?"

Jazz slammed the door with a kick, and heard a muffled "Okay, guess not," through the wood. She snorted back a laugh.

Borden, coming here. Jazz dropped folder and mail onto her desk, and sank down in her chair. She picked up a catalog and flipped through it. She stared blankly at the latest in tasers and rubber bullets for crowd control.

Pansy opened the door without knocking, sailed in and slammed a cup of coffee down on Jazz's desktop. Jazz looked up, surprised.

"I know, you told me I'd never have to get coffee," Pansy said, "but honestly, don't you think you should at least talk to him?"

"I don't want coffee, and why the hell would I do that?" Jazz asked. She tried to go back to her law-enforcement catalog.

"Because he's a total hottie who's obviously crazy in love with you?" Pansy took the catalog out of her hands and handed her a copy of *Elle*. "Here. Try to find something that looks like it didn't come out of the gang-banger collection."

"I'm not dressing up for *Borden*."

"He dresses up for you."

"Does not."

"Does—" Pansy was interrupted by the phone, switched in midstream and snatched the receiver out of the cradle. "Jasmine Callender's office, this is Pansy, how can I—oh, hey, Manny. Yeah, she's right here. Tell her to buy some new clothes, would you?"

She extended the phone without looking at Jazz, who tossed *Elle* unopened back on the desk and took the receiver. Pansy, like Lucia, had a nice manicure. Jazz studied the short, stubby nails on her right hand as she held the phone to her left ear and said, "Manny?"

"Is this line—"

"Secure? Yeah, Manny, it's secure." She rolled her eyes at Pansy, who shook her head. "What's up?"

"I have something you might be interested in. A private client brought it in."

He was being careful. With Manny, *private client* usually meant a cop who was working off the books, for various reasons—maybe because the department had shut down the investigation, maybe because the budget was too tight to run the tests he or she wanted done. Manny usually threw them a discount, and sometimes an outright freebie.

Something strange might mean something he wanted out of his lab, which meant violent crime. Jazz was not averse to that.

"Okay," she said. "I'll drop by. You still in the same place?"

"I'll bring it to you," he said.

She blinked. "Excuse me…?"

"I'll bring it to you. To the office."

"You're leaving your lab."

"Yes."

"By yourself."

"Yes." Manny—*Manny!*—was starting to sound irritated. "I do get out, you know. Sometimes."

"If you say so," she said, and gave Pansy a pantomime of a wide-eyed *what the hell?* "Today?"

"An hour."

"Are you going to be wearing a disguise, or—"

"Shut up, Jazz." He hung up on her. She took the phone away from her ear and stared at it, then replaced it in the cradle.

"You know," she said to Pansy, "there are some days when the world is just too strange for words, and this is one of them."

Pansy patted her on the hand and handed her *Elle*.

She put it back and picked up *Guns & Ammo* and, without even thinking, reached for the coffee and sipped it. Pansy grinned in triumph and left, shutting the door after herself.

Borden was coming, after a four-month absence. That made her feel warm and odd, and impatient with herself for it. She'd cut the cord with him. With Gabriel, Pike & Laskins in general. She and Lucia—she presumed—hadn't had contact with them since the last red envelope had arrived, via FedEx, and that had consisted of taking the envelope, unopened, sticking it in another FedEx envelope and sending it right back with a sticky note reading *Not playing the game*.

Maybe Borden was coming to deliver a last-ditch personal appeal. Maybe GPL—or the Cross Society—was desperate enough to try to whore him out.

Like we're that important. She didn't believe it. She didn't think Lucia believed it, either.

Maybe Borden was just...coming to see her. *Someplace nice for dinner.* She hadn't even thought about dinner with him, not since Arthur Bryant's, when everything had gone to hell with one phone call.

No. No dinner. No conversation. I want nothing to do with James Borden.

And some part of her brain added, *Well, sleeping with the enemy might be kind of fun. Not to mention informative.*

She told it sternly to shut up, sipped coffee and eyed *Elle* while determinedly reviewing the latest in zip-tie cuffs in *Law Enforcement Supply.*

Manny arrived an hour later, on the dot, looking freshly scrubbed and far neater than Jazz could remember—practically presentable, in fact. He'd forgotten to take off the lab coat, but other than that, the button-down shirt and blue jeans were clean, if a little frayed, and the tennis shoes were almost brand-new. He'd gotten a haircut—or, more likely, done it himself—and it made him look ten years younger. He'd even shaved, but as usual, the constant five-o'clock shadow made him look a bit shifty.

His eyes were nervous, trying to look everywhere, bright with terror, but he was here. Standing beside Pansy's desk, hands in his lab-coat pockets.

Shaking but upright.

Jazz stood in the doorway for a second, taking it in; there was a tight bloom of happiness inside her, seeing him. She loved Manny, she always had. He was a gentle soul, and he'd never deserved anything that he'd endured. It was nice to see him finding his strength again.

And then she saw him smile, and something clicked into focus with blinding clarity.

Ahh. He was smiling at *Pansy*. And she was smiling back, warmly. They'd been spending time on the phone, and Pansy had started taking all the drop-offs to Manny. But this was a big step forward.

No wonder Manny was out of the house and looking human again. Sometimes, the best therapy was just plain old hormones.

"Manny," she said, since clearly Manny was at a loss for words when it came to chatting up women—that part probably had nothing to do with his posttraumatic stress and everything to do with being a lab geek from way, way back. Manny looked relieved and put out at the same time. "Hey, bro, it's good to see you."

He nodded jerkily, shifted his feet and abruptly held out a package. It was wrapped in brown paper, taped securely and tied with string. The tape was evidence tape, and he'd practically hermetically sealed the thing.

She reached out and took it off his hands.

"Anything you want to tell me about this?" she asked, and got a violent shake of his head. "Who dropped it off to you?"

"A friend," he said. Which could mean anything, or nothing. "You don't need to know. Just…take a look at it. Tell me what you think."

"Anything in particular I should be looking for?"

"You'll know," he said. "If I'm right. Um, I—authenticated—anyway. There's nothing hinky about them. I checked."

He shoved his hands back into the lab coat. The package felt light in her hand. Paper, maybe. Clothing. Nothing very substantial. The packing he'd wrapped it in probably weighed more than the item.

"Want to stick around, or…?"

"No," he said, and whirled around to look at Pansy, who looked back, startled. "No, I—bye."

He hurried away, jerky movements, head down. He took the stairs, not the elevator. Pansy and Jazz watched him go.

"Huh," Pansy said contemplatively. Which Jazz supposed kind of covered it.

She shook her head, went into her office and closed the door.

Using a pair of sharp scissors and a pocketknife, it still took her about ten minutes to strip away the tape-reinforced paper to reveal…a tape-reinforced box. She slit the tape, put the box down on the table and reached into her desk drawer for a pair of latex gloves, which she donned before lifting off the top of the cardboard box. It had been designed for letterhead, she saw—plain white, no markings unless they were hidden by the evidence tape. She didn't know if it was

Manny's box, or the one provided by his "friend"—but then, she realized, Manny would never damage it by slapping tape all over potential evidence.

Inside lay a sheet of paper and what looked like three eight-by-ten photographs underneath it. She focused first on the paper, which was computer printing on plain copy stock.

Jazz: Note time and date stamp on photos

Nothing else, but for Manny, that was the equivalent of a page-long memo. She set the paper aside and looked at what was underneath.

The first picture underneath was grainy black-and-white, clearly taken in low light. The note was right, there was a time/date stamp on the lower right-hand corner in block white letters. The photo was of an alley, a part of a sign flush against a building that said *vet Palace*. Since veterinarians rarely had that kind of neon, that had to be the Velvet Palace, a not-so-gentlemanly club over on the raw side of town. There were three men pictured. Two were standing under a floodlight, and the camera caught a good shot of one of their faces. She didn't recognize him.

She stared at the picture for a moment, frowning, waiting for a penny to drop, but nothing came to her. She picked up the photo and moved it over atop the letter.

The second photo showed the second man's face. He was wearing a cheap rumpled business suit, but again, nobody she recognized. He was handing over a wrapped package to the third man, who was hidden in shadow.

The last photo was clearly taken as the meeting was

breaking up, and one of the men was already hidden by the open back door of the club, the other preparing to enter. But it had the face of the third man, who up to that point had been hidden in shadow.

She felt a short-circuit shock of recognition and adrenaline like a fist to the temple. She put both hands on the desk and stood up, staring down at the picture, which showed her ex-partner, Ben McCarthy, staring almost full-face at the camera. She even knew the clothes—a long black trench coat, dress shirt, black slacks. No tie. Ben had never worn a tie, except at trials.

He was sliding the package into the pocket of his trench coat.

She stared at him for a long few seconds, trying to slow down the beating of her heart, and then focused on the date and time.

"Son of a bitch," she whispered, and sank back in her chair.

That's what had been nagging at her about the previous photos. Date and time.

The same date and time that Ben McCarthy had supposedly been on the other side of Kansas City cold-bloodedly putting bullets in the heads of two unarmed men and a woman.

The pictures clearly showed that he'd been behind the Velvet Palace, taking a payoff.

"You son of a bitch," she amended, in a lost whisper,

and dug the heels of her hands into her eyes. "You lied. You *lied*."

He hadn't lied about being innocent—he hadn't been guilty of the killings—but he hadn't produced this alibi, either. Probably because it was nearly as bad, and would have unearthed more than just this one incident. Maybe he was protecting himself. Maybe he'd just plain believed that he could beat this thing, and then it had been too late to change his story.

Besides, two criminals and a payoff in an alley behind a strip club was probably not the world's most believable alibi.

He hadn't known about the pictures.

She stared down at them. The date and time. The faces of the men with him.

She'd been looking for evidence of Ben's innocence all this time, but she hadn't expected this. She also had no idea who had given it to Manny, or why. Why now?

Authenticate, she warned herself. *This is crap without provenance. Without testimony from the guy who took them.*

First step would be to find subjects number one and two in the photos.

She put the photos back in the box and carried them out to Pansy's desk. Pansy, on the phone, looked up, saw her expression, and apologized to whoever was on the other end of the line before she hung up.

"Boss," she said. That was all, but it was enough. Jazz set the box down on the corner of her desk.

"I need these scanned," she said. "Evidence rules. I'm going to need some copies to take with me, too."

Pansy nodded and reached in her desk drawer for latex gloves. "Did Manny already do the printing?"

"Believe me, Manny would have done everything it was possible to do to these photos, short of burning them and sorting through the ashes." She cleared her throat. Something felt tight in there. "Pansy."

"Boss?"

"It's important."

Pansy nodded solemnly. "I can tell that."

"Soon as you have them done—"

"I'll let you know," she said. "You want me to talk to Lucia?"

"No, I'll do it." Because Lucia had contacts at the federal databases, who might or might not, depending on the political climate, be willing to run the faces against their records. But for now, Jazz was burning to do it the old-fashioned way: pounding pavement. "Soon as you can, all right?"

"Doing it right now," Pansy said, and fired up the scanner. Jazz didn't wait. She was already on her way back to the office to gear up.

When the knock came on the door, she figured it was Pansy, returning the pictures, but instead it was James Borden bearing gifts.

To be exact, a fruit basket in his right hand that would have looked perfectly at home on Carmen Miranda's head, and in his right hand, a red envelope.

She blinked at the fruit basket, holstered the gun that she had just loaded and transferred her stare to his face.

Damn, he's pretty, some traitor part of her brain told her. She ignored it. She wasn't interested in pretty. She was interested in those photos telling her that Ben McCarthy had been on the other side of town when people were being murdered with his gun.

Borden raised the fruit basket and his eyebrows at the same time. "I come bearing...um, looks like bananas, papayas, some pears..."

"You come bearing trouble," she said, and crossed to take the basket from his hand. It was heavy. She deposited it on the side table with a frown. "What if I don't like fruit?"

"It's good for you," he said. "Chocolate seemed a little clichéd. But hey, there's some pear honey in there, too. And pear butter. Are you going to shoot me?"

"Thinking about it," she said shortly. "I'm on my way out."

The humor drained out of his face. "Jazz, wait. Look, I'm sorry, but I want—need—to talk to you."

"Bad timing," she said grimly, and adjusted the shoulder rig under her loose jacket. "Some other day, maybe, but this one's just turned a little more interesting than normal, so if you don't mind—thanks for the fruit, now get the hell out."

"I can't. I need to—"

She rounded on him and took a step into his space, spearing him with a glare. "Look, I don't care what you need, okay? You come here with your—your fruit basket and your stupid red envelope and just expect me to be avail-able? Well, it's not that easy. I'm an *Actor,* after all. Free will. Whatever."

"You're not the only one," he said, and it occurred to her that she'd never heard anybody say, one way or another, what exactly James Borden's role was in this little opera. Spear-carrier? Chorus? Actor? *Lead?*

Assuming she bought any of their bullshit, which she so very definitely didn't. She'd gone to the cops and put in her statement about Blankenship's murder. Lucia had put together an absolutely amazing cover story for why she'd been there on that street at that particular moment, and while detectives like Ken Stewart hadn't cared for it, they hadn't been able to poke holes in it, either.

And Wendy Blankenship's killer was in jail, awaiting trial. That was something.

Sometimes, at weak moments, she wondered how the red envelope had managed to put her there on that street at the right time, if Laskins hadn't been on the up-and-up with her. But she didn't wonder too long or worry too much.

Too busy. If everything she did mattered, then she was damn well going to make every moment count.

"Right. I'm going…and, you're not leaving," she said, as Borden walked over to her couch and sat down, all arms and legs and angles. "Why aren't you leaving?"

"I told you, I'm not going without talking to you." He'd done something new to his hair, she decided. She wasn't sure she liked it, but then, she hadn't liked his last hairstyle, either. At least he looked comfortable today, not tied up in the suit and strangled in a tie. Blue jeans and that long-cut leather jacket she remembered from before. She'd never noticed before, but he had on some academic ring or other, something large, round and gold. Harvard or Princeton or something equally Ivy League, probably. He didn't seem the type to have taken his J.D. at Podunk University.

"Okay, it's possible that I'm using words that are too short for a smart guy like you to understand, but—"

"We have something we need you to do."

"We? I just see one of you standing—"

"The Cross Society."

"Stop interrupting me!"

"Stop acting like an asshole."

"Hey!"

He uncoiled from the couch. It was probably unconscious, the way he tried to use his superior height and reach to intimidate her, but she didn't like it. She stepped right into his space, staring into those dark eyes.

"Call me an asshole again," she invited softly. "Go on."

"I said you were acting like one, not—"

"I know what you said."

Silence. She watched him breathe. Some part of her was acutely aware of him, of the warmth radiating off him, of the smell of his cologne and the matte-velvet slide of his skin. The quick throb of the pulse in his neck.

"I have work to do," she said, and reached around him for her jacket.

He grabbed her wrist.

She pivoted, came in behind him and used her leverage to bend his arm up behind his back. Slammed him against the wall with such force that the pictures rattled. That was all right, they were Lucia's choice anyway. Not like Jazz Callender had a lot of Kodak moments in her life.

She felt his shoulder muscles jumping, trying to resist, but she had the pressure point and he was off balance, and she grabbed the back of his neck and held him still.

"Seriously," she said, "don't think that just because you're a big guy you can take me. Maybe you can, if you get lucky and I get stupid, but any normal day, Counselor, I'm going to whip your ass, all right? So don't get tough with me. And don't even *try* to tell me what to do."

He moved his head fractionally, trying to get a look at her. She pressed harder. Her fingers curled into the soft hair at the nape of his neck, and God, it felt good.

"You can beat the crap out of me, and it doesn't change anything," he said. His voice was stressed but even. "And if you break it, you buy it. Assault on a lawyer—that's pretty dumb."

"Not like I've got a ton of assets you could want," she replied, and pressed a little harder before letting go and stepping back. Borden caught himself with both hands against the wall, pushed off and spun to face her.

"Foreplay with you must be murder," he said. "Fine. Do what you want, Jazz, but just read it. Please. Personal favor to me."

"You should have given it to Lucia. She might not have shoved you into a wall."

She got an adrenaline-pumped smile in response to that. He was breathing fast, watching her, and she wondered—not for the first time—if buttoned-up, nicely dressed Counselor Borden might not have some kink under there.

"No," he agreed, "she'd have thanked me and taken it and shown me the door, but that wouldn't have gotten me anywhere. Lucia's bulletproof glass. You're—"

"I'm what?"

"You listen. I might have to let you thump me a few times, but you listen while you're doing it." He took in another deep breath, let it out with deliberate slowness, and said, "I wouldn't come here if it wasn't important, you know that. There's a life at stake."

"From what your buddies tried to tell me, there are always lives at stake. Hell, there are lives at stake when I pick up milk at the store. Isn't that what it means to be a *Lead*?" She couldn't say the word without the coating of sarcasm, it just wasn't possible.

Borden shrugged. "Yeah, that's true. But this isn't about you. Not this time. This guy's got a wife and kids, and I'd rather not see this—happen."

"So this is you. Begging me for a favor."

She saw a tensed jaw muscle flutter. "Not exactly."

"Well, this is me, walking away."

"Fine. I'm still not begging. I'm asking, Jazz."

She stared at him for a long few seconds, and then reached

out and grabbed the envelope from his hand. She weighed it for a second, then yanked it open with unnecessary force. Wasn't like it was resisting arrest, after all.

Inside were the details on the daily routine of a middle-aged man named Lowell Santoro, film producer. Pictures of a tired-looking guy with male-pattern baldness chatting on a cell phone. The letter—on official Gabriel, Pike & Laskins stationery, signed by Milo himself—contained instructions to shadow Santoro for three days, starting tomorrow. Audio and video surveillance.

She focused on the address provided as her starting point.

"You're kidding me," she said, and looked over the top of the letter at Borden. "Los Angeles? You want me to fly to L.A. to shadow this guy? No way."

"It's important."

"Yeah, so you've said, and no, I'm not going. I've got things to do. I've seen the TV shows. They have private detectives in L.A."

"We want you," Borden said, which was nice but stupid. Not cost-effective.

"Sorry," Jazz said, and slid everything back into the envelope. "The answer's still no." She tried to give it back. Borden showed absolutely zero willingness to take it from her. She rattled it impatiently.

He just looked at her.

"I'm serious," she said. "I've got things to do. I'm not going to L.A. Not now. Next week, maybe."

"It has to be now. Today."

"It's not going to happen." She thought about the photos, sitting on the desk. The tantalizing thought of a lead, an actual honest-to-God *lead* after all this time. A chance to throw proof on McCarthy's lawyer's desk and demand action. A chance to sit in the courtroom and see Stewart's face as Ben McCarthy became a free man.

A chance to see Ben smile again.

Borden must have seen it in her eyes. "You're not going to do it."

"No," she said, and instead of coming out cold, the way she'd intended, it sounded regretful. "No, I'm not."

"You're going to let a man die."

She didn't have an answer to that, except to say, "If what you guys said in that car was right, there are other people out there. Other people who can stop it. It doesn't have to be me."

"You know what, Jazz? Sometimes, it does." He didn't sound angry, just sad. Sad, and a little lost. "Sometimes there just isn't anybody else to step up and do what has to be done. You should know that."

She didn't say anything at all to that. Borden shook his head.

"Fine," he said. "I'll get you copies of the autopsy photos. Maybe you can put them in your scrapbook."

"That's not fair."

"Yeah? You know what? *None of this is fair!*" He shouted it at her, and for a second she saw something flare, something hot and wild and desperate, and it jumped across to her like ignition through a wire. "This is *my friend!* Do you understand me? *My friend!* So yeah, you want me to beg? I'm begging! Please, Jazz. Please help me save his life!"

She swallowed and came a step closer to him. His pulse was beating fast along the matte-velvet skin of his throat, and his lips were parted. He looked on the edge of doing something…dangerous.

"If you don't go," he said softly, "I will."

"What does your boss say about that?"

"That I won't come back."

"But I will."

He nodded slightly.

"So it's not really just your friend I'd be saving," she said. "Right?"

No answer. He didn't move, didn't speak.

"That's a hell of a blackmail, Counselor. And it only works if I believe even a fraction of the bullshit the Cross Society is peddling."

"Then don't believe it," he said. "Go on with your important case. I can't stop you."

He started for the door, then came back and grabbed his fruit basket.

She watched in disbelief as he stalked out the door, handed the basket to Pansy, whose lips parted in a silent *O* of amazement, and kept going, heading for the elevators.

Jazz caught up to him at the reception desk. "Hey! Counselor!"

He stiff-armed through the glass doors and into the elevator lobby, where he hit the button twice before stopping. He didn't look at her.

"Borden," she said, and then, half-desperately, *"James."*

That got his attention. He glanced over at her, then away.

"I'm sorry," she said. "I don't like being—manhandled. You might have noticed that the first time we met. And I *really* don't like being manipulated."

"Yeah," he admitted. "Sorry. I'm not trying to manipulate you. I just—I just don't know where else to go."

Now that the adrenaline was wearing off, she knew that. "I'm keyed up," she said. "I've got some new information about..." For some reason, she didn't want to explain it to him. "About a case. Asking me to take three days away from it's a pretty high price to pay."

He nodded, eyes on the closed elevator doors and the lit call button. "Maybe so," he replied, "and I can't ask you what's more important. I can only tell you that my friend is important to me, and I'm willing to go if you don't. So tell me now, because buying a last-minute plane ticket is murder."

Maybe I could send Lucia... No, she couldn't pull Lucia out, not now; Lucia had taken weeks settling her cover, and she was getting close to breaking the case. Despite the jokes earlier, Lucia wasn't going to disengage, and she damn sure wasn't going to pull out of undercover work to go work for the Cross Society.

Jazz took a deep breath and held it. The pictures would keep. They'd kept all this time, three days wouldn't kill her.

It would give her time to pull the details out of Manny and verify the provenance.

"Fine," she said. "Fine, I'll go. Tell Laskins I'm cooperating."

"That would be a pretty free interpretation of events," he said, and looked at her with a trace of a smile.

"You're a lawyer. Prevaricate."

"Sorry I gave away your fruit basket."

"Please tell me that was Laskins's choice of a gift."

His smile was purely giddy. "Fruit baskets don't turn you on? Come on, Jazz. Bananas, pear honey—it's practical *and* seductive."

"Are you hungry?"

"What?"

She said it slower. "Are...you...hungry?"

"Why?"

"Because I want to talk to you about your friend. If I'm going to fly off to L.A. to protect his ass, at the very least I should know a little something about him."

Borden looked more stunned by that than by her agreement to take the case. "Um...okay. Where do you want to—"

"Wait downstairs," she said. "I'll be there in a minute."

The elevator arrived with a musical ding. She watched him get in and press the button for the first floor. Just before the doors closed, she said, "By the way? If you want to send a woman a present, chocolate's seductive. Bananas are just crude."

The closing doors cut him off before he could come up with any kind of a response.

Jazz stopped by Pansy's desk on the way back to her office. Pansy was turning the fruit basket this way and that, trying to catalog contents without unwrapping the shiny paper.

Jazz picked it up and carried it into her office.

"Pear honey," Pansy called after her. "He must really like you. That's kinda kinky. Think of all the applications..."

She slammed the door, gathered up the photos into a briefcase, added her collapsible truncheon, PDA, a few more files she needed to catch up on, and grabbed the travel bag she always kept ready in the closet, with changes of clothing and toiletries. She shouldered it, opened the door again and saw Pansy jump.

"I'm going to L.A.," she said, and Pansy's eyes went narrow with surprise.

"It's not on your schedule—"

"Add it. Three days in L.A."

"With...anyone?"

"Please. It's a *fruit basket*."

"Is it a case? Because I should open up a file if—"

The red envelope was in Jazz's briefcase. She took it out, tossed it to Pansy, and said, "Make two copies, and give one to Lucia. In case."

"In case what?" Pansy asked, frowning.

"In case I don't come back."

Pansy gave her a long, measuring stare. "You have to

come back. You know that, right? I don't give you permission not to come back."

Jazz smiled. "I have to sign bonus checks," she said.

"Damn straight."

It wasn't romantic, really, as dinners went. Maybe midway between the Formica bustle of Arthur Bryant's and some French restaurant with low lights and unpronounceable food—the restaurant was brightly lit, Italian, and full of the smells of garlic and parmesan and red sauce. Instead of soothing violins discreetly whispering through concealed speakers, this place featured waiters who sang opera. Loudly. Jazz supposed they were lucky the waiters actually *could* sing.

She politely clapped after the second aria from the guy topping off her tea and gave him a not-too-subtle bug-off sign, which he took with good grace. Across from her, James Borden was digging into a plate of chicken parmesan, with bread sticks. She stuck to spaghetti.

"Here," he said, as she was questing for a meatball with her fork. He slid an envelope across the table toward her. Not red, this time. White, but still the size and shape of a card. She raised her eyebrows and opened it up.

It really *was* a card. Flowers on the front, and inside, a handwritten note that said, simply, *Thank you.*

With a plane ticket for one to Los Angeles, leaving in— she checked her watch—four hours.

"Should give you enough time to eat, get there, check in and relax a little," he said, watching her.

"You bought the ticket this morning. Before you actually talked to me."

He substituted a mouthful of chicken parmesan for an answer.

"Am I actually that easy?"

"No," he mumbled. "I was willing to take the risk."

She studied him, twirling spaghetti on her fork, and said, "Tell me about your friend."

He did, after swallowing. Lowell Santoro. College roommate. One of those running buddies that Jazz had always wanted and somehow never really had, apart from McCarthy—someone to laugh with, raise hell with, experience life with. "He was older than I was," Borden said. "It didn't matter, we both acted like twelve-year-olds. He never met a girl he didn't try to talk into bed, but he never had one hate him afterward, either. Lowell's always been—honest. I know that sounds strange, but it's true. He's just got nothing but truth in him."

"Uh-huh," she said doubtfully, and took a sip of crisp white wine. It had a nice cool undertone to it, the perfect counterpoint to the salt of the spaghetti sauce. "So he's Don Juan and Saint Francis, all rolled up into one. And he was, what? A law student?"

"He changed after the first year, took film courses. That's how he got into producing. It was a good thing. He wasn't going to be a great lawyer. Too honest."

"Unlike you."

"Unlike me," he agreed. "He met Susan—his wife—his last year in college. They got married, moved out to L.A. He's a good guy, Jazz. What's going to happen to him—he doesn't deserve it."

"What *is* going to happen to him?" Because that wasn't in the letter. Just instructions on how to conduct surveillance. No warnings. She supposed the Cross Society thought it would predispose her toward what to watch out for.

"It's not clear," Borden said. Or prevaricated. "Something fatal. And something painful."

"Car accident? Building collapse? Bullet?"

"It's a human agency, that's all that I know."

"I hate it when you talk like—"

"Like a member of the Society? Jazz. I am one."

She knew that. She just didn't like to think about it. Conversation collapsed into silence as they ate, and the waiter came around to deliver a selection from *The Marriage of Figaro,* and it was dessert by the time Jazz said, "About the fruit basket?"

He looked up from his tiramisu, took a sip of wine and raised his eyebrows.

"Was it Laskins's idea?"

"Mine," he said.

"You're hopeless."

Borden had the good sense to look embarrassed as he shrugged. It might have been the wine, or the marinara sauce, but she felt a surge of warmth toward him, entirely unconnected to the undeniable surge of—what the hell had that been? Lust?—she'd felt in her office, when she'd had him up against the wall. That was unsettling. She preferred lust. Lust was simple—it had a beginning, middle and end to it. You could shut lust up by giving it what it wanted.

This feeling...it had more of a feeling of sticking around.

He was watching her. She realized she'd been staring back, felt a rush of blood heat up her face and turned back to the cheesecake she was not really eating.

"How's Lucia?" he asked. Which was completely the wrong thing to ask at that moment.

"Don't you know? I mean, don't you guys know everything?" She heard the edge in her voice.

"Yeah, sorry, I don't actually sit around and monitor your lives on a daily basis."

"Who does?"

He changed the subject. "I take it that she's okay."

"She's fine. Better than fine, actually. She's happy as a clam. That girl really *likes* undercover work. It's a little scary, how good she is at it, for somebody who wears a lot of—you know—designer clothes."

"What's she doing now?" he asked around a mouthful of brandy-soaked ladyfingers.

"Right now? Probably emptying trash from the sixth-floor restrooms." Jazz glanced at her watch. "Actually, I take it back. She's on her break, sitting in the lunchroom, watching Spanish-language soap operas."

"You're kidding."

"I told you. She likes undercover work. You're not going to do anything stupid like follow me to L.A., are you?" she asked, without any transition, and watched him scramble to keep up with the conversational left turn.

"Do you need me to?" he asked. Not, she noticed, *Do you* want *me to.*

"No," she said. "I don't need you there. And it would probably be easier if you stayed out of my hair. Having somebody around with a personal stake in things is distracting."

"It's just that he's—like family." Borden shrugged, but it didn't look casual. "I don't have a lot of that."

"Family? Hell, sometimes I have too much. Want a sister?"

She'd said something wrong. She saw the flinch. Unless he already knew Molly.

"I had one," he finally said, and met her eyes.

She knew that look, had seen it on the faces of too many families. Lost. Baffled. Wounded. She hadn't just made a mistake, she'd opened a vein. "What happened?"

"The usual. She was in the wrong place at the wrong time." His smile cut like glass. "Not everybody's a Lead. She never even got to be an Actor."

Not a good time to express her skepticism on the whole theory. "Any other family?"

"My mother lives in Canada. Father—" He shrugged again. "I don't really know. So, Lowell means a lot to me. He was there when I needed him."

She studied him. "Then I'll do everything I can."

He nodded, sipped wine and fiddled with his fork. "Want me to drive you to the airport?"

"Sure." She shrugged and then frowned. "You don't have a car."

"Rental. I need to take it back to the airport and catch the red-eye back to New York."

"So you weren't planning to stay."

"No, I was planning to go, but which way I was flying depended on you."

There was something underneath that, something like a cliff she could easily fall from, and she backed up fast. "Okay, then. If you could give me a ride, that would be great."

Borden called for the check. They argued over who was going to pay it, but in the end, she let him put it on the GPL tab. They exited into a rush of late commuters and a cool whisper of wind, and walked together like a couple along the sidewalk back toward the office. Borden silently took her shoulder bag; she just as silently let him. Her gun wasn't in it, anyway.

"Is somebody going to start taking potshots at me again?" she asked him. He missed a step, stumbled and lengthened his stride as if trying to leave that awkwardness behind him.

"I doubt it," he said. "Generally, once Leads are inside the Society, it's not in the best interest of the opposition to try to get rid of them unless they really present a problem. Their best chance of success is before you're fully informed, before there are others watching your back. Or to get to you first and put you on their side."

"Huh," she said. "So that's why they tried to kill us in the parking garage. Because we hadn't actually joined up yet, but we knew enough not to join them."

"Yes. It was their last opportunity to stop you without directly coming after the Cross Society."

"This thing—this L.A. thing—this isn't just to get me out of the way, right? Because something's going down here?"

He jammed his hands into his pockets and hunched his shoulders, looking lost in thought. "Interesting thought," he said, "but I don't think so. I'm not saying it wouldn't be possible, but..."

"You don't know?"

"Do I seem like the secret master of the world to you? No, I'm not sure. But I don't think they'd do that." Still, he was frowning, concentrating on his feet. She wished she hadn't brought it up. "I suppose we'd better get you to the airport."

"Yeah," she agreed softly.

They walked in silence for another few hundred feet, and then Borden unlocked a dark red rental car and handed her inside—literally, offered a hand, as if she was a lady in big skirts getting into a carriage. She was taken aback by that, but she had to admit, the warm touch of his fingers on hers was nice. And he hadn't done it to be showy; it was, she sensed, just something he did. She remembered him doing it for Lucia, at the limo door...but not her. She supposed her body posture at the time had been in the language of *touch me and die.*

The car felt small and intimate with the two of them inside of it. Borden drove competently, without any hesitation, although she knew he couldn't possibly know his way around that well. Could he? She concentrated on traffic and taillights, on road noise and the peripheral glow of his face in the wash of headlights. When she looked over, she was struck by how...*good* he looked. A little rough around the edges, a little tired, a little worried. Human.

"Hey," she said. He looked over at her, then back at the road. "I'm going to make sure nothing happens to him. You know that, right?"

"Right," he agreed. "Make sure nothing happens to you, either, would you? As a favor to me?"

She hadn't really noticed, but clouds had convened overhead while they were in the restaurant, and now big, fat raindrops began to pelt the windshield—a few at first, and then a silver shower. Borden activated the wipers. They were already on the freeway. *Ten minutes,* she thought to herself. *Ten minutes and I'm at the airport, ready to get on a plane. This is not how I wanted today to end.*

She drummed her fingers on the armrest nervously, watching the rain-smeared road, and was surprised when his right hand suddenly came down on her agitated left one, stopping her from tapping out a rhythm. He didn't say anything. His long, tapering fingers wrapped slowly around hers, exploring. More sensual than anything she'd felt in a long time. This wasn't reassurance, wasn't a quick impersonal touch of the hand...this was something else.

She looked down, watching as he turned her hand over, palm up, and began to lightly trace fingernails down the center of it. She felt light-headed. Tense. Oddly out of breath.

"Come back safe," he said softly. "That's not a request, all right?"

"All right," she agreed. Her pulse was hammering, and that was stupid, *stupid*. It was just skin, just a touch, not even a touch anywhere she could call intimate. But she could barely keep her voice level.

Borden reclaimed his right hand for the exit to the airport. She clenched hers into a fist, willing herself to stop feeling so...so...

She had no words for how she felt at the moment, except frustrated.

Borden pulled up at the curb, set his hazard lights and got out to grab her bag from the backseat. She was already out of the car by the time he'd managed it.

As she shouldered the strap, he stepped in closer and looked down at her. She looked up.

"See you," she said.

"Yeah."

She thought, for a blinding instant, that he was going to kiss her—the thought was right there, in his eyes, naked—and then something happened, something out of the corner of her eye, and she snapped around to watch...but it was just a car squealing up, a frantic father yelling at kids, people running late.

Normal life.

She turned back to Borden, but the thought was gone. He was behind a polite screen again.

"I should go," she said, and nodded toward the door. He inclined his head, too. "Right. See you. Um...thanks for the ride."

He didn't say a word. When she looked back, he was still standing there, hands in his pockets, looking after her.

After negotiating security again, Jazz got on the phone to Lucia in the waiting area, exchanging information in short, vivid bursts.

"You're sure you want to do this?" Lucia asked as Jazz watched a family of five meander its way into the gate area. Mom, dad, three kids who should have been poster children for their various age groups. Toddler in a stroller, burbling happily. Six-year-old with a neon-pink Barbie backpack, from which Barbie herself peered, battered and well loved. A disaffected preteen who sat with his face buried in his Game Boy screen, kicking the legs of his chair. "Jazz?"

"Remind me never to get married," she said.

"What brought that on?"

"Kids."

"Ah. I think you'd surprise yourself."

"Me? Hardly. Not the motherly type, me."

"Depends on your definition of motherly." Lucia sounded

amused. "I think of you as a mother wolf, defending her cubs to the death."

"Yeah, well, I think of myself more as the single wolf, defending myself. Sorry. What were you saying?"

"I was saying this is a nice chat we're having, but I've got work to do. So, you needed something...?"

Jazz hesitated, kicking a foot out rhythmically, watching the shadow move on the floor. "Lucia. Would you do me a big favor?"

"Big?"

"Major."

"Of course."

She sucked in a deep breath, let it out, and said, "Pansy scanned some photos for me. Would you put them out on the wires, see if anybody can match the images for me? Not the last one. I know who that is."

"Oh, yeah? Who?" Lucia sounded interested, not invested.

"Ben McCarthy."

Silence. Jazz listened to the distant, constant hiss of dead air, and finally said, "You still there?"

"Yeah. What kind of pictures?"

"Potentially exculpatory pictures."

"Ah." Nothing in her partner's voice now, which was something in itself. "After I put them on the wire—"

"No, you don't need to do anything else," Jazz hastened to say. "I'll take care of it."

"I could ask around."

Jazz stared hard at her shoe. "I couldn't—that's a lot of favor."

"If I can wrap up this case today, I have free time tomorrow," Lucia pointed out. "And you're not coming back for what, three days?"

"Yeah."

"You'll go nuts."

"Probably," Jazz said, smiling. "But seriously, only if you have time, right? This isn't work. This is—personal."

"I know," Lucia said.

"Be careful."

"You're the one flying off to L.A. without backup."

Good point. Jazz looked around. Nobody seemed to be watching. They'd been free of surveillance for months now, after that initial bout of scariness. "I'm good," she said. "No bullets whizzing as of yet."

"Speaking of whizzing, I'd better get back to cleaning toilets."

"Yeah, right. Listen, I'll call you from L.A., all right? To check in."

Lucia agreed. Jazz folded the phone just as the flight attendant made the first boarding call.

Chapter 8

She'd seen the picture of Lowell Santoro, and it was a good thing she had, because otherwise she'd have completely missed him. By the term "film producer," she'd have been expecting a flashily dressed, heavily bling-blinged guy, probably driving some overmuscled, overpriced convertible.

Lowell Santoro had on walking shorts, a staid-looking Hawaiian shirt and drove a Toyota. His sole concession to Hollywood seemed to be the sunglasses he wore, which were pretty fine, and made Jazz wish she'd thought to pack some, because the morning light was pretty fierce.

From the coffee shop across the street, she watched as Santoro parked in the lot of his office building. She sipped a pretty damn excellent coffee as he locked up his car and plodded up the walk to the front door of the lobby. She noted the time on her PDA, finished her coffee and got another to go. She went back to her rental car—an economy-class Ford, nice and clean, tons more comfortable than most copmobiles she'd ever used for stakeouts. Her small video camera and digital still camera lay on the seat beside her, along with her cell phone and her collapsible baton. *Add some CDs, and we've got a party,* she thought, and drummed her fingers on the steering wheel to the radio, which wasn't half-bad, really.

She'd parked to be in the shade, with a kitty-corner view of Santoro's car and a clear shot to pull out in a hurry if necessary. Not that she figured it would be necessary. This was her second day of surveillance, and she'd already gotten the clear sense that Lowell Santoro was a man of rigid habits.

She plugged in the last piece of equipment, using what was labeled as a "utility power outlet" instead of the time-honored cigarette lighter, and flicked on the tiny LCD screen on the palmtop.

It had taken some trial and error in the dead of night, and some real skills, to enter Santoro's offices and set up the video feed, but she was patient and thorough, not to mention careful. Lucia had given her a solid two-month course in electronic bugging and breaking and entering…apparently, all useful skills taught by government agencies with three letters. Jazz had been a good student.

She watched as Santoro's tiny little video figure crossed to his desk with a full coffee cup in his hand, exchanged some words with his assistant—indistinct in Jazz's earpiece—and began to open up his mail. All very normal. This was going to be another of Borden's "your presence prevents it" things, she already knew it. They'd had two before the debacle with Wendy Blankenship, besides the near-drive-by back in K.C. while she'd been recovering. One of them had been an all-night stakeout in a Denny's, watching a waitress who hadn't done anything but yawn, give bad service and drop a plate of food. The other hadn't been that exciting.

I shouldn't be doing this. Then again, this would bring in cash, and Jazz was in favor of that. She'd never been a small-business owner before. Having people like Pansy depending on her for rent money made her nervous and greedy.

Santoro's phone rang. He had a conversation about an upcoming film he was producing, and against her will, Jazz thought that was kind of cool, because they were talking about casting actors she actually recognized. The assistant came and went, bringing him stacks of correspondence once the incoming mail had been disposed of. Santoro had a pair of lungs on him, and from the language he used talking to an MGM executive, he had a pair of brass balls, too. Jazz found herself liking the guy. He called his wife and talked with her, and it sounded nice, too. Comfortable. The kind of conversation adults had who could bicker a little about what color the new refrigerator was going to be, and whether or not the kids needed summer camp or not, but still end with a *love you* that sounded heartfelt.

She never had conversations like that. Her arguments always felt so damn important…even when they weren't.

Santoro seemed like a good guy. Someone you'd want for a friend. Which told her something about Borden, too—

because, not only was he friends with somebody warm and generous like this, he *cared*. Borden had a decent heart.

Around an hour and a half later, the assistant broke into his routine to remind him he had some kind of set visit, which marked the end of the administrative portion of the day, and Jazz gulped down the last of her coffee as Santoro tidied up and prepared to depart.

Apart from having heard half of a conversation—the wrong half, unfortunately—with Johnny Depp, she hadn't accomplished a damn thing, really. She hadn't spotted a single person tailing him, watching the office or home, or any suspicious activity whatsoever.

She picked up the still camera and shot a couple of angles of his car while she was waiting for him to emerge from the building.

Her cell phone rang. She flipped it open without taking her eyes from the entrance.

"Anything happening?" Borden. She actually felt a little electric tingle at the sound of his voice, caught sight of herself in the rearview mirror and realized that she was smiling. *That* kind of smile. She wiped it off her face and glared at her reflection, as if it was to blame.

"Not a damn thing," she said. "Your friend's doing fine."

"That's good." He sounded relieved. "How about you?"

"Not a damn thing happening to me, either," she said, "except that I'm about to OD on caffeine. You know the biggest problem about stakeouts without a partner?"

"No conversation?"

"No bathroom breaks," she said. "Gets pretty difficult."

"I can imagine."

"You at the office?" Because he'd have to be, it was almost noon in New York.

"No. I was in court earlier. I have the rest of the day off."

"Do you ever work, Counselor? All I ever see you do is stroll around your office looking sharp, taking meetings, and fly around bugging the hell out of me."

"It's a filthy job, but the compensation's pretty good," he said blandly. "So I look sharp, eh?"

"Don't get cocky."

"Wouldn't think of it."

She checked the monitor. Santoro's office was empty, except for his assistant cleaning up the coffee cup and re-straightening piles of paper. He hadn't come out of the front door yet.

"I'm going to have to go," she said to Borden.

"Anything wrong?"

"No," she said. "Go help a corporation hide its ill-gotten gains in an offshore account or something. I'll call later."

Maybe Santoro had stopped off at the bathroom. Hell, she was starting to regret the second cup....

Another full minute passed. No Santoro. No activity in his office.

Jazz drummed her fingers on the steering wheel again, this time more from nerves than any enjoyment of the pop jingle on the radio. She watched the digits crawl on her clock.

He was taking way too long.

"Dammit," she whispered, and got out of the car. She grabbed her still camera—nothing odd about a tourist with a camera in L.A.—stuck her collapsible baton in her back pocket, covered by the windbreaker she threw on, and moved quickly toward Santoro's office building.

She kept expecting him to pop out at any moment, as she got closer, but all remained quiet. Something tingled at the base of her spine, like a gun pressed close. She walked faster, took the three short steps up to the glass doors and walked in.

No security in the lobby. There was a desk, but it was empty. She checked the elevators. Nothing was moving. Santoro's office was on the fourth floor, and both elevators were on the ground. If he'd come out here, he'd have walked out the front. There weren't any other places for him to have gone.

Except for the stairs.

Jazz cracked the door to the stairwell and listened, and heard a dull scuffling noise. Grunts of effort.

She shoved the camera in a pocket, grabbed the baton and snapped it out to its full length as she ran up. She took the steps three at a time, feeling the burn in her thighs and a sharp twinge in her side, but if she was right, there wasn't time to take it any easier.

She burst around the third-floor landing and saw, on the flat halfway point to the fourth floor, Lowell Santoro being strangled.

He was still alive, barely—face congested dull purple, eyes bulging, mouth open and tongue protruding. Fingers still scrabbling weakly for the cord around his throat that had dug in so deep she couldn't even see it. The cord was all that was holding him upright.

Jazz yelled—she didn't even know what—and the sound bounced and echoed sharply from the concrete all around her.

The man standing behind Santoro, both gloved hands twisting a black rope, met her eyes. She didn't know him, but she knew the type—something missing in the eyes, a kind of animal vacancy that marked a bad life and a worse end coming. He was tall, blond, California-pretty, with an off-kilter nose that had seen somebody's fist close up in the not-too-distant past.

He let go of Santoro and let him pitch forward, right into Jazz as she bounded up toward him. Santoro's weight—she didn't dare think, *dead weight*—bowled her over, and the world became a confusing, hurting blur as they fell. Jazz landed flat on her back, Santoro half-crushing her, and saw California Guy heading back up the stairs, fast.

She rolled Santoro over. His eyes were blinking, and he was whooping for breath. His mouth was bloody. He'd bitten his tongue.

"Stay here!" she shouted at him, and lunged to her feet, digging her cell phone out of her pocket as she started up the steps in pursuit. She yelled out the office's street address to the 911 operator, craning her neck to try to see where California Guy was on the stairs. She paused to listen.

No sound. Either he was waiting, or…

She hung up on the operator, who was trying to get her to give her name, and took the next few steps slowly, quietly, feeling cold sweat slide down her back. She wished for a gun, or at least a good coating of Kevlar. California Guy might like to use his hands, but that didn't mean he was a conscientious gun objector, either.

She had an unpleasant flashback of her blood glittering on asphalt, of the strange liquid feeling of being shot, and shook it off to ease up one more rising step. She was scared, she realized. Scared of being hurt.

California Guy was waiting for her around the blind corner. Or rather, California Guy's powerful kick was waiting for her, and it caught her squarely in the stomach and slammed her back against the concrete wall, seeing stars and out of breath. She hung on to her baton, somehow, and saw a black flash coming at her; she ducked, and heard his fist make hard contact with the wall, followed by a loud, yelping grunt of pain. Since she was safely braced, she yanked up a knee, missed his crotch, kept going and planted her foot flat against his chest and uncoiled with a shout. He went stumbling backward.

She blinked the last disorientation out of her eyes and took a surgical swing with the baton. *Whap.* Right in his undefended ribs, which she felt crack. As he hunched over in reaction, she gave him a hard smack to the side of the head, too.

His knees buckled, but instead of falling down unconscious, he lunged from a kneeling position, got hold of her and slammed her back against the wall again. Her head impacted with a dull thud. She tasted blood and *damn,* that hurt. She could barely get her breath, but his hands were yanking at her waistband, fumbling for a gun she didn't have, and then he pulled her off balance and down, his weight on top.

He liked to use his hands. Jazz didn't particularly mind that. She grinned at him, spit blood in his face and slammed the heel of her palm up into his crooked nose just before he managed to get a grip on her neck. It didn't drive bone up into his brain, but it certainly rearranged cartilage with a satisfying crunch and made him yowl in pain. Blood spattered her, warm as tears, and she used her leverage to flip him off.

This time *his* head hit the wall.

It was lights out, sweetheart, and he slumped sideways, breathing heavily through his mouth as his rebroken nose leaked a steady stream of red.

Jazz crawled to him, yanked him forward and zip-tied his hands behind him before letting herself collapse to a weak sitting position on the steps. The place looked like a war zone. She dabbed cautiously at her face and sniffed. Yep, she had a nosebleed, too, not to mention a split lip and a ringing bell of a headache. Her side felt tight, protesting the action. One of her knees registered as hot and uncomfortable.

Not bad, considering. Not bad at all. She'd had worse after an interesting night of barhopping.

She patted down California Guy and came up with no ID at all—not even a bus pass—but a fat wad of cash and a letter.

She paused as she slid it out of his pocket, staring, because it looked...familiar.

Big red envelope. Like a Hallmark card.

She didn't have a proper evidence kit—hadn't thought she'd need it—but this was no coincidence. Killers didn't stroll around with birthday cards for their girlfriends in their jackets. She tucked it into her windbreaker just as she heard sirens echoing up the stairwell. Heavy treads on the steps, coming up.

"Victim's on the third-floor landing," she called down. "The perp is up here. He's secured."

They came carefully, not taking her word for it. She sat against the wall, hands up, as two uniformed officers rounded the blind corner with guns leveled. When they were sure the situation was under control, she got searched. The baton got confiscated, along with the camera and cell phone.

California Guy was still out cold, bleeding all over the concrete. "Jeez," the bigger, older cop said, bending over him. "I thought you looked like you'd had a rough time, but this guy needs a plastic surgeon. Good thing he's in L.A. We've got more of them than gas stations."

The atmosphere got more congenial, when her bona fides were vetted. Ex-cops got a little more respect than bloody-faced regular citizens armed with batons, although the out-of-town private investigator status didn't necessarily win points. She went through statements to the uniforms, then another round with a blank-faced detective who didn't seem to be listening but probably was, and a third time to another detective who focused on her like he planned to marry her later. By that time, the aches were kicking in. She'd washed the blood off, but desperately needed a nap and coffee, in that order. Her cell phone kept ringing. That was probably Borden, checking in and getting worried because there was no answer.

"Look," Jazz pointed out the fourth time it rang, "if you don't want to have the FBI down here poking around looking for me, you might want to let me answer it. I'm not operating in a vacuum. I have a partner, and I have a lawyer."

Whatever they thought of that, they let her have the cell phone, and when she answered, sure enough, it was James Borden on the other end of the phone.

But what he said wasn't what she'd expected.

"He has an envelope," he said. No preamble. "Get it. Don't let it out of your sight."

"Oh, hey," she said with grim cheer. "Yeah, I'm fine, by the way, thanks for asking. Your friend's in the hospital. I don't know much about him, but he was still breathing when they carted him away."

"I know," he shot back. "But you have to keep hold of that envelope, do you understand? Don't let it out of your sight."

The cops had taken it but hadn't evidenced much interest in it. She'd said it was a card for her niece; they'd returned it without comment. It was currently a thick square reminder poking a corner into her ribs under the jacket.

"Yeah," she replied. "Thanks for the advice. Any ideas about who my dance partner was today?"

"He doesn't matter."

"You know what? He did to me. And I'll bet he did to Santoro, too."

One of the cops got called from the room for a whispered conversation at the door, nodded, and came back. Jazz's eyes tracked him, watching body language. She didn't much care for the change. He was boring a hole in her with his stare. She hunched her shoulders a bit as she paced the small, dingy room. It was a standard interrogation room—a battered industrial table, some sturdy chairs, a camera in the corner and an observation window.

"I'm coming to get you," he said. "I should be there in a couple of hours."

She swallowed a sudden surge of relief, and said, "I'm sorry. Sorry for all of this."

Another hesitation from him. "You tried."

"I said I wouldn't let anything happen to him."

"You saved his life."

That was it. No hearts and flowers, not even a fruit basket, just a quick disconnection. She stared at the cell phone for a second, then shrugged and handed it back to the hard-eyed detective, who—from the way he was watching her—must have talked to somebody back in K.C. with a less-than-glowing opinion of her. Probably Stewart. Somebody who'd filled his head full of crap about corruption and murder and drug running, probably. And cited Ben's trial to back it up.

"Who was that?" the cop asked, weighing the phone in his hand.

"Wrong number," she said, and smiled as brilliantly as she could, under the circumstances.

It didn't get more pleasant as the day went on. She got another phone call, this one from Lucia, who was coldly furious and torn between kicking LAPD ass or Cross Society hiney. That felt oddly bracing. Jazz had quite a time convincing Lucia not to come flying to the coast, and in the end had only succeeded because Borden was already on his way and Lucia was convinced she was about to break the industrial espionage case within the day.

Toward the end of the day the cops finally informed her that Lowell Santoro was resting comfortably. He wouldn't be giving any speeches soon, but he'd narrowly avoided a fractured hyoid bone and a nasty death. His trachea was seriously bruised but intact.

She'd saved someone. She'd actually, finally, saved someone.

Not that you'd know it from the continuing barrage of questions from two increasingly unfriendly LAPD detectives named Weston and Cammarata. Weston was thin and dressed in old, unfashionable suits; Cammarata was more the dress-slacks, snappy-tie, crisp-white-shirt type. He could have walked the halls of corporate zombiedom and looked utterly in place, if he'd taken off that clip-on badge from his belt and stuck a business ID in its place.

Of the two, she found she preferred Weston, who was at least honest in his dislike. Cammarata kept trying to make her think he liked her. She kept reiterating facts to them, stubbornly refused to reveal who'd hired her, and finally reverted to the old standard, "I'll wait until my lawyer gets here."

Borden arrived looking, well, like a lawyer. A damn fine one, too. Navy blue tailored suit, crisp off-white shirt, power tie, shiny shoes, a briefcase that looked expensive and was probably worth twice whatever she would guess. He looked L.A. spiffy, in a New York kind of way.

And he had her out of the police station in forty-five minutes, which she figured had to be a new world record for intimidation in a town that had more or less invented the fast-talking lawyer.

"So," she said as he walked her down the steps to a waiting black chauffeured car, "you don't do criminal cases. Because you seemed to do that all right, Counselor."

"Shut up," he said darkly. She could already tell he was in a towering bad mood, which was weird, because after all, she'd saved his friend. Weird, starting on annoying.

"Is that legal advice?"

He firmly directed her into the car—backseat—and walked around to climb in the other side. He'd gotten another limo for a reason, she saw—better leg room. Not so critical for her, but his knees were an absurdly long distance from his hips.

He flicked the locks, engaged the privacy screen between them and the driver—evidently *not* a Cross Society insider—and without looking at her said, "You could have called the police instead of going in."

"Oh, please, what's the nine-one-one response time in L.A. when you call and say, hey, I'm on stakeout and my subject hasn't come out of the building yet? I'm guessing it's twenty-four to forty-eight hours, if they don't laugh you off the phone."

"You could have called them when you knew something was happening."

"By that time, your friend was about ten seconds away from choking to death on a broken throat. Look, what do you think you sent me here to do? Knit doilies? Run and hide when the going gets tough?" She shrugged. "Borden, you know me better than that. If there's a fight, I'm in it. That's who I am."

"I didn't send you here to stage the first annual Stairwell Smack-down and nearly get yourself killed. Again." His voice sounded tight and grim, and as she stared at him, she saw the tension in his shoulders. In the hard line of his jaw. "You like this, don't you? The adrenaline rush. Kicking ass at every possible opportunity."

"You think I did this for fun?" she asked, and felt her hands trying to make fists.

"Tell me what was going through your head, then."

"The subject went out of the range of electronic surveillance," she said. "The subject didn't reappear on schedule. I went in to check it out, which was exactly what you knew I was going to do. And if you think maybe I should have checked on him, discovered him being choked to death and gone back to the car, well, maybe you don't know me very well."

Borden raised his head, finally, and looked straight at her. "I know you better than you think," he said. There was something odd in his eyes. "I'm not the only one. Take out the envelope."

She didn't. She looked at him, frowning, and then reached into her windbreaker and pulled it free.

"Open it," he said.

She slit it with a fingernail and pulled out the letter folded neatly inside.

"Read it."

She didn't want to, suddenly. It felt as if something was wrong, something was *very* wrong, indeed, and if she just slid this letter back in the envelope…put the genie back in his bottle…then maybe things would be different.

Instead, she unfolded the crisp paper, and saw the letterhead of Eidolon Corporation. It was a bold red logo, a world in an hourglass. It read in neat typewritten lines:

To Jasmine Callender,
Should you read this, you will have taken matters into your hands that would have been better left to others. We have no choice but to take steps. In acting today, you have forfeited what little protection the Cross Society could offer you. Inform them.

She read it through twice, numbly. There was no signature. She finally looked up mutely to stare at Borden.

"It says—"

"I know what it says," he interrupted her. "Laskins got a fax two hours ago and read it to me on the plane. Jazz, you were just another Actor before, but they know what you are now, and you've proved a real threat. They've moved you up to the top of their hit list. You're not safe now."

"But they addressed it directly to me," she said. The words felt strange in her mouth. "How the hell could it be to me, when I took it from the other guy? Why—?"

"They must have known there was a chance you'd do this. I think—" He paused, licked his lips and looked very, very sick. "I think the Society knew, too. They…"

"Let me guess," she said. "You heard Santoro was on the hit list. They decided to let him get taken out for strategic reasons, and you decided to act on your own. You didn't fly out to deliver an assignment from Laskins. That's you. You decided to produce the paperwork and bring it to me in a red envelope, just like the rest of them. And they told you not to do it."

He didn't answer. He was pale to the lips.

"Did they fire you?"

"Not yet," he said, and she saw some of the stiffness leave his shoulders. He slumped against the window and closed his eyes. "Santoro—he's a good guy. He does good things. His wife and kids—"

"So we saved him," she said. "I'm not upset about that, believe me. I don't believe all this fortune-telling horseshit anyway."

He reached out and touched the unfolded Eidolon Corporation letter still in her hand. "No? Then why does that have your name on it, when you took it off a guy you'd never met who was trying to kill you?"

"People try to kill me all the time," she said. "Not like it's new."

He hit an intercom switch and said, "Let's go," and the limo glided into motion. "There's somebody I need you to meet."

She groaned. "Not more of this crap. Look, Borden, just let me go home, okay? I have things to do." The photos. McCarthy, waiting for freedom. Every day he sat behind bars now was another day that she couldn't take back, and could only regret. If anything happened to him...

"If I let you go home, you're dead," Borden said. "I realize that might not mean much to you, because you think you can win any fight, but I'm not as brave. Not with your life."

He looked tired. As well he should, she realized; he'd

come all the way from New York, and for all she knew he'd done it on little or no sleep.

"Borden," she said. He opened his eyes, which had drifted nearly shut. She wasn't sure if he was even aware of it. "I'm sorry."

"Don't apologize," he said, and there was a gray leaden weight to his words. "I did this. I made the decisions. I changed the rules, and now you're a target. I need—I need to find out how to fix it."

"So we *are* going to see somebody from the Cross Society."

"Not exactly." He turned away and looked out of the smoked-glass window. "Not exactly."

She realized, belatedly, that he hadn't even asked if she was okay. That pissed her off to an unreasonable extent. She glared at him and read the letter again, silently. It was dated for today. She'd pulled the envelope out of Surfer Killer's jacket herself, and had hardly let it out of her sight since. It was dimly possible—*dimly*—that one of the cops might have switched it while they'd been holding it, but she didn't think so.

She rubbed her aching forehead, folded up the letter and jammed it back into the envelope. Too late to worry about fingerprints or any other useful forensics.

It has my name on it.

That was a whole new level of creepy. The Cross Society was way creepy enough for her tastes; she felt out of her depth in dealing with them. This was...

This was crazy.

"Where are we going?" she asked.

Borden didn't answer. After a few seconds, she looked over and saw that his eyes were shut, his breathing light and even. He couldn't be asleep, could he? No, he was just trying to piss her off.

He was succeeding brilliantly.

It was a long, long drive, and L.A. traffic was everything everyone had always said it would be. Being in a limo made it palatable but boring. Jazz stared out at the unmoving traffic. People in other cars were checking out the limousine's tinted windows, trying to imagine what celebrity was hiding within. She'd have been right there with them, imagining George Clooney or Meryl Streep.

Borden actually *was* asleep. Ridiculous as that seemed. She'd been on the verge of shaking him awake to shout questions at him, but the truth was, she didn't think it would do any good, and she had an odd little soft spot for watching him this way. He had a lock of hair falling over his forehead, and her fingers itched to do something with it. Yank it by the roots, maybe. Or move it gently aside, light as a feather. The jury was still out and deadlocked.

She was off balance, leaning forward to see what was available in the minibar—because, what the hell, how often was she actually going to be in a limousine and have unrestricted access?—when the limo moved forward, then jerked to a sudden stop. She ended up being pitched forward across Borden's knees.

Well, that was embarrassing.

She slowly straightened up without looking at him, although she could feel the sudden tension in the legs under her hands, which meant he was wide-awake.

"Something you wanted?" he asked neutrally. His voice sounded rough and tight.

"Yeah," she said. "Soft drink." She straightened up without actually looking at his face.

They negotiated over brand names. He clinked ice into a crystal glass better suited to holding Scotch or bourbon and poured her a short little can of cola. He handed it over without comment. She drank, grateful for the syrupy rush, the liquid on her dry throat, and for something to do with her mouth other than get herself in even more trouble.

Borden, awake, was much less readable than Borden, asleep. He looked at her from time to time as she drank, and stared out the windows. They hit smooth sailing after about fifteen more minutes, and Jazz made her drink last as long as possible before passing him the empty glass and last few melting cubes. He stowed it away without comment.

"It's not your fault," she said to him.

"No?" He sounded so damn *neutral.* "How do you figure that?"

"If somebody above me had said, no, you need to lay back and let your friend get horribly murdered? Guess what. I would've been forging documents and persuading you to help me, too. And I don't think you were wrong to do it. It's never wrong to save a life."

"No?" he repeated. "You'd pull, say, John Wayne Gacy out of a river and start chest compressions."

"It'd be easier if I didn't know he was a crazy murdering bastard, but yeah, that's pretty much the size of it."

"You'd do it even if you knew. Even if you knew he was killing people."

"If I knew that, I'd revive him and slap handcuffs on him before he could figure out what I was doing," she said. "I'm—I was a cop, Borden. I never tried to make myself judge, jury and executioner. That's a responsibility I don't want, and nobody should have unless they have checks and balances. That's what scares me about your dear friends in the Society. How do you know what they're doing is right? How can you really tell? Save that guy, let that guy die—" She shook her head. "I don't care what they *think* they know, I can't really believe they're ready to play God."

He shook his head. "I'm not feeling guilty about saving Lowell," he said finally. "I'm angry at myself that you had to put yourself in danger to do it, and I'm scared that this saving one life is going to cost me another, and I—I'm not ready to play God, either, Jazz. And if you die because of what I've done—"

"Hey," she murmured, and reached over to rest her hand on top of his. His fingers twitched, but didn't move to caress hers like they had in the car on the way to the airport in Kansas City. She missed it. "I'm a big girl. Even if I'd known it would paint a target on my butt, I'd have done it. You understand that, right?"

He shook his head and didn't answer at all. But he didn't move his hand from under hers for a long moment, either. When he finally did, when he folded his arms into a touch-me-not kind of defensiveness, she settled back in the opposite comfy corner and watched scenery flash by in silence. Desert. Lots of desert.

She wanted to sleep, but something wouldn't let her. Borden didn't doze, either. She shot him looks from time to time, but his eyes were on the horizon, his face utterly blank and composed. Nothing to see here, move along.

She saw a road sign flash by as the limo exited the freeway, and turned back in a futile attempt to be sure she'd gotten that glimpse correct. "Borden? We're going to a prison?"

"Yes."

"Federal or state?"

"Federal."

"Do I have to do the animal, mineral, or vegetable part of this quiz, too, or can we jump to the part where you tell me where the hell we're going and who we're going to see?"

Borden looked at the blank screen dividing them from the driver, evidently decided it was okay to talk, and said, "We're going to see Max Simms."

"Simms?" she echoed. "Max Simms, the serial killer?"

"No, Max Simms, the interior decorator. Why the hell do you think he's in prison? Yes, he was convicted of being a serial killer." Borden looked angry and ever so slightly sick. "I helped defend him, remember? He's not guilty. I know he's not."

She had a flash of sitting across from Ben McCarthy, separated by scarred Plexiglas, staring at his weary face and saying, *It's okay, it's going to be okay,* and knowing that it wouldn't be, knowing that every day he was behind bars was another day he'd risk his life, his body, his mind. She felt responsible for that, and it hadn't been remotely her fault that he was imprisoned. If Borden felt the same, if he really believed Simms was innocent, that was a kind of slow, endless torture that she couldn't quite imagine.

"Do you think you lost the case? That it was really all your fault?"

"No. Anyway, I was second chair. Laskins lost the case, if anybody did." Borden's tiny shrug went for casual and missed by a mile. "Truth is, I don't think anybody could have gotten him acquitted. The evidence was too good."

"But you still think he's innocent."

"I didn't then," he admitted. "I do now."

"Because…?"

"I've seen things," he said. "I know things. I know how easy it is for events to be manipulated to someone else's gain, and I've seen how ruthless Eidolon Corporation is. Simms was involved in a power struggle for control of the company. And he lost."

She frowned, watching him, but he didn't have any more light to shed. The limo glided on until it braked to a smooth stop, and the door opened on golden sunset.

The air held a tang of bitter sage and dry air, and as Jazz stepped out, dazzled, she had to shade her eyes from the glare. Everything looked bleached here—the sand, the pale uniforms on the guards, the buildings. Unlike some of the older prisons, no attempt had been made to make this one look like anything more than what it was: a big, solid concrete block to hold people inside. The exercise yard—a big flat paved expanse radiating waves of heat—was deserted, and a basketball roamed aimlessly around the tarmac, pushed here and there by swirling winds. The fences were chain-link topped with at least two feet of razor wire, with guard towers at regular intervals manned by snipers. Jazz hoped they had air-conditioning up there. The heat down here on the ground was murderous.

"This way," Borden said, and led the way to a gate manned by two armed deputies. They viewed her impersonally and checked a list for names, then buzzed her and Borden into a claustrophobic walkway. More chain-link and razor wire. Even McCarthy's prison didn't seem this daunting, but then, he was a state inmate, not federal.

Two more checkpoints, and they were inside a dim, cool room that smelled of industrial cleaner and sweat. Three more deputies on duty, one a petite black woman who gestured Jazz over to one side. Jazz, without being asked, emptied out her pockets. The deputy lifted an eyebrow at the baton but said nothing. The pat-down was fast and professional. Jazz risked a glance over her shoulder to see Borden receiving the same treatment from a guy big enough to qualify for a Russian weightlifting team; he didn't look as if he was enjoying it much. His briefcase didn't make it. Neither did the contents of his pockets, or his cell phone.

They joined up on the other side of a gate, where another deputy led them along rows of silent, darkened cells.

"What's with all the empty space?" Jazz asked. "Or are you telling me crime's actually down in California?"

The deputy—his name tag read Manning—gave her an unreadable look. "Most prisoners have already been moved out to another facility," he said. "Upstate. We've only got two active pods right now. Your guy is in the second one."

They weren't heading to the cells, though. The deputy turned them to the right, through an open iron-reinforced door, into a visiting room.

Jazz felt a definite creep along her back. The place was deserted. It even *smelled* deserted. A soft-drink machine glowed and hummed at the far wall, but the lights were at half power, and the kids' area at the far side of the room with all its grimy, battered plastic toys lay silent and abandoned. The deputy grunted softly and flicked on a switch; fluorescents snapped on overhead, blindingly white.

"Where?" Borden asked. He looked informal. She couldn't figure it out for a second, then realized that his tie was missing. Were they expecting him to hang himself? Or her to strangle him with it? Granted, the second part of that wasn't out of the question....

The deputy gestured widely toward the cubicles. There were six of them, all doors gaping open. All empty.

"Whichever," he said. "Go on in. Press the button when you want out."

Meaning that once they were inside, the door locked behind them. Jazz forced a smile and headed for cubicle number one. It didn't feel too bad until Borden crowded in with her, and then it was instantly too small, his heat too vivid against her skin. Their knees bumped as they tried to jostle their cheap plastic chairs for position. He muttered an apology as he elbowed her. She glared back.

They both froze for a second as the lock snapped shut behind them, and their eyes darted into a shared gaze. In his, Jazz read the same undertone of panic and frustration she felt. She deliberately forced herself to relax, nodded at him and folded her hands in her lap.

They sat in silence, waiting. The Plexiglas was scratched and warped, muddy with fingerprints. Some woman had kissed it at some point and left a smudged hooker-red imprint; Jazz itched to clean it. *And if I want to clean it,* she thought, *this place really must be filthy.*

"Jazz," Borden said.

"What?"

He was looking down at his right hand, which was curled into a loose fist on his knee. The top two buttons of his shirt were open, cotton hanging loose and limp around his long throat, and the skin there looked exposed and sleek and vulnerable. "I got angry with you, before. I'm sorry."

Her lips parted, but nothing came out. She just stared at him.

"You need to quit doing this to yourself," he said. There was a strange tension in his voice. "Hurting yourself. Jazz, you keep putting yourself in danger, and there's no reason for it. You throw yourself in the way of every speeding truck hoping to get run over, and sooner or later, you're going to—"

"You think I'm suicidal?" she asked, astonished. His loose fist tightened.

"I think you blame yourself," he replied. "For McCarthy either being innocent in prison, or being guilty in prison, and that's a no-win scenario. I think you don't see a way it isn't your fault, and that's bullshit. You need to quit assigning yourself the blame."

She felt anger fill her up like boiling water. "Look, *Counselor,* you don't know me, and I don't need your Psych One-oh-one crap about what I do or don't feel. You don't know Ben McCarthy, you don't know anything about—"

"What makes you think I don't know Ben McCarthy?" he interrupted, and met her eyes. Held them. "What makes you think I don't know you?"

She had no defense for that. She resorted to pure fury, to reaching out and grabbing a handful of his jacket lapel and pulling him closer, but then the heat from his body washed over her and the smell of that warm, edible cologne, and the gentleness in his eyes…

"Jazz," he said, and she'd never heard anyone say her name like that, with such infinite tenderness. "If you hurt me again I'm going to have to hurt you back. So please. Don't punch me, okay?"

She felt herself flush. "I'm not—I wasn't going to—" She let go of his jacket, but they were still too close together, alarmingly close, and her heart was racing so fast she could barely feel individual beats. "Back off, Counselor."

"You use that like a shield," he said. Still low and calm. "My title. You can use my name, you know."

"Borden—"

"I've got another one."

"Fine, *James*. Back the hell off." But it didn't sound right, even to her ears. It sounded weak and fragile and oddly uncertain. "Don't do this to me. Not now."

He was so close his breath was stirring the hair around her face. His eyes were tired and bloodshot, his freshly shaved face pale with exhaustion.

His smile, when it came, looked wounded. "Do what? Worry about you? Care what happens to you?"

"James—" It slipped out before she could stop herself. *Counselor* and *Borden,* those were things she flung at him to keep him at bay. *James* was a name that felt intimate on her lips, and from the sudden flash in his eyes, he knew it. "I don't need your help."

"I know," he said, and it was almost a whisper this time. "You never need anybody's help."

It was utterly insane, but she couldn't stop herself. She moved forward, a bare three-inch lunge, and kissed him. She felt him tense in surprise, then deliberately relax, and those lips she'd been staring at for the past long minutes were warm and baby soft and damp against hers, and the heat she'd been feeling that she thought was anger was turning into something else, a white-hot flare that burned down her spine and melted bone along the way. She started to pull back, but then Borden's lovely manicured hands slid up her arms and ruffled her hair and cupped the back of her head and, *oh, my Lord,* his mouth opened and his tongue, *his tongue* like hot velvet stroking her lips, then sliding inside…

Somewhere on the other side of the Plexiglas came the harsh clang of a metal door slamming open.

Jazz gasped and jumped back, shaking, tingling all over, staring at Borden, who looked just as stunned and ruffled as she felt. His lips were damp, still parted, a little swollen and red. She wanted to touch them. No, she wanted to devour them. Again.

She swallowed hard, looked away and moved as far from him as it was possible to get in the narrow confines of the tiny cubicle. She heard him pulling in deep breaths, and out of her peripheral vision making fussy, nervous movements, smoothing his jacket, his shirt.

I can't believe I did that.

It already seemed like a strange daydream, and she might have convinced herself it hadn't happened at all, except that she could still taste him, still smell him on her skin and, oh, that felt so…good.

"Later," he said quietly.

"In your dreams," she shot back. Unsteadily.

"Yeah, I'm almost certain that will happen, too."

On the other side of the barrier, she heard jingling metal. Shuffling shoes. And then saw a shocking orange blaze of a jumpsuit—Jazz thought irrelevantly that Ben McCarthy was wearing the same color, right now—sidle awkwardly into the frame of the window.

The legendary Max Simms had arrived.

Where McCarthy filled out his prison garb in flat planes and intimidating angles, Simms was entirely different. Slender, lost inside the ill-fitting outfit, with giant blue eyes and wispy white hair and a face that looked gentle and sensitive and old before its time. He stood maybe five foot five, at most, and his shoulders were stooped like an arthritic ninety-year-old. It looked like his restraints weighed more than he did.

He fixed those mild blue eyes on Borden, who had risen to his feet, and nodded. Borden returned the gesture and settled back on the very edge of his chair…and then Simms turned his attention to Jazz.

It was like having all the air sucked out of the room. Like being in the center of the brightest spotlight in the universe, a beam so bright that she felt one instant away from combusting, so bright that there was no hiding in any corner because there were no shadows left, anywhere.

Simms blinked, mild as milk, and settled into a plastic chair that a deputy thumped down on concrete for him on the other side of the glass. He rested his elbows on the table and flicked on the old-fashioned intercom on his side of the barrier.

Borden reached over to turn on the one on their side of the glass.

"Mr. Simms," Borden said. "Thank you for seeing us, sir. How are you?"

Simms nodded slightly, still staring at Jazz. She no longer felt that appalling rush of—of what? Focus? Intensity?—but she could feel herself shaking from the aftermath. "It's good to see you again, James," he said. He had a pleasant, quiet voice, nothing remarkable. A little deeper than she'd expected. "I see you brought Ms. Callender with you."

"Had to," Borden said. "There was a letter—"

"Yes, I know," Simms said. "May I see it? Just flatten it against the glass, if you don't mind."

She fumbled it out of the envelope in her pocket, unfolded it and slapped it against the barrier for him to read. He had fussy little reading glasses that he fished out of his jump-suit pocket and placed far down on his nose. His pale blue eyes moved in short jerks down the page.

"Ah," he murmured, and removed the glasses as he sat back. "That's interesting, don't you think?"

"The part about me getting killed? Yeah. I think it's pretty damn fascinating," she said, and folded the letter back into the envelope. "Thanks for agreeing with me."

He smiled. It looked like a nice, kindly sort of expression. "I like you," he said. "Why do you think I had them hire you?"

"I don't understand how a guy who's behind bars for killing five people has the right to hire me to do anything," she said. "And furthermore, you don't pay me, so far as I know."

"I set up the Cross Society," Simms said, eyebrows raised. "Where did you imagine that money might have come from? Investments I made, with my own funds. So in a way, you continue to be paid by me, but you're quite right in legal terms. I haven't hired you. I have no assets, no rights, no existence beyond these walls, Jasmine. I rely on the friend-ship and goodwill of others."

He sounded like the worst kind of con artist, the religious kind, the one bilking Ma and Pa Kettle out of their farm money while diddling little Ellie May out behind the barn. "You don't get to call me *Jasmine,*" she snapped, "and I've got no friendship and no goodwill for you, so let's cut to the chase. It was a long drive out here, I'm tired, and I got myself pretty well beat up today, so if you don't mind—"

Simms looked up sharply, and the image she'd been form-ing of him dissolved under the force of that gaze again. What the hell *was* that? It was like a storm in her head, a white-hot merciless laser boring right through everything she thought, everything she was....

"Do you understand what an eidolon is?" Simms asked, and didn't wait for her answer, as if he already knew it. "It's the essence of a thing put into another form. The Greeks thought it a god made flesh, but it doesn't have to be a god, it can be anything that *acts* as a god. An avatar of power."

"Eidolon Corporation," she said. "You named it that."

"I did," he admitted. "I hired incredibly smart people to do research. To put some scientific framework around what I already knew to be true. I set the agenda, I directed the research, and I created a monster. A monster which turned on me, as you might have guessed."

"Fascinating," she said. "What does that have to do with me?"

He blinked at her. "You mean nobody's told you?"

"Told me what?"

Simms's blue eyes took on a liquid shine, something eerie and strange.

"That you are one of the two people that I believe will bring down the beast. Bring down Eidolon, before it's too late."

She cocked her head, shot a look from him to Borden and back. "Too late for what?" She was sure she was going to be sorry she'd asked.

She wasn't wrong.

"Too late to stop the end of life as we know it," Simms said, as if that made all the sense in the world.

Crazy. This was crazy talk, and she felt trapped in this tiny airless room with Borden and this crazy man across from them. She ached all over and wanted to go home, crawl into bed and forget all of this. Give back the damn money, call it a day—

"How?" she asked.

"Does it matter?" Simms shrugged. "It's the sort of thing you can't prove, Jasmine. If it happens, then there are no witnesses to testify. If it doesn't, well, no one can ever be certain I wasn't crazy."

Crazy. Even he had the word in his head—or maybe he'd picked it up out of hers. Maybe he really was some sideshow freak mind reader. "Humor me," she said.

"Very well." Simms leaned his elbows on the table on his side of the glass, and the light slid over his pale, thin skin. She could see the cold pulse of blue veins underneath. "I suppose you expect me to say something very movie-of-the-week, the new hot disaster terror in all the tabloids. Ebola, or some such. In fact, it's much more prosaic than that. War."

"War won't destroy life as we know it. It might kill a large number of people, but—"

"Forgive me for my inexact description," Simms interrupted her, "but I meant the destruction of human civilization. The world, of course, will continue. Damaged, fragile, but certainly not shattered beyond repair. But humans? It will take thousands of years to recover. Or, if there is another catastrophe, never."

"War," Jazz repeated flatly. "That's it? Just war?"

"You forget, Jasmine, we live in a time when killing has become a matter of engineering as much as brute force. We are only a few years from the implementation of machines capable of slaughter on a scale undreamed of fifty years ago, which was a quantum leap forward from the slaughter of fifty years before that. We live in an age of rapid acceleration." He shrugged again. "I told you, it doesn't matter. Either it will happen or it won't, but in any case, it won't matter to the course of this conversation."

Borden, next to her, was still and quiet and steady, as if he'd already heard all this. Maybe he had.

"Okay, then," Jazz said. "Tell me something concrete. Tell me why Lowell Santoro had to take one for your team.

That's what it was, right? The Cross Society decided he was expendable. That's why Borden had to get me to help."

"Mr. Santoro's role is a bit complicated to explain, but I'll try. In six months, he will be instrumental in the making of a motion picture that changes the course of political campaigns in certain key states. That means that there will be increased funding in those key states to the military suppliers. Those suppliers will develop the weapons that I'm speaking of. And so on."

Jazz leaned back in her chair, staring at him. "You're willing to kill a guy over a movie? Why not just kill the movie?"

"I understand the concept of Actors and Leads has been explained to you?"

"For all that I believe in it, yeah."

"The movie itself cannot be stopped. In every permutation of timeline that I have examined—and I have examined a vast number of them—the movie exists. What changes is the credibility of the movie. The people associated with it. And Santoro is the key to forming that group." Simms leaned even closer to the glass. His eyes looked almost transparent now, at close range. "Understand me, Jasmine, I would have done it differently if I could have. We researched this for years, growing more and more desperate. Nothing changed. Santoro couldn't be separated from this project, nor it from him, with anything but lethal force."

Jazz opened her mouth, but Borden beat her to it. "So you got the opposition to do it for you," he said. "You manipulated them into killing him."

Simms didn't reply. He didn't even look at Borden, whose voice was low and tight with anger. He seemed fascinated by Jazz's stare.

"I manipulate everyone, my dear counselor," he said. "It's all I have, you know. The power of suggestion, and responsibility. So yes, I did manipulate them. If you'd left well enough alone, we wouldn't be having this conversation, but..." Simms smiled, and there wasn't anything really kindly about it at all. "But I thought you might do something like this. The odds were low, but definitely present. The others didn't see it, but I did. And that's a great pity, you know, because now Jasmine will pay the price. There's nothing I can do about it."

He leaned back, eyelids lowering to hood his stare.

"You're saying—" Borden began.

"I'm saying that you've ruined years of work," Simms said, "and I'm not pleased, James, not pleased. There are ways it can be fixed, but they'll cost me. I'm not at all looking forward to the work."

Jazz stared at him for a few seconds of silence, then reached up and pressed the red button. Somewhere, a buzzer went off. She stood up, banging her chair into Borden's knees, bringing him upright with her.

"What are you doing?" he blurted, frowning. Simms merely looked at her, placid and unmoving, on the other side of the glass.

"Getting the hell out of here," she said. "I'm sorry, but this is bullshit. This guy is talking about *seeing the future.*

Are you getting that, or does he have you so brainwashed you believe everything he says? Because frankly, *Counselor,* you seemed like a smarter guy than that to me."

She slapped the red button again, impatiently. The buzzer continued to rattle somewhere outside.

Simms said, very quietly, "Don't be foolish. I knew where to find you, Jasmine. I knew where you would be when you didn't know you were going there. I know things about you that even your closest friends don't know. I can recite them to you, but I doubt you'd want Counselor Borden to be privy to—"

She slapped the button again, rounded on him and leaned on the table to put her face close enough to the glass to fog it with her breath. "Save it, asshole, I'm not buying your side-show crap. You had somebody follow me to the bar. Hell, for all I know, you had somebody switch envelopes on me just now at the police station. It's all crap, all right? And you're not going to convince me otherwise—"

"At precisely ten-oh-two tonight," Simms said, "Flight eight-oh-two, the plane you will be flying back to Kansas City, will suffer an engine failure. There will be two possible outcomes. One, the plane will rapidly lose altitude and crash into a row of suburban tract homes just short of the runway. There will be two survivors, a blond woman named Kelley Walters and a businessman, Lamar Qualls. Kelley will be traveling to visit her sister in Kansas City. Lamar will be visiting the city on business, to sign a contract for a grocery-store supply chain."

She froze, staring at him. His eyes looked pellucidly clear. Sky blue. If he was lying, he was the best liar she'd ever seen in her life. "Bullshit," she said. But she wondered if it was. It was too specific, too definite. Liars liked to talk in generalities, not specifics that could be checked and disproved.

"Two," Simms continued as if she hadn't spoken, "the pilot will be able to compensate for the loss of the engine and land the plane safely, without incident. There is an eighty-two percent chance that will be the case. I hope you find that comforting."

"So you're giving me a doom-and-gloom prediction that won't come true," she said. "How convenient for you."

"I'd say it's more convenient for you, actually," he said, "considering that if I'm wrong, you won't be one of the two survivors being carried out of the wreckage." He shrugged. "I'm not a fortune-teller. When I tell you these things, I'm simply relaying what I know to be true based on my survey of possible futures. You can act on them, or not act. But altering the future is a delicate thing. If I send someone right now to the airport, for instance, and remove a certain mechanic from duty who is about to forget to tighten a bolt, then the engine problem doesn't occur at all. However, that sends events down another path, and I can't always see the consequences clearly from where I stand. Sometimes changing things makes them worse."

"What's worse than a plane crash?" she asked.

"I assure you, you don't want to know," he answered, and craned his neck. "Weren't you leaving?"

The buzzer shut down abruptly outside, and she felt a change in pressure and cool air on her back as a deputy yanked open the door behind her. It would be the easiest thing in the world to stalk out of here, leave Borden twisting in the wind.

"Don't you know what I'll do?" she asked him.

Simms smiled. "There are a very few people in this world who are blank slates to me," he said. "Those people bring random action to the game. You are one, or rather, you are one now. I predicted your actions somewhat accurately up until the night Laskins sent Borden to you with the offer, but unfortunately, you have grown more opaque since then. Your decisions drive events, Jazz. Yours, and Lucia's. That's why we call you Leads."

"Why?" she flung at him. "Why us? We're not important, are we? We're just—"

"Pawns?" Simms's mouth stretched in a wider smile. A much more unpleasant one, to Jazz's revulsion. "Pawns win games, you know. And I'd call you...knights. Perhaps one of you might even prove to be a queen, before this game is over."

She balled up her fists on the cold, cracked Formica of the counter. "If you're playing a game, who are you playing? Why can't you stay ahead?"

"It should be obvious to you by now that I have an opponent," he said. His eyes flicked to focus behind her. "I believe Officer Sanchez is waiting on you."

Behind her, the deputy said, "Yeah, I am. In or out, miss. I've got things to do."

She allowed herself to relax back into the chair, took a deep breath, and said, "I'll stay. For a while."

She felt the guard's shrug. "Not going anywhere," he said, and the door clicked and locked again behind her.

Bad decision, she thought instantly, and wondered from Simms's crazy point of view what kind of futures had just imploded or expanded. What factors had shifted.

Which was just…nuts, wasn't it? To believe in a thing like that?

"You think you're playing Eidolon Corporation. Right?"

Simms glanced at Borden, who leaned elbows on the narrow table beside her and said, "When Simms started trying to change the course of futures that he thought were dangerous, some people at Eidolon disagreed. Some of them for idealistic reasons, some for practical economic reasons. Eidolon is an inside-trader's dream. When you know the course of events, imagine how much profit there is to be made…but Simms didn't agree. So when push came to shove, Eidolon needed to lose Simms but decided that Simms's abilities were too valuable to let go. They found somebody as backup. Somebody with similar, ah, abilities."

"His name is Gilbert Kavanaugh," Simms said. "Gil for short. You'd like him, he's actually very amusing, for a psychopath."

"And let me get this straight. You claim to be able to see

the future, and you didn't see it coming when he, what, framed you for murder?"

Simms nodded, a neat, economical motion.

"I told you. Certain people—"

"Yeah, blank slates, yadda, yadda. You can't read his future?"

"No."

"Or your own, I'm guessing."

Simms's smile was thin and discomforting. "No."

"Or mine."

"Not at present. There are times yours is clear, and at others, not. Like Mr. Borden's. Like Lucia Garza's."

"Explain to me why you want to hire people whose actions you *can't* predict. Assuming this isn't a giant steaming pile of crap, of course."

"Of course. Because," Simms said very calmly, "the ones I *can* predict cannot change anything. Their fates are set, for better or worse, unless one of the random pieces acts. I have gone to considerable trouble to hire all that I can, but of course Eidolon has deep pockets, as well."

"You're delusional."

"No." Simms shrugged. "But I do think it is a wonder I'm not insane, don't you?"

"Five bodies buried in your backyard say different."

Simms stared at her for a long, long moment, and she had that sensation again, as if a floodlight had swept over her and illuminated every cell in her body, every dark thought, every secret. It made her dangerously angry.

"Take her home, Counselor Borden," Simms said. He sounded suddenly tired, and not at all happy. "I've had quite enough excitement for one day, and I believe Gil is going to attempt another clever move before bedtime. I will need all my concentration to undo the mistakes of today."

Borden reached across Jazz and punched the button. She knocked his arm away, rose to her feet and leaned both palms flat on the table, staring at Simms's small, pale face. "I think you're full of crap," she said. "We make our own choices, and you're just a con man and a murderer."

Simms didn't smile this time. He looked thoroughly exhausted, as if the life was draining out of him. "Part of that is always true some of the time," he said. "And part of it is true all of the time. I leave it to you to decide how to divide the statement. It's been lovely to meet you, Jasmine."

"It's not mutual," she said, and turned toward the door as it opened behind her. Moving into the larger room with its harsh fluorescent glare and empty ringing silence felt like escape, as if she'd been under some threat she hadn't identified.

She looked back. Borden was still standing there, speaking softly to Simms. As she watched, Simms nodded, stood up and shuffled away with a deputy at his side.

Borden looked grim and angry, and he didn't say a word as they followed their own deputy back past empty cells and through sally ports. They both spoke in monosyllables as they signed papers and collected their belongings again, then were escorted back into the harsh desert sunshine. The car was still waiting, idling in the falling darkness.

When they were back on the road, Borden clicked open his briefcase, rooted around in it for a second, and then handed her a plane ticket. Flight 802. Los Angeles to Kansas City.

"He didn't know," Borden said. "I didn't tell him we were flying back tonight, and there's no way he could have known which flight we were on. Think about that."

She gave him a long, considering look, and said, "And if I were a half-decent con man, I might know how many flights there were to K.C. from LAX in a day, if my mark was heading there. I might make a pretty educated guess as to which one she'd be on, given the time of day. Looks like magic. Smells like crap, Counselor. Sorry. No sale."

He shook his head and avoided her eyes. She licked her lips and suddenly—shockingly—remembered the warm pressure of his mouth, and felt something in her plummet again, lost and liking it. *It's a long ride back to L.A.,* some part of her whispered. She tracked it down and throttled it into silence.

Borden said something under his breath that sounded like, "He said you'd be like this," and they spent the entire ride back in silence.

Not touching.

To Jazz's well-concealed disappointment.

Chapter 9

Jazz had done such a good job of putting Simms out of her mind that it wasn't until she was queuing up to the ticket line behind a petite blond woman dressed in a fuzzy pink scarf and heard the ticket agent say "Ms. Walters? May I see your ID please?" that the whole thing came rushing back, like ice through her veins. Simms's cool, precise voice whispered in her head. *There will be two survivors, a blond woman named Kelley Walters and a businessman, Lamar Qualls. Kelley will be traveling to visit her sister in Kansas City.*

The blond woman moved off. Jazz stared after her for a few seconds, then moved up and handed over ticket and ID. Borden was right behind her. No hitches. They breezed through security and took seats at the gate with twenty minutes before boarding.

If Borden had heard the woman's name, he didn't give any indication. He'd stopped along the way to buy a copy of the *New York Times* and was deep into the business section. He'd stopped looking at her at all. Jazz, for her part, felt ancient and creaky, thanks to the day's exertions. Her muscles were telling her they badly wanted a rest, and she was pretty sure she looked like she'd gone a few rounds as a punching bag. She told her various aches and pains to shut up, and strolled over to the restroom when she saw the blond woman get up and head that way.

It's crap, Jazz told herself. She did her business in the stall and came out to find Ms. Walters—Kelley, no doubt— washing her hands. She was a lovely pink rose of a woman, neat and friendly, flashing an immediate smile when Jazz took the sink next to her.

"Late flight," Jazz said, and yawned as she yanked paper towels from the dispenser. The other woman nodded.

"At least we get to sleep," she said. "And there's no traffic at the terminal when you get there. But there's something really eerie about looking for a cab in the middle of the night, you know?"

"Nobody meeting you?"

Kelley shook her head, causing blunt-cut blond hair to brush her cheeks. "I'm visiting my sister and her family. No sense in getting them out of bed at oh-my-God in the morning. I'll just take a cab and get a hotel. I was supposed to be on the six-o'clock flight, but I got bumped. What a pain flying is these days."

Jazz was good at reading people, good at sensing setups and deceptions, and she felt nothing. Heard no false notes.

If Kelley Walters was a plant, working as part of the larger con orchestrated by Max Simms, she was the best damn liar Jazz had ever seen.

Jazz went back to her seat. Borden had finished the business section and moved on to sports. She picked up the paper and scanned it without really reading, watching the other passengers who were getting ready to board. Not a huge crowd, this time of night—maybe thirty, altogether. A few college-age kids, with the ubiquitous backpacks. A gaggle of businesspeople who must have all worked for the same firm—they had the look of people who'd traveled together so often they no longer had to make conversation. One middle-aged man, overweight and prematurely gray, sat slumped in his chair reading a mystery novel. His battered, much-traveled carry-on roller case had a large tag that read Qualls.

Jazz felt a sense of unreality close around her. Walters, she could dismiss as a deliberate setup. Qualls, being part of a group, wasn't so easy. Still, Simms and the Cross Society *could* have gotten hold of the passenger list....

Flight 802. She stared at the number and found it suddenly hard to swallow.

"Borden," she said, and stopped. He looked up. His brown eyes were tired and bleary.

"What?"

"Maybe we should—"

He folded his newspaper. "What?"

"Nothing."

The boarding call went out for business class. Qualls and the rest of the flock of suits headed for the ramp. Jazz checked her ticket. She and Borden were in business, as well. She shouldered her bag and followed his long-limbed stride past the checkpoint, through the hollow booming tunnel, up to the accordion end pressed against the smooth skin of the airplane...

She stopped. Just...stopped.

This is stupid, she told herself. *Move. Get on the damn plane.*

Borden had heard the same things she had. He wasn't hesitating.

She took a deep breath and edged past the tired smiles of the flight attendants to her seat. Borden eased in next to her with a sigh and buckled in tight.

"Borden," she said again. "Listen, what he said—"

"About the crash?" He sounded utterly calm. "You weren't listening, Jazz. There's an eighty-two-percent chance it won't happen. Believe me, the longer you're around Simms, the more you'll trust his odds."

"But—" *There's a woman named Kelley Walters back there. And that guy over there, he's named Qualls.*

Borden went back to the sports section. "Just stay buckled in," he said. "Trust me. You'll either believe soon, or you won't. And there's an eighty-two-percent chance it'll actually still matter in the end."

The engine blew out, by Jazz's watch, at 10:03 p.m., California time. She was next to the window and had a view of the sudden flare of fire. She hadn't gone to sleep, though the plane was nearly silent and most of her fellow passengers—including Borden—had nodded off.

They all woke up fast when the loud *bang* shuddered through the aircraft, and the plane lurched sharply to starboard. Jazz gasped and punched fingernails into the armrests, wishing the damn plane came with crash harnesses instead of ridiculously inadequate lap belts; next to her, Borden snapped awake and grabbed for support, too. "Hold on," he said.

She stared out the window at the whipping fire and smoke pouring from the ruined engine. The plane hit rough air and tilted again, waking screams from the back cabin. The engines growled, shaking the airframe, and Jazz felt her ears pop.

She grabbed for Borden's hand.

"Eighty-two percent," he said. It sounded like a prayer, or a chant. "Eighty-two percent. We'll be okay."

It didn't feel like that. It felt like her stomach had dropped somewhere out of the cargo bay and was falling, weightless, to earth. About to crash into a row of sleeping suburban houses. *He didn't say how many of them it would kill,* she thought, *how many more innocent victims.* Maybe, to Simms, nobody was innocent.

She felt her fingers twine tight with Borden's. His were shaking. A whine built up at the back of her throat, and she felt the plane falling, falling, tilting…

And then, suddenly, there was a surge of power, and it leveled out. They were saved.

She let out a startled gasp and heard the cries behind her fade out. Borden was still holding her hand, but he wasn't crushing it anymore, and she could hear him breathing again. Deep, deliberately slow breaths.

"See?" he said. His voice sounded an octave higher than normal. "Eighty-two percent. We're going to be fine."

She turned toward him in the dimness as the Fasten Seat Belts sign flashed on with a belated *ding,* and the captain announced in a businesslike voice that no, they were not going to die.

"He's not bullshit, is he?" she asked. "Simms. He really can do these things."

"Well," Borden answered, "the alternative is that he has enough power sitting in a maximum-security prison to have arranged for a commercial airliner to be sabotaged just to convince you. Which one would you rather believe?"

She managed a pale, shaky smile. His fingers wrapped around hers, warm and comforting, and she let them stay there all the way to the terminal.

It was nearly five in the morning by the time Jazz flipped on the lights in her office and dropped bonelessly onto the couch. She let her head drift back against the cushions and stared at the ceiling, blank and drained, and saw Borden's long, sharp-chinned face bend over her.

"Okay?" he asked. He hadn't ever put his tie back on, she

realized. His suit jacket was off and tossed over the arm of a chair, drooping just the way she felt, and his once finely pressed shirt was a mass of wrinkles. Unbuttoned about one too many fastenings to qualify as businesslike.

"Yeah," she said. "For somebody whose head exploded several hours ago."

"Believe me, I understand." He sank down on the couch next to her. "Remember the night I walked into the bar with your letter?"

She wasn't likely to forget it. "You looked like an idiot."

"I felt like one."

"Did Simms tell you what to wear?"

He didn't answer. He reached out and smoothed a stray lock of hair back from her face. She turned toward him, cheek resting on soft cushions, and met his eyes.

They both froze.

His hand was still brushing her skin, fingers light and warm, but there was nothing casual about the look on his face. Dangerous, that look. Especially here, in the dark, after adrenaline and a hard day and the destruction of the universe as she knew it, with a comfortable couch to lie back on.

Really, really dangerous.

Jazz moved away a little. Just enough to put space between his hand and her skin. He took the hint and leaned away, elbow on the back of the couch, staring at her but not quite as nakedly hungering. "I should call Lucia," she said.

"This early?"

He had a point, and the couch felt far too comfortable. "I should go home," she said. "Then again, I should be here in three hours."

"Sleep," he advised her, and pulled her legs into his lap. She couldn't honestly remember when it was she'd allowed him to get that close to her, allowed herself to be touched with that much freedom. His hands felt huge and burning hot through her clothes, points of fire on her skin. She closed her eyes, sucked in a deep breath and concentrated on the sensation of his palms moving lightly across the backs of her calves, massaging. He stripped off her shoes and let them drop to the floor.

She didn't mean to fall asleep, but there was something so achingly soothing about the warmth of his body near hers that she dropped into a field of black behind her eyelids, and was gone.

Jazz woke up alone, to the blaze of overhead lights. She blinked, coughed and dragged herself upright, wishing for hair-trigger reflexes and managing more like a blunt object.

Lucia was framed in the door, paused in the act of walking into the room, staring at her with an expression of utter surprise.

"Hey," Jazz muttered, and ran both hands through her hair. She didn't even want to think about how she looked. There were bag ladies going through Dumpsters who probably looked better.

"Hey," Lucia said cautiously, and closed the door behind her. "Ah...were you supposed to be back today?"

"No. Change of plans." *I'm marked for death,* Jazz started to say, and decided to hold that back for later, after coffee. "Where's Borden?"

"Was he here?" Lucia set her purse down and swung dark hair back over her shoulder with a practiced swing of her head, smiling like the Mona Lisa. "And is there something I should know about this?"

"Nothing interesting."

Lucia pulled a chair up and sat down, elbows on her knees in a pose Jazz realized was a mirror of her own. Only, of course, Lucia was dressed in an olive-green pantsuit with a peach silk blouse, flawless makeup, and didn't look as if she'd ever in her life had a black eye, a chipped nail, or a short night's sleep on the office couch.

"What happened?"

Jazz didn't intend to tell her all of it, but that's what came out. All of it. From the saving of Santoro's life—which, if one believed Simms, wasn't the greatest of all possible good deeds—to the creepy prison conversation, to her own new-found status as Eidolon's Most Wanted, which by extension endangered all of them. She dug out the letter and handed it over. There was a lipstick smudge on it that baffled her until she remembered the lip print on the Plexiglas in the visitor's cubicle. She'd forgotten about it when she slapped the paper to the surface. It looked now as if somebody at Eidolon had given her a sloppy, openmouthed kiss as a parting gift.

Lucia took it in without comment or question, until Jazz finished, and then looked up. "Do you believe it? Any of it at all?"

That was a tough question. At five in the morning, she'd believed a hell of a lot more than she did sitting in the office, with morning light streaming in through the blinds and the smell of coffee beginning to percolate through the air-conditioning system.

"Some," she finally said. "Look, one thing's for sure—he didn't arrange that demonstration last night with the plane, and the chances of it being a lucky guess? Zero. Well, probably so close to zero that you couldn't see them without a microscope."

"And the thing about trying to prevent the end of life as we know it?"

"I have no idea," Jazz admitted. "Combine delusions with an actual weird ability, what do you get?"

"Something scary. Something very scary."

"No shit." Jazz mussed her hair again, and saw Lucia grimace. "What? Don't I just look like the hottie of the month?"

"You look like you could use a bath," Lucia said, with brutal honesty. "And another haircut. I've never seen anyone who can grow out of one as quickly as you."

But Jazz could tell that Lucia's mind wasn't on fashion and hair, not anymore. She looked stone-cold serious behind the frivolous words, and her mind was racing a million miles an hour. This was the Lucia Jazz knew and liked.

The one who could shoot the eye out of an ant at a hundred feet.

"Precautions," Lucia said. "First things first, you don't go anywhere without Kevlar. They've taken shots at you before, they will again. Also, we start with standard risk-assessment protocol. You never get into a car without it being checked for explosives or sabotage—"

"Lucia, come on. Seriously."

"I'm being perfectly serious. You never get into a car with anyone you don't know. We upgrade security on your apartment...no, scratch that, we abandon your apartment and move you someplace safe. No forwarding address."

"Safe? Like where?"

Lucia's smile flared impossibly white and gorgeous. Whatever she'd been about to say was interrupted by the arrival of Pansy, who poked her head around the door and waved a good-natured hello, then opened it wider as she said, "Guess who's here?" She looked like a canary-fed cat. A well-satisfied canary-fed cat.

Standing with her, shuffling his feet uncomfortably and looking desperately as if he wanted to be anywhere else on earth, was Manny Glickman.

"Manny?" Jazz got up so fast she felt her throbbing head swim. "Everything okay?"

"Yeah," he mumbled, raised his muddy green eyes to hers for a bare second, and then looked down. "I, um, was just—on my way to—"

"Manny," Lucia said slowly, and got up, too. She took a

couple of steps in his direction, and stopped when he backed up a little in alarm. He liked her well enough, Jazz knew, but Manny didn't like *anything* coming at him that quickly. "Sorry. Listen, maybe you can help. You know something about security."

"Pretty much everything," he agreed, without any arrogance. "Why?"

"Jazz needs secure accommodations."

Manny looked up sharply, and fastened a laser stare on Lucia. "What's going on?"

Careful, Jazz thought, wishing she was telepathic. If she was going to be so god-awful *special,* she ought to at least have some particular power beyond getting thumped on and kind of enjoying it.

"Jazz has somebody after her," Lucia said. "I don't think she'll be safe in her home as it is right now."

Manny's stare transferred to Jazz. "After you?"

She sighed. "Yeah." Any second now, there would be a cloud of dust and an end to her relationship with Manny Glickman. Danger was something Manny just didn't do. Not that he'd ever been Adventure Man, but his turn under the ground had stripped away whatever bravery he'd once pretended to own. Not that she blamed him. She knew she wouldn't have survived it at all. "Never mind, Manny, don't worry about it. You go on and—"

"You can stay with me," he said. A simple, declarative statement. No shifting, no stuttering, no nervous flutters.

He was rock still, his eyes steady and his face set. "There's no place safer in this city than mine."

Oh, God, Jazz thought, and a wave of hilarity cascaded over her. She saw Lucia bite her lip, eyes wide. *Manny Glickman as a roommate....*

"I won't let you down," he said, and suddenly all of the funny stuff fell away, and she was looking not at the screwed-up Manny she'd known for years, but at an entirely different person. Somebody who might have been able to pass the FBI's stringent tests and personality profiles and background checks. Somebody who had strength and dignity and courage.

Somebody who'd always been there, underneath all of the panic and worry and tics.

"I won't," he repeated, and took a step toward her. "Jazz, let me do this. I want to help you."

She had no idea why he was offering. "Manny, look, you don't understand. People may be trying to hurt me. Kill me. This isn't a game."

He swallowed hard. She saw his Adam's apple bob up and down convulsively, and he squeezed his eyes shut. He was trembling a little, but only a little, and he jammed hands into the pockets of his tan raincoat to hide it. "Fine," he said. "Just, you know, leave it outside. Don't bring it in."

Lucia stepped smoothly into the silence. "You set the time and method for us to move her," she said. "Just let us know."

"Hey!" Jazz said. "Don't I get—"

"No," Lucia answered without looking at her. "It's

Manny's call, not yours. Let's face it, Jazz, you gave up the right to make the decisions when you decided to run off to L.A. and get a contract put out on your life. So from now on, you go nowhere without me. You live in Manny's house. And you *do not* get a vote."

Jazz's temper—never far from the surface—flared into bubbling lava. "I'm not living like a prisoner!"

The window behind her exploded in a shower of bright, sharp-edged glass, and she felt a rush of wind that blew her hair forward violently. Lucia was heading toward her, but she was already diving for the carpet, squirming to get under the desk, twisting on her side to see if anybody else had been hit.

Manny was still standing, staring uncomprehendingly at the shattered window and the clanking, wind-tossed blinds. Pansy screamed something unintelligible at him and tackled him; they tumbled together, off balance, back out into the reception area between the offices. Lucia hadn't gone for cover. She'd hit the carpet, rolled gracefully, and fetched up against the far wall under the windows. By the time she made the last rotation, she had her gun out and in both hands. She shook hair out of her face, panting, and stared at Jazz. "You all right?" she shouted. Jazz made an okay gesture with one hand as she yanked open her desk drawer with the other and felt around in the depths. She found a cold metal box and pulled it out to thump on the carpet next to her head, then punched in the combination with trembling fingers. The lock snapped open.

She took the Sig Sauer and scrambled to join Lucia at the window. They sat there together, backs to the wall, guns ready, and exchanged a look.

"Now," Lucia said, and rolled right, over the broken glass, coming up on one knee and aiming out the open window. Jazz angled to cover her own side. There was a second's tight silence as they searched for targets.

"Clear," Lucia announced.

"Yeah, here, too."

"If he's any good, he's already gone," Lucia said. "Snipers don't hang around waiting for a second chance. They take the shot and go without seeing how it came out. If it doesn't work, they come back for another try."

Jazz nodded jerkily and narrowed her eyes against the glare, still looking. The morning looked bland and bright. Traffic crawled along outside without incident. Nobody seemed to have noticed a thing, so far, though there was a nice glittering spray of glass on the sidewalk below.

"Get out," Lucia said, still maintaining a rigid focus outside the window, gun at the ready. "Stay low."

There wasn't any reason to argue about it. Jazz did a combat-crawl across the floor, keeping close to the wall, and when she was far enough, rose to a crouch and moved fast out into the darker area beyond. Manny and Pansy peered at her from the cover of Pansy's desk.

"Over here!" Pansy whispered, and gestured her urgently on. "Get down!"

"There's no reason to keep your voice down, they're not

stalking the halls with Uzis," Jazz said in a normal tone, and straightened up. "Also, there's no way they can see in here from any of the windows. We're fine."

"Thanks, we'll just—stay here," Pansy said. "I called nine-one-one."

"Good idea." Jazz realized her heart was still pounding, and she was breathing too fast, and reached up to run her hand through her hair. Something bit in a sharp hot line on her finger, and she bent over and shook her head. A rain of glass fragments came out and bounced on the carpet. "You both okay? No holes in you?"

"Fine," Pansy said. Manny wasn't speaking, evidently. "Jazz? I'm thinking I might, you know, take a personal day."

Jazz nodded calmly, ejected the clip from the Sig Sauer and checked it before slamming it back in and ratcheting the slide to put one in the chamber. "You know," she said, "I personally think that sounds like an excellent idea. But wait for the police."

"Don't worry," Manny said. Like Jazz, he sounded extremely calm. Unnaturally calm. "I'm not moving until there's three-hundred-sixty degrees of Kevlar."

She had no doubt that was true. She expected the next time she saw Manny, he'd look like the Michelin Man, only in black body armor. "Pansy. You didn't see Borden when you came in this morning?"

"No, was he here?"

"Yes." No need to go into details. "I'm going to check the rest of the offices."

"Um…" Pansy made a vague gesture toward Jazz's legs. "You might want to put on some shoes first."

She'd forgotten, but it came back to her in a weirdly warm rush of feeling, Borden sliding her shoes off her feet and dropping them to the floor…they must have landed next to the couch. She turned back to the office but met Lucia at the door coming out. Lucia had holstered her gun and was holding Jazz's shoes in her left hand. She thrust them out without a word and slammed the door behind her.

"Off-limits," she said flatly. "You said Borden was here somewhere?" As Jazz bent to slide on the shoes, she turned her attention to Manny and Pansy. "Wait there. I don't care what you hear, don't come running, all right?"

Two nods. Jazz straightened up, and Lucia performed that magic trick again, the one where she started empty-handed and ended up with that gleaming little gun in her hand. Only this one, Jazz noticed, wasn't so little. It was at least a .38. Still elegant looking, though.

"Do you match your guns to your outfits?" she asked. Lucia threw her an exasperated look. "Kidding."

"Go left," Lucia sighed. "No heroics."

Borden was nowhere in their offices. Nowhere, as it turned out, in the building. Police arrived within five minutes and turned the entire place inside out, coming up empty. They also turned up nothing on the sniper. Jazz wasn't shocked. As she and Lucia finished giving statements, she felt her cell phone buzz against her hip, and stepped away to answer.

"Borden?" she asked. It was his number lighting up on the panel. "Where the hell are you?"

It wasn't his voice that answered. "Go to your secretary's desk. Right now."

She froze for a second, mind racing. She didn't know the voice, had never heard it before, but it had a ring of authority. She turned away from the cops and Lucia, trying to look casual about it, plugged a finger in her left ear and tried to make it look as if she was seeking a quiet place. Pansy and Manny were still behind the desk, watching the cops move around. Jazz stopped at the low counter on the other side of the barrier from them.

"I'm here," she said. "Where's Borden?"

"Shut up and listen. Look through the mail. There will be a FedEx envelope."

There were three, in fact. Jazz spread them out quickly on the counter, looking at addresses.

One was from Gabriel, Pike & Laskins.

"Open it," the voice said.

She picked up the GPL envelope, jammed the phone between her shoulder and ear, and ripped the tab. When she turned the stiff cardboard upside down, a familiar red envelope fell out.

"You have the envelope?" said the voice.

"I'm holding it," she said. "Want me to open it?"

"If you break the seal on it, your lawyer friend dies. I

want you to turn and walk with it to the stairs. Proceed down to the lobby, go outside and turn right. Walk exactly two blocks, then turn left and go one block. No cops."

She tapped the red envelope on the counter, staring at Pansy's frown, Manny's worried expression.

"Any particular reason I need to take this stroll? Other than for my health?"

A shockingly loud scream burst out of the phone, wild and full of agony, a full-throated bellow. She flinched, nearly lost the phone and slowly straightened up. She felt the blood drain from her face.

"You know what I call a half-dead lawyer?" the voice asked. "A good start. Move your ass, bitch, or he gets something else cut off. Maybe something that he can't live without."

The phone went dead in her hand. She closed her eyes for a second, felt a hot bead of sweat trickle down her back. She turned slowly, keeping the phone to her ear as an excuse to stay where she was, and looked at the cops and Lucia.

Lucia, who was talking, glanced over at her, away, back again to stare. She paused for a breath, smiled at the cop and murmured something that sounded like a graceful apology. Then she walked over to where Jazz stood, red envelope in hand.

"What?" she asked softly.

"Borden," Jazz replied. "They have him. They want this." She moved the envelope slightly, drawing Lucia's attention to it. "They sound real serious."

Lucia nodded. Something sparked bright in her eyes, and her expression smoothed into an unmoving mask. "You want to get real serious?"

"I do." She was still vibrating from the force of the scream. *Maybe that wasn't him,* she thought, but she knew that was a stupid wishful lie. She'd felt that scream go deep. She'd *known* it. "I want to get real fucking serious, right now."

"We have visitors." Lucia crossed her arms and tilted her head toward the cops.

"I go first. You back me up." Jazz fixed a hard stare on her. "I need you on this."

"I know. I'll be there."

Jazz nodded once, took the envelope and shoved it into her coat pocket, then walked, in no great hurry, around the corner.

"Where's she going?" one of the cops asked behind her.

"Bathroom," Lucia said. "Do you think we should get away from the windows? In case he's not really gone?" She suddenly sounded vulnerable and scared.

"Sure. No problem."

Jazz heard them moving away, and grinned without humor. She was just moving for the stairs when someone hurried around the corner and almost collided with her. She jumped away, ready to punch, and Pansy staggered back to catch herself against the wall, hand flat against her chest and an expression of shock all over her face. She straightened her glasses and fanned herself.

"What?" Jazz demanded.

"Here!" Pansy pressed something into her hands. "Manny gave it to me. Give me this one. Go!"

She hurried off, back the way she'd come. Jazz, mystified, looked down at what she was holding in her hands, and felt a sudden surge of wild, strange glee.

She shoved it into her pocket and hit the stairwell door at as much of a run as she dared to keep noise to a minimum. Rocketing downstairs on tiptoe was a trick, but she managed, checking her momentum with an outstretched hand raking the walls at the turns. At the lobby door she paused and risked a look outside. More cops down there, but they were all on the street by the patrol cars. She eased open the stairwell door, hurried across the lobby and made it to the service entrance.

Loading dock. Deserted. She left at a flat-out run, breathing deep, feeling a burn in her knee where bruises hadn't begun to heal from her fight the day before. It was easy enough to dodge the cops on the street, and then she kept running, moving as fast as she dared to cover the two blocks. As she waited for the light to cross to the left-hand side, she looked behind her. No sign of Lucia. No sign of cops looking for her, either. She supposed that was a wash.

She pelted across the street the instant traffic paused, bounded over the curb and jogged another block, past the blank side of a long windowless building. Cars were parked at meters on the side. She passed a beat-up Ford, two trucks, a panel van…

The sliding door on the van slapped open when she was even with it, and she darted backward, hands up, as the muzzle of a gun slid out in her direction.

"Against the wall," a voice barked. She couldn't see into the van. Too dark. Sun glinted on window glass, blinding her. No markings on the van, *dammit,* she needed to see something, describe something.... "Do it. Now."

She backed up until her heels and shoulders pressed against brick, hands still high.

"Where's the envelope?" The voice sounded different in person than on the phone, but she was still sure she'd never heard it before. "You have two seconds or I start shooting."

"Here," she said, and pointed down at her pocket. "Let me get it out."

"Go. Slowly."

She reached in with two fingers, showed him the red envelope. Still sealed.

"Pitch it to me." A gloved hand beckoned from the shadows.

"No," she said. "Let me see Borden first."

There was a flurry of movement inside, and the van rocked on its springs. A limp body rolled half out of the door, head knocking on the curb; she winced when she saw it was Borden, pale and unconscious, blood trickling from a cut over his eye. His shirt was ripped along the seam to bare most of his bicep, and was saturated with fresh red blood. There was a wound there, but it was too bloody for her to see what it was.

She concentrated on the pulse in his throat. It was still moving. His chest was still rising and falling, shallowly.

"Time's up," the man inside the van said, and she heard the dry metallic sound of the gun preparing to fire.

"Okay!" she shouted, and tugged the envelope out of her pocket, waving it between two fingers. "Okay, here! Take it!"

She pitched it. It fluttered in the wind and fell short, slapping facedown on the pavement next to Borden's limp, bloody hand. She immediately turned both hands palms out, pleading, and lunged forward to grab it and offer it to him. "Don't shoot, okay? Sorry! I'm sorry!"

He reached to take the envelope.

She threw it edge-on into his face, and as he flinched, she grabbed the barrel of the gun and forced it aside. It went off, hot and violent in her grasp, and she felt a burn on her leg from cement fragments as the bullet dug into the sidewalk, but then she was lunging inside, throwing herself on the unseen opponent, trying to twist the gun out of his hand.

It was a massive miscalculation. She didn't have a chance. She'd lunged into the unknown, blindly trusting, and now she had two problems.

One, the guy was about twice her size and three times her upper-body strength, and he easily slammed her to the side, against the steel wall of the van.

Two, there was another man in the van, and he threw an iron-hard forearm across her throat, holding her in place tight enough to make her gag for breath. She instinctively grabbed for his arm, and he pressed harder as she clawed at a smooth nylon windbreaker. She saw spots and stars in the dark.

"Bitch," the first man said raggedly, and stepped in to plant a fist hard in her stomach. She couldn't double over, but her knees jerked upward, trying to protect her midriff; that just increased the choke hold on her throat. "We're done playing with you."

He reached down and retrieved the red envelope from the floor of the van. In the dim light of the door, it had a boot mark on the back. He ripped it open and slid the contents out—

It was a Hallmark card. Flowers and hearts. Jazz's eyes were watering; still she couldn't help but bare her teeth in a bloody grin and mouth, *Gotcha*.

He turned, threw the card at her, and began ripping at her coat, trying to find the right envelope.

There was a popping sound, and a rapid flicker of blue-white sparks, and he froze in place, head back, muscles trembling, then slumped to the floor.

Lucia stood behind him with a taser the size of a particularly nasty sex toy. She kicked the gun out of his reach and lunged forward to stab the taser hard into the side of the man holding Jazz to the side of the van.

Snap, crackle, pop...down.

Jazz slumped, coughing, gagging, rubbing her throat, and looked up at Lucia, who tasered them both again for good measure, looking grim. She stooped and picked up the red envelope and card from the floor of the van, studied it and extended the open card to Jazz.

It read, in Manny's neat, almost calligraphic handwriting, *Thanks for not hating me.*

Jazz barked out a painful laugh and shoved sweaty hair back from her face. "You've got the right one?"

Lucia nodded. Jazz moved around her, grabbed Borden under the arms and heaved him out of the van onto the sidewalk. He flopped limply, then groaned and rolled over slowly onto his side and curled in on himself. His bloody arm smeared dark red onto the cement.

"James?" She dropped to her knees next to him, breathless, and pushed aside his torn sleeve to see what the damage was. She felt sick when she saw it—a long strip of flesh cut out of his arm, baring muscle. Still bleeding. She stripped off her coat and jammed it against his arm, saw his eyelids flutter, and brushed her fingers greedily across his forehead, his face, his lips. "James!"

His dark eyes flickered open, pupils too large and too slow to contract. Drugged, maybe. Or concussed. "Jazz?" His tongue came out, pale, to wet his lips. "Turn the light off."

She let her breath out in a rush and, for no particular reason, kissed him. Hard. Felt his lips curl up under hers, vaguely smiling.

"Jazz!" Lucia was beside her, and the red envelope in her hand was open. A sheet of crisp paper was in her hand. "Jazz, we have to go. Now."

"I can't leave him here. He's bleeding."

"He's fine. Jazz, the cops are about a block away. He'll be okay—we've got to go *right now!*"

Jazz grabbed the sheet of paper and scanned it. Directions to an address and a time—ten minutes away. Two Polaroid photographs, one of a girl about ten years old, one of a nondescript-looking young man, maybe twenty, twenty-five.

Two words:

Stop Him.

"What the hell?" She looked up at Lucia, who handed her one more thing. A newspaper clipping.

"It was in the envelope," she said.

Third Victim Found Dead, Killer Still At Large. Black-and-white newsprint photos of three children, two girls and a boy, all smiling eagerly for the camera, their lives ahead of them.

"Oh, God," Jazz murmured. She looked down at Borden, whose eyes were at least partly comprehending now. "James—"

"I know," he mumbled. "I'm good. Go."

Lucia grabbed her by the collar and dragged her upright, pushed her into a stumbling run, heading farther down the block. Jazz tried to stop, to turn back, but Lucia shoved her again.

"The car's back that way!" Jazz yelled, just as a huge black SUV roared around the corner, taking it on two wheels, and squealed to a stop next to them. Jazz fumbled for her gun, but Lucia lunged for the passenger door.

"In!" she screamed, and clambered up. Jazz, breathless, followed.

As she slammed the door, the SUV took off with a sudden jerk, and she nearly slid off the bench seat before she could brace herself with the panic strap over the door.

Manny Glickman was driving. *Manny.*

"What the hell...?"

"Bulletproof glass," Manny said, and reached out to tap a knuckle against the thick surface of the side window. "Reinforced steel. The ride's custom, but I think the President has one like it."

"Manny!"

"What?" He looked honestly puzzled, staring over at Jazz. She just blinked, unable to think of a single thing to say.

Lucia, ever practical, unfolded the paper and read off the address. Manny reached over and pushed a recessed spot on the wood-grained dash; a section of it glided out, revealing a keyboard and a small plasma screen. "Put it in," he said. "We have GPS navigation."

Even Lucia paused at that, then nodded and began typing. The SUV felt smooth and comfortable, after the initial jerk; Jazz let herself relax a little. Enough to gulp in some air-conditioned breaths, and say, "'Thank you for not hating me?' Jesus, Manny, is that really the best you could do?"

The GPS navigator's smooth female voice said, "Right turn at the next traffic signal."

"Well," Manny said, and glanced down at his speed, "I

figure having a woman not actually hate me is a pretty big accomplishment. All things considered."

He whipped the wheel. The SUV raced around the corner, straightened out, and smoothly avoided two lumbering trucks, a taxi, and two sedans before the navigator read off another turn.

Lucia had her eyes on the clock. "We're not going to make it in time," she said. "Dammit. Why didn't we know about this? Why didn't Simms tell you?"

"I don't know," Jazz admitted. "Maybe he thought we already knew."

Lucia cursed under her breath, a steady stream of Spanish. The computer recited another fast set of directions. Jazz clung to the panic strap, swallowing, glad that they'd left Borden behind; she couldn't imagine this kind of thrashing around could be good for a head injury. It wasn't doing much for her sense of claustrophobic panic, either.

"Where's Pansy?" she asked. Lucia checked the directions on the paper against what was appearing on screen, then tossed the paper aside and pulled the gun from its holster behind her back.

"Distracting the cops," Lucia said. "Did you know she has a cousin in uniform? His name is Ryan. Kind of cute. We're almost there. You good to go? No broken bones?"

Jazz nodded. "I'm fine."

Lucia shot her a distrustful look. Jazz supposed, on balance, her croaky, damaged voice wasn't exactly the traditional definition of *fine*.

Manny made the final turn onto a suburban street and cut his speed to something less than enough to break the sound barrier.

"There!" Lucia yelled, and pointed. A car was just pulling away from the curb ahead, an electric blue boat of a car with black-and-yellow plates. It was the same car. Jazz remembered it, remembered seeing it accelerate down a street just like this one, the day they'd done the surveillance on the woman loading boxes.

There had been kids playing, she remembered. Kids playing two yards down.

"Oh, my God," she whispered. "They were wrong. They were wrong about who to watch."

They'd managed to disrupt an abduction by accident, rather than design.

She threw a desperate look over at Lucia, then at the house where the car had been parked. The front gate was open, still swinging. A neon-pink backpack lay abandoned on the sidewalk, books spilling out of it.

"He's got her," Jazz shouted. "Manny, go! Follow him!"

He applied the gas, and they rocketed after the disappearing taillights of the Pontiac.

The idea that Manny Glickman, of all people, was some kind of stunt-car driver was so weird that Jazz couldn't get her head around it.

Luckily, her belief—or lack thereof—didn't seem to matter much. Manny drove like a maniac, keeping them within sight of the Pontiac as it dodged and danced in and out of traffic. Lucia got on the phone to the cops and fed them directions and information. Jazz just kept wishing she'd paid more attention to what Simms had been telling her in the prison. *If everything we do makes a difference, is this right? Are we doing the right thing? Should Manny be here? Should I have left Borden back there?*

You could make yourself crazy, thinking these things.

A turn slid Lucia down the bench seat to collide with her. Lucia muttered an apology and put one hand on the dashboard to anchor herself in place. Jazz belted herself in, not willing to risk it any further. Sure, maybe it was a matter of fate that they wouldn't wreck and die, but there was no sense tempting it.

Manny rounded a corner with a squeal of rubber, and they all scanned the road ahead. "Not there," Manny said, slowing. "I think he lost us."

"Dammit, he turned." Lucia scanned side streets on the left, while Jazz took the right. "Anything? See anything?"

"Nothing," Manny said grimly. "There's no sign of him up there. He must be down one of these side streets."

It seemed to take forever.

"We've lost him," Manny finally said. "He's a ghost."

"No, he's here, he's got to be here," Lucia said. "Back up."

Manny hit the brakes, shifted gears, and glided the giant SUV backward into shade. A narrow alley stretched on the left. At the end of it was a dilapidated tin shed, some for-

gotten warehouse that had clearly missed a demolition notice or two.

Jazz saw it first. "Paint." She pointed to the corner of the
alley. There was a fresh-looking scrape on the brick there,
and a glitter of electric blue.

"I can't fit the Hummer down there," Manny said.

Jazz released her seat belt, popped the door and jumped
down, drawing her gun before her feet hit the ground. "Stay
here," she said. Lucia slid out after her.

"Wait!" Manny looked scared out of his mind again, the
cool, calm stunt driver entirely gone. "Look in the back.
Get whatever you need."

Lucia sent a questioning look at Jazz, who shrugged and
led the way around to the rear of the vehicle. She swung
open the gate, and…

Wow.

"Manny," she said slowly, "someday, we've really got to
talk about how that therapy thing is going."

She reached over the racked shotgun, the assault rifle,
and the assorted handguns to grab two flak vests, standard
black. She handed one to Lucia, who looked it over, eyebrows climbing higher.

"FBI standard issue," she said. "Only these don't have
insignia. I'm guessing Manny's friends with the supplier."

They got into the body armor quickly, sealing the Velcro
as they went. Behind them, Jazz heard the snap of locks
engaging on the SUV. Manny probably had some kind of

stunning electrical field on the damn thing, too. She didn't put much past him, at this point.

Lucia had taken the shotgun. Jazz stuck with her pistol. Together, they moved slowly down the alley, covering each other, keeping focused on the closed double doors on the tin shack at the end of the alley.

"Careful," Lucia murmured.

"Screw careful. This guy knows he's been popped, and he'll kill her as soon as he has the chance." Jazz moved faster, reached the end of the alley and paused, looking both ways around the corner.

It was deserted. If the cops were on the way, they'd be late. She remembered what Simms and the Society had said about Actors and Leads. Most of the cops clearly didn't qualify. They wouldn't affect events, whatever transpired.

It was up to the two of them, and the guy in the shed.

And just maybe, the little girl.

She ran across the open space, light-footed, and put her back against the tin wall, careful not to make any noise. Lucia followed and mimed walking around back. Jazz nodded.

She counted to ten, took a deep breath and used one foot to kick the sliding door on her right. It slid open easily, rattling like a tin can full of marbles; if he hadn't heard that, he had to be deaf or dead. She waited for any gunfire, heard nothing, and ducked low and around the corner, darted immediately into shadow.

The inside of the place was dark, cool and apparently

deserted. No sign of Lucia, either. Jazz held her breath, listening, moving silently across the open concrete floor and constantly checking the shadows for anything that might give her a warning.

She was starting to think that they'd been wrong when she caught a glint of chrome in the far shadows, and heard the ticking of a cooling engine.

And then, very faintly, the muffled whisper of a child's sob.

She froze, listening, trying to locate the source, but the place was an echo chamber, a terrifying trap of a place, and she just knew that she was looking the wrong way, that he was behind her, creeping up...

She spun, unable to resist the feeling, and brought the gun up. Saw a shape move and nearly fired before she saw a gleam of highlights on long, dark hair and knew she'd nearly shot Lucia.

Lucia put a finger to her lips, half in shadow, and motioned Jazz to the right. She disappeared into the left-hand shadows.

Jazz had only gone three steps when she heard a man's curse, a child's full-throated scream and the patter of feet, all coming from off to the left on the other side of the parked car. Something lunged out of the dark, small and ferocious; Jazz reached out, got a handful of sweater and swung the kid around into her arms. She picked her up and backed up fast. She felt the girl's breath hot against her face, tears dripping

onto her skin, got a mouthful of curly brown hair and jerked
her head out of the way to try to see what was going on.

Just in time to see a muzzle flash. Not a shotgun, a handgun.

She heard a body hit the floor and metal clatter.

Lucia. Lucia was down.

Get the kid out. Get the kid out first.

Jazz ran backward, gasping for breath, keeping her gun
trained on the spot where the muzzle flash had briefly lit
up the shadows, nearly tripped over a pipe, and managed to
somehow get her balance back without falling full-length.
At the door, she set the girl down and crouched next to her.

"What's your name, honey?" she asked. She spared one
second to glance into her face, into honey-colored eyes and
a heart-shaped face, tanned golden by summer.

"Marla," the girl said. "He—he tried to hurt me."

"I know, Marla, but he's not going to do it again. Now,
you see that big black truck at the end of the alley? My
friend Manny's in it. When I let go, you run as fast as you
can straight for Manny and get into the truck, all right? I'll
be behind you in a minute."

Marla nodded, tears streaming down her cheeks. Jazz
reached up and wiped some away, managed a fast smile,
and pushed her gently out the door.

"Run," she said.

The kid pelted for the SUV.

Jazz was just turning back to the darkness when she

heard a man's voice whisper, "You can't do this. Nobody can stop me. They told me, nobody can stop me."

And then her chest exploded in pain.

She fell back, unable to breathe, waves of red-hot agony sliding over her, trying to pull her down into the dark, and she couldn't breathe, couldn't speak, couldn't do anything.

He came out of the dark, a dull shadow, gray, colorless. Too small a man to be making so much of a difference in the world.

She couldn't breathe.

He raised the gun, sighted on her, then shook his head and whipped it up, taking aim at Marla, who was running down the alley.

I told her to run. I told her to do that. She remembered Simms saying, *Everything you do matters.*

She couldn't fucking *breathe.* Her whole body felt numbed, destroyed by the impact in her chest.

Kevlar. He shot you in the vest. You're fine, you're just fine.

Something was very wrong.

Her heart.

She couldn't feel her heartbeat.

Everything was going dark.

She saw a blinding flash of blue-white light, like a spotlight. An intense glare bright enough to make her want to close her eyes, but she had no control over that anymore, no control over anything, and there was so much silence inside of her.

Simms. Simms was staring at her, and he was saying, *Everything you do matters, Jasmine.*

She couldn't breathe.

The light got brighter. Brighter. Overwhelming and burning, like lightning, like lightning racing along her nerves.

Listen.

Everything you do...

A single hard jerk in her chest. A thud.

Everything you do, Jasmine...

Her heart beat a second time. A third. She raised the gun. She didn't even know how she managed it, because she couldn't feel her arm, couldn't feel anything but disorientation and pain and fear, but then her gun was up and she was looking into the face of a killer as his eyes widened.

Everything you do matters.

I know that, she told Simms.

And she fired.

Chapter 10

"Ow," Jazz whispered. "Don't make me laugh, okay? It hurts to laugh."

Borden, his arm swathed in approximately a mummy's worth of bandages, smiled at her and shook his head. "No, I'm completely serious. You and Mooch are all moved in. Manny said he'd give you the alarm code the next time he drops by, because he can't trust it to anybody else."

"Not you?"

"I'm guessing especially not me."

Jazz, propped up on two pillows, squinted at the morning sunlight and pulled her hospital gown away from her neck to take a look at the spectacular bruising. It looked better than it had yesterday, the blacks turning a sickly dark blue-green, the reds fading. But still.

Colorful.

"Manny for a roommate," she said sadly. "My life is

really not turning out the way I'd hoped, Counselor. I think I might have been better off drinking my future away at Sol's."

He didn't smile at that one. He leaned forward and captured her hand in his, rubbed a thumb over the scraped and bruised knuckles, and said, "If you'd done that, at least three more people would be dead right now. Including me and Marla." Marla had dropped by earlier with her mother, a very pregnant, very scared lady who'd still been prone to dissolve into tears over the near tragedy.

The cops who'd been by had been, if not tearfully grateful, at least cautiously pleased by the whole thing, and more than willing to accept the explanation she'd come up with as to how she, Manny and Lucia had come to intercept the killer. She figured there would be more questions, but nobody seemed too unhappy with her just now.

Not even Laskins, who'd called to gruffly inform her that the Society would be picking up the medical bills. Again.

"Hey," Borden said, and leaned forward. "Rest. You look wiped out." He pressed a warm kiss to her forehead, moved to her lips and brushed them very lightly with his own, and she felt a surge of lightning heat that had nothing to do with the painkillers pumping through her system. "I'll see you tomorrow."

"Hey. Counselor."

He paused in the act of retrieving his jacket from the chair. He looked nearly back to normal. The cut on his forehead had been sutured, and his color was good. There'd be plastic surgery coming, for the skinned part of his arm, but he seemed to be dealing pretty well with that.

Better than she was, with the memory of his scream on the phone.

"You never told me how they got you."

"I went outside," he said. "I was going to get us coffee."

"There's coffee in the break room. You know that."

He shrugged slightly. With his good arm. "I wanted to get you Starbucks. Kind of a joke."

The smile melted her like butter. She watched him go, smiling, and shut her eyes to savor the warmth of the sunlight slanting over her face.

Naturally, the room didn't stay quiet long. She heard the door swing open again, and cracked an eyelid. Lucia was moving slowly, but she was moving on her own, and dressed in street clothes instead of backless gowns. A distinct improvement, though it was, Jazz thought, the very first time she'd ever seen Lucia without full battle-dress makeup.

She looked young and very, very vulnerable. There was a livid purple bruise on her cheek where she'd hit the concrete in the shed after taking a bullet in her flak vest.

"Hey," she said, and leaned against the wall as if she was either too cool or too exhausted to make it across the room to the visitor's chair Borden had last occupied. "How are you feeling?"

"Like I took a double-barreled shotgun blast to the chest," Jazz said. "By the way, remind me to send thank-you notes to the Kevlar people."

"You're taking it easy, right? Cardiac bruising's nothing to take lightly."

"I'm fine," Jazz assured her. "No exertion for me for at least two weeks before they let me out of here. And then I'm on light duty for a month, they say."

Lucia nodded and tucked her glossy straight hair back behind an ear, then walked over and seated herself. "They said you could have died. *Commotio cordis.* Sudden non-invasive impact to the chest, disrupting the heart rhythm."

"Yeah, well, I didn't die," Jazz said. She didn't really want to talk about it, or about that moment when she'd felt her heart stop, or the light and the visions.

"You heard about the envelope they found at his house, right? The one postmarked yesterday morning?"

The killer—his name had been, prosaically, Dave Jennings—had never opened it. The police had, in their forensic analysis. It was a red envelope. It had said, on clean white paper that carried no logo or watermark of any kind, three words. *Use head shots.*

"Good thing he doesn't check his mail," Jazz said somberly.

"I think all this happened at the last minute," Lucia said. "There was a voice mail on your cell phone telling you to check FedEx as soon as you got in, but it came while you were in the air."

"Yeah, and I was a little busy panicking over the plane hurtling toward the ground," Jazz said. "I'm guessing the people sending us the messages? Not Actors. At least, not Leads."

"You think?" Lucia smiled slightly. "Presuming we buy any of this crap."

"Presuming."

Not that either of them would admit to it.

Jazz shook her head and let herself sink down on the pillows again. The world seemed soft-edged. Gentle. Quiet. Trees rustled outside of the hospital window and blended with the sound of turning pages as Lucia settled in with a book.

"Sleep," she heard Lucia whisper, as her eyes drifted shut. "I'll be here."

Two weeks later, on the day she was scheduled to leave the hospital, Jazz had a new visitor. Lucia was gone to get the car; Borden had disappeared for a meeting with some attorney or other to go over paperwork. Even Manny was MIA, although he'd dropped by to furtively provide her with the password to get into the loft. After some persuasion, she'd also gotten him to give her the new address rather than send it to the dead drop.

She supposed that meant he was improving. That, and the love bite on his neck that without a doubt must have come from the lips of Pansy Taylor. Who didn't hate him.

She was getting her clothes together, heartily ready to get the hell out of the hospital, when the door opened behind her.

It was Kenneth Stewart.

The KCPD detective leaned against the closed door for a couple of seconds, staring at her, and crossed his arms. "You don't look so bad," he said. "Heard you took one in the chest."

She tapped her breastbone lightly. "Flak vest."

"Heard you damn near shot the face off a baby-raper."

She didn't answer that one. She wasn't happy with that memory, even knowing who the man had been, what he'd done. Even knowing that firing that shot had allowed a beautiful little girl to return safe to her mother.

There was no way to avoid seeing it, over and over again, in her nightmares.

"Bet you think you're the golden girl, don't you?" Stewart asked, raising his eyebrows. He looked pale and doughy and unpleasantly shiny, as if he'd been jogging. His eyes were open wide, his pupils too small. She'd always wondered if he took drugs. He never quite looked right in the head to her.

"Is there a point you're going to get to, or are you just here to kiss my ass?" she asked. She wished she had a gun, because Stewart made her feel the lack, but of course that wasn't possible in the hospital. Though she strongly suspected Lucia was always packing.

Stewart pushed away from the door and came toward her. "What's the crap I'm hearing about photos that show McCarthy across town at the time of the murders?"

"It's not crap," she said, and folded up a black hoodie before stuffing it in her canvas bag. "They've passed every test. My partner also found one of the guys in the pictures. He's willing to testify to their authenticity."

"It's crap," Stewart repeated. He was closer now. She could smell a sharp, metallic scent coming off him, like gun oil and sweat. "I know exactly where he was. Pumping rounds into the backs of the heads of three people."

"Pictures say different."

He was way too close. In her space, trying to get her to react, and boy, she wanted to. She wanted to slam her fist into his face, but she knew better, knew he was waiting for it and besides, she'd promised the doctor she'd be good.

"The pictures are fakes," he said softly. "I'm going to prove it. McCarthy's not getting off on this one. Not ever."

She gave him a slow, liquid smile. "Evidence is going before the court next Tuesday," she said. "It's exculpatory. The conviction's going to be vacated."

Stewart's eyes flared heat, then narrowed. "Maybe he doesn't make it to Tuesday."

She *almost* hit him. Almost reached for his throat.

She said nothing.

Behind him, the door opened, and Jazz looked over his shoulder to see Lucia standing there, tense and ready. "Jazz?" she asked.

"I'm fine," she said. "Detective Stewart was just dropping off—what was it you were dropping off?"

"Congratulations," he snapped, and turned and walked away, brushing past Lucia as if she wasn't even there.

Jazz let out a slow breath, tilted her head and got a similar wide-eyed look from her partner.

"Well?" Lucia asked.

"I think we'd better go warn Ben," Jazz said. "Just in case."

Jazz hadn't given it much thought, really, about how much time Lucia had spent in and around Ellsworth during the investigation. How many times she must have dropped in to talk to McCarthy.

But when they sat down at the table in the visitor's area—no claustrophobic booths here, it was just open plain tables with preformed benches, much more accessible—and McCarthy walked in from the prisoner's door, the first one of them he smiled at was Lucia, and that look…

That was a look Jazz had never seen in his eyes before.

She glanced sideways at Lucia, who was staring back, and caught the same glint.

Well, she thought blankly. *Huh. That's…interesting.* She couldn't decide if it was interesting-bad or interesting-good. McCarthy had always been her territory, more or less…not in a romantic sort of way, but in a proprietary sense, anyway. He'd been her partner. Her friend.

She cut her eyes toward Lucia again as McCarthy walked over and slid onto the bench across from them. Yes, that was the look. A hungry look. Something open and—odd, for Lucia—vulnerable.

"Hey." McCarthy nodded at Lucia, and then—with reluctance, it seemed to Jazz—transferred his smile to her. "Jazz. You look good. How you healing up?"

"Not so bad," she said. "I guess there can't be too many people who've taken it like that and lived to tell about it. Even with a vest."

"Not too many," he agreed. His hair had grown out more, and was curling on the ends. Silver threads gleaming all through it like hidden treasure. His eyes flicked over to Lucia again, as if he couldn't keep them away for long. "But you're taking it easy, right?"

"Yeah, yeah, everybody interrogates me about that. I'm fine, okay? How about you? How's the arm?"

He extended and flexed it. "Healed," he said. "Ribs, too. Collarbone's still a little tricky, but it'll do."

"We want to make sure you keep them that way," Jazz said. "Stewart came to see me this morning."

McCarthy went still, arm still flexed, fist clenched. She heard tendons crack, but his face had gone expressionless, his eyes hidden and dark. "Yeah?" he asked neutrally. "Dropped off hearts and flowers?"

"Not exactly. He said you might not make it to the hearing on Tuesday," she replied. "You're going to watch your back, right? Night and day?"

"Jazz, no way I'm letting them get to me now. Too much to hope for." He looked at Lucia again, a little longer this time. "What about the pictures? Any leads on who sent them to Manny?"

"No, but we authenticated them," Lucia said. "The photographer's name is Harrison Rohrman, he's a private investigator out of Michigan. He got the pictures by accident, actually. He was photographing everybody who came out the back door because he was waiting for a husband to duck out with one of the strippers. Divorce case. He had no idea the pictures were important."

"But somebody knew," Jazz said. "Somebody who recognized you in them and dropped them to Manny, knowing he'd be able to do something with them."

"Meaning?" McCarthy's hands stretched out flat on the table. Jazz thought about reaching for them, but before she could, Lucia's hand moved and stroked lightly over his knuckles, then retreated.

As if she couldn't help herself.

McCarthy's hands moved after hers, then stopped.

Neither of them willing to commit, not in front of Jazz. She felt heat in her face, felt like an outsider, and hated it.

"Meaning," she forced herself to say, "it was probably somebody from the force who doesn't want to be identified as helping you out. Somebody Stewart might go after out of sheer revenge."

McCarthy nodded. "Yeah, there are still a few guys who'd step up and do that, at least anonymously. Hell, I don't care who did it. So long as the judge admits the evidence, I'll just be grateful."

"You know this won't mean you get reinstated," Jazz said. "The payoffs—"

"Yeah, my lawyer talked about it. There's a deal on the

table, if the evidence gets admitted. I get time served on the extortion. Community service, and I lose my pension, but Jazz, I deserve that. We both know it." McCarthy shrugged. "I should've been better than I was. I will be, from now on. If I can't be a cop anymore, that's okay. I'll find another way. The important thing is that I'm not stuck in here anymore. That I can have a life again."

His eyes flicked to Lucia, then away. Not quite an admission of interest, but...

Jazz swallowed, forced a smile, and said, "Yeah. That's great."

On Sunday, Jazz woke to the sound of gunfire, and came bolt upright in bed. Mooch shot off the comforter with a growl and stalked away. She rolled over, grabbed her pistol from the nightstand and shrugged on a robe over her white T-shirt and sweatpants before easing open the bedroom door.

The door read, Jazz's Room, in shiny black letters, along with Authorized Personnel Only. Inside the room, things looked like a normal bedroom—like her old bedroom, in fact, down to the curtains and the battered furniture—but outside, it was still disorienting to see that it was a freestanding cubicle sitting in the middle of a concrete warehouse floor.

Not that the place was empty. Over to the right was the freestanding kitchen, to the left was the curtained-off en-

tertainment room, and beyond that was Manny's private
space where even she didn't dare go.

The lab, however, was directly in front of her, and as she
looked in that direction, she saw Manny pull off a pair of
safety goggles and make safe an automatic pistol. He spotted her standing in the doorway, and waved, then looked
awkward.

"Um—did I wake you up?"

"With the gunfire?" She gestured at the pistol he'd just
put down, and the ballistic tank of water he'd fired into.
"Oh, no. Had to get up anyway."

"Sorry. It's just that—"

"Never mind, Manny. Really. I'm awake." She stretched,
realized she was still armed and dangerous, and went back
to replace the pistol in its drawer next to her bed. When she
came back, Manny was in the kitchen, pouring a cup of coffee. He handed it to her and leaned on the counter, staring
at her with one of his puppy-dog expressions.

"Manny, why are you test-firing a gun? Since you don't
do violent-crime work?"

"Yeah, well…" He shrugged. "I've been thinking of getting back into it. A little. This is nothing, though. The insurance company wants to prove that the owner of the gun
shot up his own house and then claimed it was a drive-by.
Oh, here. Message." He reached over for a pad of paper and
slid it across to her. Written in Manny's neat calligraphy was
Call Borden cell phone. "He didn't want to wake you up."

She yawned and nodded. "What time is it?"

"Six o'clock."

She froze, blinking. *"In the evening?"*

"Yeah," he said apologetically. "I thought you—the doctor said you should sleep as much as—"

"Manny, I was supposed to go to the office!"

"Yeah, well, you really don't need to go until—"

"Manny!"

"Sorry." He held up his hands and turned away, shoulders hunched. She glared at him for a second, then shook her head and grabbed the cordless phone from the counter as she headed for the bathroom.

It was impossible to stay mad at Manny, especially in the bathroom, which was very possibly the most heavenly place she'd ever seen. Marble, massaging jets of water, a tub big enough to hold three or four…it was hard to hold a grudge. She still thought of it as Manny's bathroom, but really, it was hers now, too. For the time being.

Weird.

As she toweled her hair dry with one hand, she dialed Borden's cell phone one-handed. He answered on the second ring.

"Are you in town?" she asked.

"Well, across it," he said. "Meeting with some corporate clients. Just finished."

"I was planning on going to the office, but Manny's blown that by forgetting to tell me to wake up."

"That's his job now?"

"Shut up."

"Who's a grumpy late riser?"

"I'm starving. And I want dinner. I heard you eat, some-times."

"When the company's agreeable," Borden said. "I'll be there in—twenty minutes. Tell your boyfriend not to shoot me on the way in, okay?"

She smiled and hung up on him, but he had a point about Manny. Not the boyfriend part, the shooting part. Manny was taking guard duty way too seriously. Even Lucia thought he'd gone a little loony on the subject.

She put extra time in at the mirror, experimenting with makeup and blush and eyeliner, and when she was finished, she decided it wasn't too humiliating. She still looked like Jasmine Callender. Just not the one who got drunk and beat up truckers.

After some thought, she chose a black pantsuit with a plain white French-cuffed shirt—Lucia's shopping influence—and some mid-heeled shoes. By the time she was slipping them on, Borden's rental car appeared on the security monitor, and she had to race to tell Manny not to activate his more extreme self-defensive measures.

She met Borden downstairs, in the garage, and found him leaning against his sedan, looking tall and lawyerly. Very legitimate.

His eyes widened at the sight of her, and he straightened up. She deliberately slowed down, enjoying the effect.

"Counselor," she said, and gave him a long, measuring look. "Something wrong?"

"Yes," he said. "I'm pretty sure there are some laws being broken, I'm just not clear on which ones."

He walked around and opened the door for her. Handed her in, fingers warm around hers.

She didn't let go. She tugged hard on his hand, tipping him off balance and down to her seated level.

Grabbed his tie and kissed him.

Warm, slow slide of lips, just as hot and sweet as she remembered from that strange, dizzying day at Simms's prison. His lips parted, and she plunged her tongue into the opening, tasting coffee and caramel. His tongue scraped hers, teased, stroked. She moaned, deep in her throat, and grabbed a handful of his hair to try to get him deeper into her. It was unbelievable, really, how much she wanted this.

Wanted him.

She let him go, but he didn't go far, one arm draped over the car door, staring at her with those warm eyes. He licked his lips slowly, tasting her, and said, in a voice she hardly recognized, "What was that for?"

"For—" She couldn't think of a single thing to say, and suddenly it came to her, foolish and charming and strange. "For not hating me."

He reached down and fitted his hand along her cheek. His thumb brushed over her damp, parted lips. "Who says I don't?" he asked. "Sometimes."

"Are we going to sit here all night?" she asked.

"Maybe."

"You're a complete bastard."

He smiled. It was such a satanically beautiful smile that she felt herself light up inside, light up and burn, and he stood, shut her door and walked around to the other side.

"I'm taking you someplace special for dinner," he said as he backed out of the garage.

"Is it quiet?"

"No, it's very loud. Mariachi bands. Small children screaming. People talking on cell phones. And there's a buffet—"

She grinned. "Sounds perfect."

He was staying at the Marriott, the nicest one, and valeted the car and ushered her into the lobby with a hand at the small of her back. Like they were about to dance. Guided her to the elevator and pressed the button for the ninth floor.

She watched him in silence as the floors flashed by.

"The restaurant's on the ninth floor?" she asked.

"Best in town," he agreed. "Very exclusive."

They didn't touch. He led her down the carpeted hall once they'd arrived on the right floor, down to a door at the end of the hall, and opened it with a flourish.

It was a suite. A nice one, with a king-size bed and a respectably sized bathroom and a view.

He shut the door, watching her.

"Where's the food?" she asked.

He reached over and swung open the minibar. Tiny little bottles of liquor. Miniature champagne. Candy bars.

"Screw the food," she said, and then he was on her, hands in her hair, pushing her back against the wall, and she couldn't believe she'd ever thought he was weak, because there was no way on earth she had the strength to push him away, not now.

Not ever.

His hands moved under the jacket, trailing fire, tugged the hem of her shirt free and found a path beneath it. She gasped into his mouth, arching against him, as his palms stroked over her breasts and circled her nipples into hardness, then slid around to the small of her back to pull her tighter against him.

His mouth was hot and hungry and all over her, all over her neck, traveling down, tongue tasting every pulse point as she gasped for breath.

He moved her hands back, pinning them up against the wall, and she felt something fierce and hot shudder through her. Something powerful.

He felt it, too, and raised his head to meet her eyes. This close, his eyes were enormous, hot, full of something too dangerous and too violent and too perfect.

She moaned and let her head fall back, surrendering.

Just…finally…for the first time in her life…surrendering.

Everything we do matters.

She lost thread of that in the stroke of his skin on hers, in flashes of heat and light and a fast, almost brutal rhythm thudding in her head, in her heart, her back against the wall, climbing, struggling…

"James," she whispered, and felt him shudder and spiral

into her, heat and light and a perfect crime of passion, committed in hot blood and without regret.

Guilty as charged.

The next morning, she woke sore and exhausted and utterly filled with light, and rolled over to find Borden sitting on the edge of the bed, already dressed.

"Hey," she murmured. He smiled. It looked sad, that smile. Not what she'd expected. She sat up, instinctively pulling the covers close over her skin. "What?"

He reached out and touched her hair, pushing it back from her eyes, caressing the tender skin at her temples. Long, gentle fingers. His thumb brushed her lips, a soft echo of the need in the night.

"We missed the hearing," he said. "McCarthy's hearing. They held it off-schedule, because he was designated at-risk in the prison. The judge admitted the photographs into evidence and the prosecution moved for the conviction to be vacated."

She felt an odd stab go through her. "We…we missed the hearing? What happened?"

"Ben's out," Borden said. "He walked away a free man an hour ago."

She let out a cry. It was half fury, half joy. He'd been set free, and she hadn't been there, hadn't been there—how could that have happened? How could she have missed that moment, after all this time? All this work?

Had he looked for her? Been disappointed not to see her?

"We have to go," she blurted. "We have to go see him—"

"Jazz, he's okay. Lucia was there, he's with her," he said. "There's something else. Lucia got a red envelope thirty minutes ago. Hand delivered."

"And?"

"So did you," he said, and turned to pick it up from the foot of the bed. "Someone slid it under the door while I was getting dressed."

She took it from him and pulled out the sheet of paper. It was on the letterhead, not of Gabriel, Pike & Laskins, but of Eidolon Corporation.

And it said, in printed, plain block letters, ONE OF YOU HAS MADE A MISTAKE.

She looked up at Borden. Thought about the night, about the fury and perfection of it.

Thought about Ben McCarthy, walking free from murders he didn't commit.

About the look in Lucia's eyes at the prison.

Everything you do matters.

"Why would they send this?" she asked. "It's nothing, right? A mind game?"

Borden shook his head and reached out to pull her head close and plant a burning kiss on her forehead.

"I don't know," he murmured against her hair. "I don't know."

* * * * *

MY FATHER'S RULES. I'VE NEVER BROKEN THEM...UNTIL NOW.

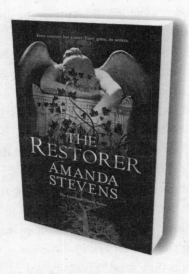

My name is Amelia Gray. I'm a cemetery restorer
who sees ghosts. In order to protect myself from the
parasitic nature of the dead, I've always held fast to
the rules passed down from my father. But now
a haunted police detective has entered my world
and everything is changing, including the rules
that have always kept me safe.

www.mirabooks.co.uk

THE WORLD IS GONE
THE DEAD ARE WALKING
HER DAUGHTER IS MISSING

Cass Dollar vaguely recalls surviving something
terrible. Around her is barren wasteland where cities
once stood. Her body is ravaged. Her daughter has
disappeared. Her eyes are unwilling to believe
what they see…

People turned hungry for human flesh by a
government experiment gone wrong. Everyone is
out for their own survival. There are no rules.
No morals. No hope. And for Cass, the
nightmare has only just begun.

HARLEQUIN® MIRA®
www.mirabooks.co.uk

M291_A

In a future world, vampires reign. Humans are blood cattle…

In a future world, vampires reign.
Humans are blood cattle.
And one girl will search for the key
to save humanity.

Allison Sekemoto survives in the Fringe, the
outermost circle of a vampire city. Until one night
she is attacked—and given the ultimate choice.
Die…or become one of the monsters.

www.miraink.co.uk

Join us at facebook.com/miraink

THEY DESTROYED HER WORLD. BUT SHE'S THEIR ONLY HOPE...

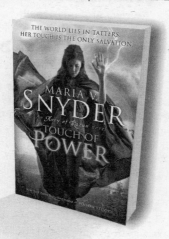

Avry's power to heal the sick should earn her respect in the plague-torn land of Kazan. Instead she is feared and blamed for spreading the plague.

When Avry uses her forbidden magic, she faces the guillotine. Until a dark, mysterious man rescues her from her prison cell. His people need Avry's magic to save their dying prince.

Saving the prince is certain to kill Avry. Now she must choose—use her healing touch to show the ultimate mercy or die a martyr to a lost cause?

HARLEQUIN®MIRA®
www.mirabooks.co.uk

BC 06/15

www.mirabooks.co.uk

The mark of a good book

At MIRA we're proud of the books we publish, that's why whenever you see the MIRA star on one of our books, you can be assured of its quality and our dedication to bringing you the best books. From romance to crime to those that ask, "What would you do?" Whatever you're in the mood for and however you want to read it, we've got the book for you!

Visit **www.mirabooks.co.uk** and let us help you choose your next book.

★ **Read** extracts from our recently published titles

★ **Enter** competitions and prize draws to win signed books and more

★ **Watch** video clips of interviews and readings with our authors

★ **Download** our reading guides for your book group

★ **Sign up** to our newsletter to get helpful recommendations and **exclusive discounts** on books you might like to read next

www.mirabooks.co.uk

HMIRA_WEB